LEGENDS AND LORE

THE LIGHTHOUSE KIDS

Spirits of Cape Hatteras Island

LEGENDS AND LORE

Jeanette Gray Finnegan Jr.

First Printing

CONTENTS

FOREWORD

This unusual history continues. So many events would not have happened had it not been for the opportunities that Hatteras Island afforded. This second in the series—*Legends and Lore*—tells what we were told. These events happened, and the stories are old. The children begin to uncover facts about the island, ones that were usually shared only among the "old people." These families survived quite well living away from most of the modern conveniences. In their lives, conveniences came one at a time, with usually a little time between. Therefore, they not only appreciated the change but brought about change of their own.

Most characters carry an island name. Some are still alive, some not, but their footprint stays. The dream sequences allow the island to speak for itself, about what it and its people have experienced. Being separated from everyone else, one learned the art of communicating with one another. The islanders lived a communal life. They knew the land and the sea. The chapters on the ocean reveal what lives in tandem with the people, like a neighboring city. The inhabitants of the ocean celebrate life in unique ways. In their existence they are both formidable competitors, and loyal friends. They live in an underwater world where size matters. Those who live by the ocean celebrate its gifts, understand its nature and respect its power.

It has been fun to recall the many stories and experiences, both enjoyed and related to me by others who lived it. The tragedy of the books is the inability to allow the reader to hear the thoroughly English brogue that permeated this island. There is no more beautiful accent on all the continents of the world than the Hatteras Island dialect.

★ 1 ★

Whale Watching

There must have been at least twenty whales slowly making their way south toward The Point. The water was dark with them as they lumbered along—bulls, cows, and their calves, all traveling in unison through the water. One or two of them would breach the waterfall that streamed from the top, indicating that the whale was getting ready to dive. As each whale made the plunge, it threw up its huge tail and slipped under the ocean for a few minutes, then rejoined the group in the herd. All the whales did that at least once before passing the lighthouse going south.

The children could see them coming from far down the beach. Luke saw them first.

"Look!" He pointed north up the island.

Blake and Ellie stood from their perch atop the lighthouse walkway, leaned on the railing looking in the direction Luke indicated, and gave a collective gasp at what they saw. The herd of right whales made their way down the beach toward the lighthouse. Watching the spectacle at the top of the tower were three eager children, scrambling and tripping all over themselves to get down the 268 steps to the bottom. Luke made it first, and Blake edged his way around Ellie to hit the grass at the bottom second. Then the race was on to see who could make it across the dune to the sandy beach. When they reached the waterline they did not sit long. They threw off their shoes and socks and just stood in awe as the herd of whales along with their calves slowly skimmed the surface of the ocean heading southeast.

This was an unusual sight, although not an unusual happening—just one seldom seen by island residents. The crisp November air was light, not even slightly cold, just energizing. Luke fingered the small whale replica in his pocket, whittled for him by Mingan, the old Indian carver they met during their last dream venture, the one that took them on a visit to their ancestral Indian family. In Luke's excitement he was trying to connect. He was jumping up and down waving his arms and shouting greetings to the huge leviathans of the deep. Blake followed suit, but his antics were almost disturbing. Ellie, on other hand, had another idea to connect.

As dream travelers, Ellie, Luke, and Blake had visited the Indian tribe of the Croatoan, historically the first known inhabitants of Hatteras Island. History records that the Indians had been on this island since AD 500. In this meeting, Ellie learned that she was a direct descendant of the tribe's chief, Weroansqua, who as a woman was not a typical leader. Weroansqua was mother of the great Manteo, and she had special mental powers that even the shaman of the tribe, Powwaw, envied. These unusual gifts of the mind were passed down through the women of her line by way of spiritual blood. They were so powerful, and the blood so strong, that when Ellie's mother, Annie, inherited them, she was not physically capable of enduring their potency. The very existence of the bestowal proved to render her frail rather than strong. She lived long enough to give birth to a girl child. As her baby drew her first breath, Annie drew her last.

Annie was the youngest daughter of Captain Charlie Gray and his wife, Odessa Jennette. Ellie's father was Joseph, who died before she was born, so it was left to Annie's parents to take the orphaned child home to raise as their own. This home was a beach lodge at the foot of the mighty Cape Hatteras Lighthouse, where Captain Charlie served as the main lighthouse keeper. Here Ellie grew up with her grandparents and the extended Gray family. This included her aunt Jeanette, Captain Charlie's oldest child, who, with her husband, Bill Finnegan, the assistant light-keeper, lived in the assistant keeper's quarters next to the main house, along with their two children. Luke was two years older than Ellie, and Blake was three years younger.

The three children were inseparable. The complex surrounding the Cape Hatteras Lighthouse was several miles east of the main village of Buxton, which made for a possibly lonely existence. This should have been the case, but nothing was further from the truth. Also in the area were the Coast Guard station and its inhabitants. For the children, every-thing in the vicinity was centered around the lighthouse—and them.

Grandmom's family, the Jennettes, could trace their ancestors back to the mid-1600s, and they were direct descendants of the Croatoan Indians who had originally inhabited the island. Grandmom Odessa had the same blood intensity and potency of gifts as the chief, Weroansqua, but in Odessa they were not as spirited and lay dormant except when seen in a vision. Grandmom Odessa knew of her mental prowess but was informed that, in its active form, the powers were to be passed on. She had fully expected to see these powers embodied in her daughter. (Odessa had been told in a dream that her child would be the most powerful female since Weroansqua, but that dream had not yet material-ized.) When her two oldest daughters, Jeanette and her sister Iva, did not display any of the traits of the mind powers, she waited for them to appear in the youngest, Annie. They did, but Annie was not able, nor did she desire, to use them. Imagine Odessa's surprise when her granddaugh-ter, Ellie, approached her with her first experience relating to the legacy.

Weroansqua's granddaughter, Kweepi, married an Englishman, one descended from the first white settlers on Roanoke Island. They had escaped the wrath of the local tribe, led by Wanchese. The English had been rescued by Manteo and taken to live with them on Hatteras Island. Research showed that the English family name was Jenet, which later evolved to Jennett, then Jennette. From Jenet's union with Wero-ansqua's granddaughter, the women inherited the gifts of the island's ancient people. These powers lay dormant for many generations, and only surfaced in a few of the women, usually many generations apart. Since Weroansqua, there had been only three times where the legacy had manifested itself into a "special" child. Men and women of the Jennette family were carriers, and the powers were passed through both, but the accomplishments were only revealed in the females, never the males. Even though both passed on the legacy, historically it only demonstrated true strength every 100 or so years. Grandmom Odessa had exhibited a few of the psychic forces, but Ellie was to have them all.

In Weroansqua, the powers were prominent: telepathy (thought transference), astral projection (the ability to travel outside the body or follow the "dream body"), telekinesis (moving an object through space), clairvoyance (the ability to see persons and events that are distant in time or space), and being able to communicate with fish, fowl, and animal. When in a trancelike state, Weroansqua could also see the future and the past. Ellie would have all of these, but she was only ten and just now learning to recognize and use a few. Watching the whales, she decided to try one that Weroansqua had indicated was already in evidence: the power to communicate with creatures.

As the children saw the herd draw closer, and as Luke and Blake struggled to make contact, Ellie did just that. She thought hard, and her heart pounded. She filled her lungs with the fresh sea air and held it as she developed a stare. Without blinking she sent her first message ever to a nonhuman being: "Hello." She repeated the exercise, but this time she opened her eyes and looked. The first whale breached the water, took in his air, and blew out the excess water through his blowholes. Then the next whale, as he passed the children, repeated the motion—coming to the surface, gulping in air, going under again, and blowing out the excess water through the two blowholes in the top of his mighty head. Soon in their staggered line they all acknowledged the figures on the beach as they passed. Even the little calves swimming close to the fluke of the mother cow blew a stream of recognition at the greeting he was receiving in his inner ear.

When Ellie became conscious of her thoughts and the reactions to them, she also became aware that both Luke and Blake had stopped their flailing around and stood stone-faced, staring at her.

"Did you do that? I know you did that," Blake blurted. "Do it again!" he pleaded. "I will help. What are you saying to them? I want to help. Weroansqua said we would be more powerful if we all did it together."

"Ellie, what are you sending?" asked Luke.

"I'm only saying, 'Hello.' I can't think of anything else. Just 'Hello,'" she replied quietly, trying not to break her breathing and concentrating.

"How are you doing it?" asked Luke.

"I'm holding my breath and sending it." Ellie once again gathered her stare, and the other two became quiet and concentrated.

The line of whales responded. Seeing the constant stream of water shooting up in the air was exciting, and the children watched in wonder at what they saw. As they stood at the water's edge, they reached for one another and held hands while they collectively greeted the herd as it passed their tiny island heading south to the birthing grounds, wherever they were. Nobody else would see or ever hear of this sight, because who would believe it? But the children did, and they had each other. This was an experience they could share, so it didn't matter if anyone else knew. However, Ellie would eventually tell Grandmom, because Weroansqua had said that Grandmom would know what to tell her if she were ever troubled by the power. The great chief said that she would send Odessa a dream explaining how to protect Ellie, and that Ellie should go to her grandmom anytime and tell her anything. Ellie felt like her grandmother should know that she was practicing.

When the entire herd had moved past and began to head farther out to sea to avoid the part of the island that made The Point, the children turned to get out of the wash of the ocean and settled down on the dry sand. They began to giggle. What they did not know was that the whales were singing their song under the ocean—a beautiful sound. The songs of whales were soulful and mesmerizing, but only the whale would hear it.

"I'm happy we saw them from the lighthouse. We would never have known they were going by if Luke hadn't spied them coming down the beach. Good job, Luke," said Blake as he skipped beside his older brother. "You are taller. That's why you saw them first. Do you think there are more?" Luke put his arm around his younger brother and gave him a squeeze.

"Let's go tell Grandpop," said Ellie. "He will know if it always happens. Maybe he has seen them, too. After all, he is old, and he seems to know everything."

The children hurried to find their grandfather. They found him in the barn where the horses were kept. He was rummaging around in the empty boxes sent by the government when upgrading the equipment for the light. Luke rushed up to Grandpop and sat down on one of the boxes, preventing Captain Charlie from opening that one.

Blake, realizing what was about to happen, was quick to avert Grand-pop's attention. "Grandpop!" he said with a little too much volume. Captain Charlie gave a start and turned away from the box where Luke was sitting and faced Ellie and Blake.

"What in the world has you three so worked up?" Grandpop questioned.

"Grandpop, we saw a herd of whales, maybe a hundred, maybe more," said Ellie excitedly.

"Well, now, young-uns, I don't think there could have been that many. That would make the water rise, but I'm sure you saw a few. This time of year they migrate south to give birth to calves in the warm waters off the coast of Florida. And yes, I have seen them before, but you have to be watching all the time, because it is never certain when they will come by. The ones passing through this part of the Atlantic are called the 'right whales,' because they are the 'right' whale to catch. They have more blubber than other species of whale—and they do not have teeth but rather long plates of bone called baleen, which is like a rake, with little hairs in between so that they can sift through small shrimp and other prey from the surrounding waters to feed. When a whale has two blowholes, it does not have teeth, but if it has only one blowhole, it has teeth. Those are sperm whales, beluga whales . . . and believe it or not, the dolphin is considered a whale and has teeth and only one blowhole."

"What's a blowhole for, Pop?" asked Luke.

"It is a nostril, like your nose. It keeps water from entering them when the whale is underwater. The blowhole is located on the back of the whale's head and used for breathing, like your nostrils."

"How come they don't drown?" Blake asked, puzzled, knowing that when he was underwater, he couldn't keep the water out of his nose.

"They have a flap that covers the hole when the mammal is diving down." Grandpop had not anticipated teaching a lesson on whales, but as he was a curious man and one connected to his island surroundings, he made it his business to study his ocean neighbors.

"This island used to harvest the blubber for oil to burn in lamps and the long bone for sturdy staves. Those baleen bones were used for staves in the early days when men needed a sturdy structure. Now we use wooden staves and other oil. But it was the right whale to have around. I have seen them several times over the years, usually while I am cleaning the lenses of the light. From the tower, the water is actually black with them. Purdy sight, I must say. They are unique because they like to hug the shore, especially here. They remember the shoals in this area, and instead of going out to sea where the shipping lanes are, they move closer to the beach. They are smart. You wait, they'll remember you. They make their deep-water move when they pass the lighthouse, to get around The Point. They know to slip through the underwater valley between The Point and Diamond Shoals. You will recognize these particular whales because of the strange horny growths on their heads, with each whale having a different pattern."

"I saw that, Grandpop. I thought they had polka dots on their head," Blake chimed in, making Captain Charlie again think that his little critters here were some kind of smart. Charlie Gray was an educated man. He had a degree in engineering and was a reader and a smart observer of the life around him. He drew great pleasure teaching these eager children about nature and character. He was proud of what he had molded, and Blake just cemented that pride.

"This is the time of year they would come, sometime before Christmas. I always counted it as an early Christmas present. I am sure glad you got to see it," Grandpop smiled, turning back to his survey of the boxes he had saved.

Luke stepped forward and gave Grandpop a hug around his middle, with his head on Grandpop's chest.

"What's this? You do something wrong? You didn't hurt those whales, did you? No throwing shells or anything like that. They are gentle giants, and they have feelings. They can also sense feelings in you, and they have memories, so as close as you three are to the animals on land, best you be that connected to the creatures of the sea. They are your neighbors." Grandpop scowled at them, hoping this sudden display of affection wasn't a confession of sorts. But it was, just not the one he was expecting.

Luke stepped away and held out his hand to give a strong squeeze to the one his grandfather extended back.

"Grandpop, we did not hurt the whales. We love them, and we also know they remember us, so don't worry about us bothering the friends we have in the ocean. We are their protectors. Right, men?" and he turned to his brother and cousin.

"Right!" they responded in unison. They looked at each other and braced for the rest of Luke's story. They just didn't know how he was going to tell it. They all had been waiting for the right time to tell Grandpop about the sword they had found. It had been wearing on all of them that they had not already told him, so now was as good a time as any— because if Grandpop opened the box Luke had plopped down on, he was going to know anyway.

Luke squared his shoulders, and Ellie and Blake moved close to him. They were not about to let him take all the blame. This was something they all would get punished for, and they were all ready for the switch.

"Grandpop, I have something to tell you, and you might get mad, but I'm gonna tell it anyway, and it is all my fault. I am the leader, and these two just followed orders, so I am the only one to get punished."

"Sounds like I better sit down, son. Spill it." Grandpop settled down on the very box where the sword was hidden, waiting for this great confession.

Luke began. "Well, remember that day we went to Mr. O'Neil's house for you to fix the roof, and you said we could walk home? Well, we kinda did that, and we did something you said not to do, but it was an accident, and we just didn't know how to tell you."

"I'll cut the switches," said Ellie. "I know which ones we need, so you don't have to get mad. We are ready!" she said with determination.

"Lordy be! What in the world are you three talking about?" Captain Charlie was having a hard time following what was going on, all this talk of switches and anger and punishment. He wondered what these three little angels had done to merit such a deep regret in all of them. He began to worry.

"Well, we kinda went too near the water, down back of Miss Lilly's house, and there was this shiny thing blinking at me from the edge of the water, where the tide had come up in the hurricane. Wel-l-l-l-l," Luke was drawing it out, scared to get to the meat of the matter, but he knew he had to go there. "Well, I got down near the water to see what it was, but Grandpop, Ellie and Blake told me not to. They didn't want to—they reminded me what you said about gettin' near the water, and I did it anyway. I took my shoes off, so Mom wouldn't have a mess, and I pulled out the shiny stick from where the tide had washed it up."

At that he put his hand under the captain's elbow and gently urged him to get off that box. Now the captain was really perplexed, but he slowly rose and stepped away from where he had been sitting. Luke pried up the lid of the telescope box, only to find it empty. The shocked look on his face was heart-stopping.

Blake stepped up and said, "Not that one, Luke. This one." Luke moved over to the box Blake had indicated. Meanwhile Grandpop was just looking from one child to the other, thinking it was all a joke—until Luke reached inside the box Blake had pointed to and brought out a beautiful, shiny, ancient sword polished to perfection.

"Lordy be!" Grandpop exclaimed as he was handed the precious object. "You found this?" he asked in amazement.

"We were gonna tell, we were, but we knew you would be mad, and we didn't want a whipping. Then it was my birthday, then it was the play, then it was Thanksgiving, and, and. . . ."

Luke was talking so fast he couldn't remember exactly what he had been thinking as to why he didn't tell his grandfather right away.

Captain Charlie was speechless for one of the first times in his life. He turned the sword over and over in his hands, looking at the golden cuff, embellished with old designs, the length, the whole amazing thing.

"Son, you got yourself some treasure here," he said. "Some treasure!"

"Grandpop, I'm sorry," Luke choked back the tears. They were all two steps from crying. What a sorrowful group faced their grandfather.

Captain Charlie gently put the sword down and gathered the three of them to his chest and gave them a mighty hug. "Son, you haven't done anything wrong. Don't you fret. And Blake, there will be no smiting today. Ellie, save your switches for some other time. You have uncovered something very valuable, and it now causes me to think on what to do about it. But while I'm thinking, what say we show it to Grandmom and your parents and just look at it for a while."

At that there was a little pause, and all four of them broke into a huge grin, with Blake dancing around like he was an Indian.

"Oh, Pop, I was so scared, I wanted to tell—," but his grandfather stopped him.

"It's okay, son. We'll get this sorted out. Let's go see Grandmom," and off they all went to the main house. Ellie skipped along, so-o-o glad she wasn't going to get switched.

Grandpop was anxious to show Grandmom Odessa the sword. They both marveled at it. It was beautiful, all shiny and old. Grandmom had a feeling, which Grandpop had known would happen. If there was something to this piece, Odessa would know it, and she did.

As wonderful as it was, it obviously was a part of the background connected to the island. They decided that it must be turned over to a museum, and historians could follow through with researching its origins. But until the historians let them know the best place for the sword, Grandpop and Grandmom would be good caretakers. For now, the sword was theirs, and it was a welcome sight over the mantle in the keeper's quarters.

★ 2 ★

The Jennette Women

Odessa Jennette Gray was born into a line of women who were destined to receive a spiritually endowed power passed down from a psychic female Indian chief of the Croatoan tribe. Weroansqua, the chief, was directly descended from an ancient clan that came from a mystical island in the East many thousands of years before. Earliest memories claimed that they came to escape a natural disaster and find a safer place near the water. Water helped to amplify their mental powers, allowing those who possessed them the power to be formidable, but only if the power was used with love and respect for all living things. The tribe had learned its lesson in the past, as power and greed had corrupted their ancestors.

They settled on Cape Hatteras Island at least 1,000 years before the first white men ever landed on its shores. These unusual people, who had already adapted to an island style of living, were watchful readers of nature. This ancient tribe was more spiritual than other human civilizations, and they drew energy from nature. The island fostered and enhanced their innate *knowing*, the legacy passed down the Jennette clan bloodline through the women. All of the descendants had a little,

13

some more than others. Only three were named as having an abundance of the power. Weroansqua was not connected to the white man except through her granddaughter Kweepi's marriage to an Englishman named Jenet, and whose line later produced two gifted women: Rhetta and her daughter Sabra. The inheritance was predominant in those three. Grandmom Odessa was sure that the most gifted of all would be one of her daughters. She was told in a dream that it would be her child, so she presumed that when Annie, her youngest daughter, demonstrated gifts from childhood, she was the answer to the prophesy. But the force was so powerful that Annie in her frail condition could not control the psychic part or the bodily strain on her as she experienced the physical elements of the gift. Annie died giving birth, passing all these spiritual gifts and so much more to her child, Eleanor "Ellie" Wilson Gray.

Weroansqua was the apparent vessel of the practices of an ancient society—a civilization whose study of the mind and all it could do through the earth's energy was advanced far beyond the development of today. This gifted nation grew so mentally powerful and aggressive that they became land greedy, using their superior strength and intellect to conquer others. The ambition for more and more control led to their final disappearance in a mighty flood that covered all the land, leaving only shoals where an island state used to thrive. The region where the civilization had been was, for a while, only soft sand from the upheaval of the ocean. Pockets of unfathomably deep gullies of water were scattered about, and eventually the entire domain disappeared under the sea.

Some escaped the destruction, carrying the knowledge with them, but by that time they realized it should be kept secret to avoid the wrath of those whom they had formerly enslaved. It became clear to the survivors of the flood, who took with them their gems and crystals, that the powers were only to be used for good. Weroansqua was descended from that group of people, as were several other tribe members. She was determined to protect the spirit energy she was blessed with by passing it on to future generations. So she and the last remaining knowledgeable shaman of the teachings used fire, smoke, the glowing gemstones, and crystals to transfer their legacy.

Weroansqua and Powwaw huddled in the old shaman's cave and, surrounded by their earthly conductors, lit a sacred fire. Powwaw sprinkled the flames with the dust of crystals, and both deeply inhaled the blue smoke that rose in the air in a funnel-shaped cloud. They placed the precious gemstones in a circle around the priestess and prayed and chanted, addressing their spirits, until they felt the power surround them. They picked up a long pipe made from the hollowed-out antler of a deer, which had both bear and wolf fur encircling the stem, and feathers of the raven hanging from its bowl. The bowl was made from another hollowed-out antler, smaller than the first, and filled with herbs and elements from the forest around them. A waft of silver reached down and mingled with the blue smoke of the fire in the pipe and the fire in the hearth. In this circling cloud, shaman and priestess drifted up, spiraling in weightless suspension toward the smoke hole in the top of the cave, lifting them to the misty sky above. In the clear heavens the clouds became feathery with threads of silver and gold, shot through that night with comets streaking across the sky. From here, in the open air, they spun in a circle slowly, higher and higher, until they could survey the camp below them.

As the spell began to fade away, the Indian priestess floated to the ground and found herself at the mouth of an empty cave located in one of the crevices of the grotto. She stumbled in a daze, feeling along the path until the walls grew damp to her touch. Here beside the underground stream she finally closed her eyes and rested. The sound of running water soothed her into a calm sleep, as a large white wolf stretched out beside her in watchful reverence.

Powwaw's spell was also gently broken. He spread his massive robe and floated over the sound until he was no longer visible. Suddenly a raven appeared over the water and flew to a tree outside of Powwaw's cave. As dawn broke, the raven faded from sight and Powwaw slept soundly on his fur pallet.

Weroansqua had summoned a psychic spell that would sift down through her bloodline forever, evidenced only through the female. The old shaman Powwaw helped her, and together they crafted the spiritualistic powers to flow through Weroansqua's lineage, resulting in the women of the Jennette family inheriting concentrated psychic potency.

The grand chief of the Croatoan watched as his young priestess wife walked across the compound to their living quarters. He saw a special glow about her, and he knew. He was most proud of his wife. She was young and gifted. They would have many children. He had chosen well.

One of the most vivid and memorable Jennette females was Rhetta Jennette. Rhetta was born to her elderly parents around the early 1700s. Her parents died when she was twelve, and she went to live with her brother, Jabez, who was wealthy and had servants who could help raise her. Jabez had inherited, through a grant from the King of England to the Jennettes, a tract of land deep in Buxton, the Trent Woods, on a high pine-covered knoll. The land included many acres of thick forest for about a mile on all sides. He began to build what was to be a stately mansion on top of the hill. The structure of the house originally was three stories with spires and lookout windows on the top floor as the height overlooked both sound and sea. He needed to survey the property and keep watch over shipping in the area. Jabez was a buyer of pirate booty. He bought what they had and resold it, sometimes to governors from whose people it was taken, also making himself quite a profit.

He and Rhetta did not socialize with the extended Jennette family, even though it was large and welcoming, nor did they cultivate friends. They were alone in that ever-growing house with all of their acquired wealth and the secrets they were bound to keep.

The mansion, not built in the style of the typical island house, rested on a stone foundation, provided by the quarries near what is now Mount

Airy, North Carolina. The stone was floated from the Yadkin River to the PeeDee River and down to Charleston Harbor, South Carolina. From there, it was destined for the Caribbean Islands, but pirates captured it on the way. In addition to the quarry stone, the ship carried expensive furniture, silver services, and other trappings for a fine house. It was intended for one of the rich government mansions of the Caribbean.

The stone was a cumbersome bounty for pirates to unload, but they wanted the riches of the cargo as well as the ship that carried it. Jabez agreed to buy their stone for a minimal price. The pirates were more than glad to unload it, and after several days the supply of stone was moved to the wooded area where the house would stand. First, Jabez built a small two-room bungalow where he and his younger sister would live while the estate was being built. The project would take many years to complete, but the materials used were of the finest woods, brick, and stones available at the time. Nothing on the island was quite like this. It was as elaborate as the elegant mansions in Charleston. From the East, the ship carried woods of mahogany, bamboo, expensive rosewood, and cherry, and from the mountains, cedar, juniper, and maple. Since none of the woods were suitable for ships, it needed to be sold, and Jabez was buying.

The deliveries from the pirates of materials unavailable on the island were large and frequent. Most took place at night and required borrowing horses and wagons from merchants in the village. All of the locals knew what Jabez did. At times they were recipients of his bounty in thanks for their willingness both to help and keep their mouths shut. The islanders were not at war with the pirates of the time, who were mostly generous to the inhabitants.

Rhetta was boarded at the finest schools on the mainland, only coming home for vacations, until she met and married a gentleman from Richmond, Virginia, and had a child, Sabra. The marriage lasted until the gentleman became embroiled in a political scandal that caused him to be caught up in fighting a duel. He was shot and killed, even though his friends as well as his enemies looked on him as a man of honor.

In that day duels were a common way to settle disputes. As a result, Rhetta and Sabra were left to their own devices in a strange town and state. When they came back home to live with her brother, Jabez was delighted. He found no pleasure in his wealth without anyone to share it with him.

The death of her husband resulted in Rhetta being shocked into her psychic mind, causing her to spend most of her time with the child in seclusion on the property. Rhetta and little Sabra both seemed to be gifted with the legacy passed on by Weroansqua, and it appeared to Jabez that they could communicate with each other mentally. Their glances said volumes, and their ability to understand the animals that roamed the property was a constant marvel to him.

Rhetta could sense danger before it happened, which was invaluable to Jabez in his clandestine activities. On many nights Rhetta slept outside in a secluded part of the estate frequented by the wolves when they birthed their cubs. First Jabez worried, but after a while he accepted that his sister was different. He also recognized strangeness in the child. He came to appreciate the warnings that Rhetta provided to keep his business safe. His was a dangerous occupation. He dealt with unscrupulous men on both sides of a deal: those who sold and those who bought. Because of Rhetta, the rumors of the house being haunted began. Those who did see her said she was always accompanied by a wolf. The gossip kept people away. Sometimes late at night, the sounds of dark and mysterious music echoed through the woods to the village beyond. What they were hearing were the strains of either the grand piano or the pipe organ Jabez had also acquired, as Rhetta played late into the evening. The haunting sounds strangely continued even after Rhetta died.

Jabez could see from the top lookout when ships were ready to empty out. They signaled him from sea, and he hitched up his team and went down to the inlet in the darkness with only a sliver of a moon to guide him. Landings were always planned for the time when the moon was

in its waxing crescent—the beginning or first quarter—or waning crescent—the ending or last quarter—as this was when the night was the
darkest. After the booty was unloaded and the pirates were paid, they
quickly went their separate ways.

The pirates went to the nearest tavern, usually on Castle Rock—
sometimes called Shell Castle for its foundation—located in the inlet
between Portsmouth and Ocracoke Islands, as it was easy to get to and
easy to get away from. Jabez went to the mansion where he and Rhetta
organized the treasure. First they chose what they wanted to keep, and
then they decided on what to sell. Jabez knew his customers and was
aware of what they would buy. After determining what to keep, he sailed
off to the mainland with the rest. Always he came back with something
for Rhetta and Sabra, like the grand piano; dresses and dolls for the
child; and once, a huge pipe organ, and with it, enough men to assemble
the instrument. Once the task was finished, the men left, probably on a
ship from the many involved in trade from the island, stopping only long
enough in port for a transfer.

There was a lot of shipping going through to the mainland between
Ocracoke and Portsmouth Islands. Ocracoke at the time was connected
to Hatteras Island by a small sand bridge. Portsmouth Island was a busy
port, functioning as a lightering port—one where freight from ocean-
going vessels could be transferred to smaller, lighter vessels that drew a
more shallow draft, resulting in moving cargo more efficiently through
the many shoals present in the inland waters. Thus goods were delivered
to the cities of North Carolina.

One of the most unusual stopping points in the area for transferring
cargo was the Shell Castle, a man-made island comprising rock, sand,
and oyster shells, built so high and wide that it supported a small trading
post and a lighthouse. This was one of the largest shell middens known
on the East Coast and was the result of the collection of materials for
thousands of years. As hard debris washed in and out of the inlet, it

amassed and accumulated on itself, become a hazard. Once the midden reached a certain size, men began to build it into the substantial rock it had become.

The lighthouse was fifty-five feet high, looking like an obelisk and shingled all the way to the top. Also located on this large expanse of oyster rock island was a wharf, long warehouse, grist mill, lumberyard, general store, ship's chandlery, and a tavern. Shell Castle was also a transfer post for ships drawing too much water to get through the shallow and shoal-ridden Pamlico Sound. Vessels docked here, unloading cargo to smaller and lighter barges and boats that carried the freight to the inland cities of Bath and New Bern, North Carolina. These were the earliest ports of entry from the sea to the North Carolina interior.

Portsmouth Island Inlet did not lose its importance as a shipping port until just before the Civil War, when in 1846 a hurricane opened a new, larger body of water between Hatteras and Ocracoke Islands, partially filling the channel between Ocracoke and Portsmouth Islands. The inlet became impassable to any vessel carrying freight.

Those living on the narrow strip of land between Hatteras and Ocracoke escaped in time to see the ocean wash over their homes and send them to the middle of the Pamlico Sound. This closing of the channel at Portsmouth Island made it necessary to reroute ships carrying freight south to Charleston, South Carolina, which then became the major East Coast port, especially before and during the Civil War, when the export of cotton to Europe was a necessity to fund the war for the South. The coast of Charleston, with its rivers and inlets, allowed the South to run the blockade set up by the North to keep the South from trading. Blockade running became a talent, a sport, and a necessity.

Jabez's grand house was a masterpiece of intrigue. It was said to have such thick walls that stairways were built between them, with hidden rooms located behind false walls. It was built partially over Old Buxton, and he had an escape tunnel built far under the house that connected to a stream running through the caves to a grotto. He was quite aware that the same governments that wanted to destroy the pirates would eventually come after him for aiding them. He did not stop building on the house until the day he died, as it became his life goal to build the island's strongest house, which he did. He was also energized by his sister and her precocious child.

Probably the most famous of the recipients of the unconventional *knowing* was Sabra Jennette Austin, Rhetta's daughter. Being raised by one with psychic powers, who was the first gifted of the females to exhibit the talents since Weroansqua, her demeanor was a strange thing to Jabez, who was gaining in years and possessed no knowledge of such things. Rhetta noticed the legacy in the child at an early age, and unknown to Jabez she used her time with the youngster to educate her in the secret ways. Rhetta was pleased with the progress made as they practiced the arts of the mind. Sabra was schooled in the dark arts, but even with instruction her knowledge did not exceed that of her mother. Rhetta lived the mysterious. Sabra only dabbled in it.

When Sabra was seven years old she acquired a wolf pup. Rhetta tried in vain to hide the animal from Jabez, but the child and her companion were inseparable. She named the pup Luna, because the little thing was always howling at the moon, and she taught him to always hide at the approach of others. Besides Sabra, only Rhetta and the pup's mother were allowed to be in the cuddly young wolf's company.

Once Jabez realized the strong pull that nature had on the child, he and Rhetta felt it necessary for Sabra to attend school with other children. Even though they knew the risks, they both wanted a normal life for her. Jabez took her to school in the village to a one-room schoolhouse that went through eighth grade. When Sabra was old enough she rode her Palomino horse to school and back. So the little redheaded girl rode out of the woods every morning and back into the woods every afternoon. Her life became the horse, the wolf, and books, and she appeared to be quite content. Meanwhile her lessons into the psychic world continued with her mother.

Once her schooling on the island stopped at the lower grades, Rhetta sent her to continue her education on the mainland at an exclusive girls' finishing school. Here she lived in a dormitory with other well-to-do young ladies, learning how to be a lady herself. On her trips back and forth from the docks of Hatteras Village, usually for holidays, she met and befriended the son of a prominent shipping family that did business with her father. When she completed her education at the boarding school she and Jimmy Austin were married. Sabra was only eighteen, and Jimmy was twenty-four.

Their life was happy and normal, unlike her childhood. Sabra was content to stay away from all the drama. Her childhood, she learned, had not been very conventional. Living with other young ladies her age and hearing of their experiences, she was aware of her uniqueness. Eventually she and Jimmy had two children—twin boys. They were delighted to be together and raise a family. Jimmy worked in the shipping business with his father, and Sabra saw her mother whenever possible. The boys were fascinated to play in and around the huge old mansion. Here they had horses to ride, trails to follow, and many rooms in which to hide.

One afternoon Sabra and Jimmy were coming back from a horseback ride on the beach. As they returned through the short brush and reeds leading to the village from Hatteras Inlet, Jimmy's horse was spooked by a cottonmouth moccasin uncurling from the tall grass near the marsh beside the dirt track road and beginning to cross to the other side. The horse reared and threw Jimmy to the ground. Jimmy's head hit the side of the angled dune pushed up from the track, and he broke his neck and died. Sabra was devastated. She lived in the village for two more years, even moving in with Jimmy's family and working at the shipping business office, but she longed for the comfort of the mother, who was now alone taking care of her elderly brother. It was time for Sabra to return to the mansion in the woods. She packed up the children, kissed her in-laws, and returned to the house in the forest.

Within several months, her father-in-law convinced her to continue with the business, as she was needed, and Sabra, also wanting to have something to occupy her time, went to work, taking over where Jimmy had left off. Soon her sharp natural aptitude and the inner knowledge she possessed led her to devise a scheme that eventually made both her and the Austins wealthy.

Sabra was aware of other people's thoughts, and in business, anticipation is always valuable. She lived around the time when the country was going through the Revolutionary War, with English ships positioned up and down the coast. These enemy ships sat at anchor in anticipation of unrest on the mainland. The patriots of the thirteen colonies were dumping precious imported tea overboard in harbors all down the coast to protest the English over taxation of it and other products. Sabra was an island girl who grew up on the tasty Yaupon tea grown in the areas of Buxton and Kinnakeet. This leaf of the Yaupon bush was high in caffeine like coffee and later came to be known as loaded with antioxidants, making it quite healthy.

Within months, Sabra built a factory to cure and package the vast Yaupon crop on the island, and she began, through her husband's family, to ship the tea to ports for inland distribution. This tea became a badge of resistance for many, and Sabra's business flourished. On the hill she could survey her property and keep watch over her ships as well as those of the English. Living back at her uncle's house she began to help her uncle in expanding the mansion, made repairs to the main structure, added outbuildings to the grounds for horses and other livestock, and reinforced the security of the surrounding areas leading to the estate.

When Jabez died, Rhetta spent more and more time in her rooms as a recluse, using only her mind for communication. Sabra was on her own in dealing with the threat of the British finding out what she was doing and protecting her aging mother. She especially shored up the underground part, as the Revolutionary War, though not immediately concerned with the island, was a worry that everyone felt. Because the English ships could not navigate the sound to get inland to major cities, they basically left the islanders to their own life.

The caves were where Sabra could hide should the English discover her clandestine business and attempt to capture her or her family. Even the boys, who were in military academy on the mainland, knew of the secret passage. They did not worry about their mother. They'd bet against anyone who came after her, and they felt secure when they were home.

Her venture continued to flourish, offering her something to occupy her time after her mother's death. Having never remarried, Sabra and her children lived alone in the woods until her own death. At that point the boys stayed on the property, continuing in the shipping business. Because of the early death of their father, and the life growing up with the Jennettes, the boys were considered the Jennette brothers, rather than Austins, whose business was shipping. The house continued to be occupied by the family until after the Civil War, when it passed to Odessa's father, who bequeathed it to her.

The house was vacant when Odessa began her life with Charlie, and they decided that, rather than live there, they would act as caretakers until they needed it. Because of its grand appearance and the pack of wolves that lived there, the mansion had a reputation as a haunted house. When she married Charlie, he made sure it was kept in relatively fair condition. Odessa loved to visit it. Most people had no interest in it, as there seemed to be wolves in that area. Sabra passed on her legacy through her boys, who also continued to pass on the gifts. And as expected, the powers lay dormant, to be rebuilt later and exhibited further down the bloodline.

Some said that Rhetta was the ghost of Frisco Woods, but most knew different—or at least it was whispered as such behind Ellie's back. They called Ellie's mom, Annie, the real ghost of Frisco Woods. They said that she died and didn't want to leave behind a child, so she kept coming back. The island's children heard these stories, and Ellie was bullied about this all her life. It didn't seem to ever go away. They said that travelers on the road from Frisco (Trent) to Buxton encountered a beautiful young woman in a flowing white cape, standing on the side of the road, beckoning the vehicle or wagon to stop and pick her up. Each time, when someone stopped and offered a ride, she appeared even more beautiful than one had noticed before, as she stood shivering in the translucent hooded cape. Somebody always gave her a coat. She seemed pleasant, wanting to go to the lighthouse road and always got off there. On closer examination, the borrowed coat was always left on the side of the road.

The story's details were always identical, regardless of the teller. Some people say that the dead who remain behind as ghosts are trying to finish something, that they were not on "this side" to commit evil. Usually they needed to complete some mission before they "crossed over."

Many stories persisted about the Jennette women—nothing grand and some not even unusual—but legend has a way of growing, and the reputation of a few of the women fueled the myth. As it turned out, the stories had some truth. These women seemed more than most to have a certain *knowing.* But they were a quiet lot—not as prominent in business as Sabra had been, equally as psychic as Rhetta, and always as intuitive as Weroansqua. Something was to be said about the women of Jennette blood.

Weroansqua had set up Ellie to receive special mental powers, which she had inherited from a previous past-life connection. Because Ellie was so young, Powwaw wanted to give her confidence. While Powwaw had been quite impressed with Luke's keen mind, and he was the perfect carrier for the legacy, the bequest only manifested itself in the females of the Jennette line. The male was only a vessel for passing on the sacred blood to the female of his lineage.

Powwaw and his old friend Mingan, the carver, also had cell memory, and they possessed some of the same teachings and mental prowess as Weroansqua. She had secured a place in her lineage for the secrets to pass. They decided that they wanted to protect Ellie by passing on a protective shield in the form of her male cousins, Luke and Blake. Both also, through their mother, were of the Jennette clan. The three shamans—Weroansqua, Powwaw, and Mingan—implored the spirits of the smoking fire and glowing crystals to give extra perception to Luke and Blake. It was decided that when in Ellie's presence, the boys' power magnified. Alone, they were simply talented, but together they could accomplish most anything.

The spirits who accompanied the children through life were also chosen. They knew their charges were exceptional, and their job was to guide them for the greater good. Ellie's spirit was Travis, a strong power. Luke's Spirit, Micah, was the most experienced, and Blake's spirit, Brendan, was an often revered Irish saint who proved to be as mischievous as his charge. He suited Blake's personality.

The wolves came to the island along with its first inhabitants. They held a strong place in the psychic civilization from which they came. They were the protectors. They were the key to the pull of the full moon. Hearing the wolves howl at the moon gave comfort and a sense of well-being to those who heard. The spirit wolf was a creature of great wisdom. Luke's wolf, Rafe, whose name meant "wise," was just such an animal. Even though he was beta to Twylah, Ellie's alpha wolf, Twylah always consulted Rafe for decisions. Twylah respected him, as he was the brother wolf to St. Francis of Assisi, the patron saint of animals. Legend told of St. Francis taming the wolf and presenting the animal to the townspeople as a protector. Theo, Blake's guardian wolf, was just like Blake, and had to be controlled by the other two wolves, in the same way as both Luke and Ellie attempted to direct Blake. But they both considered Theo a good companion to themselves and to their young sidekick. His view of the world was new, and sometimes new ways were needed. Also, Theo could run farther, faster, and longer than the others.

The wolf shadows were protectors, but they stayed in the background until needed. They had the ability to camouflage themselves with ease and blend into the landscape. On nights of the full moon, the wolves were particularly active and their howling more intense. Those nights, the children were allowed to sleep together in the same room so that the experience of the wolves' music would be spiritual rather than fearful. The whole family had lived with the wolfpack's close attention since the night of Ellie's birth. With all the other stories passed on by the Gray clan—of Indians, powers, English refugees, and pirates—the story of the white wolf licking baby Ellie was always told.

The Sea Creature

The chilled November winds were hitting up a breeze along the low dune in front of the lighthouse. Saturday beachcombing before breakfast was in full push. Luke's hair was blowing sideways, and Ellie's kerchief was flapping around as she tried to protect her face from the weather. Little Blake was leaning in against the wind. They were looking for signs of the new loggerhead hatchlings from this year's turtle crop. They had been marking the days since they saw the irregular groves in the wet sand leading to and from the area below the dune line where they suspected the turtle eggs had been deposited. It would be any day now. Sixty or so days. They marked it on the calendar.

The kids were there to flail away at any birds that thought they could swoop up a struggling hatchling on its journey to the ocean. Helping the babies actually get to the water was not a good practice. The fully formed tiny turtles were not supposed to be picked up, although they sure were cute enough. Pop said they needed the struggle to help them get ready to face the sea. It was hard to watch them making their way to safety, with all the gulls around screeching and screaming to each other about trying to catch one for breakfast. The children were unaware of the sets of green eyes watching them from the deep. The adult turtles were also concerned about the treacherous break for the sea, and it was not lost on them that, along with the waiting foe, they also had friends in this area.

Today was not the day, though. They were waiting for the first signs of the hatchlings, because when that happened, the contest was on. They would have to fight the ghost crabs who scurried about the beach at night, leaving their deep holes in the sand to feast on what the tide brought in. Also, there were the raccoons who seemed to have a taste for tender little turtle babies. With no signs of a conflict that would indicate one creature trying to gobble up another, the kids began to gather together special pear whelks—conchs—that had washed up whole on the beach. Picking one up, Ellie could hear the roar of the ocean. Luke thought he could hear a cry for help when he listened to his conch. The plea was so real to him that he strained his eyes toward the beach, to see if he could find someone or something in trouble. He looked and looked but did not see anything. He listened again—same thing. He knew it was a cry for help.

He kept the conch and would try again and come back. Maybe it was a cry from the sea, but the plea was in the conch itself. He could hear it every time he put the conch to his ear. He got Ellie to listen, then Blake. They only heard an ocean's roar, not a cry. They did not get to go back to the beach that day, as a threatening nor'easter came in howling and threw its mighty weight against the shore in a violent rage. The water surrounded the lighthouse, as well as the main and the assistant keeper's quarters. The kids stayed upstairs in the assistant keeper's quarters, watching the fury of the oncoming waves from the window facing the sea. As the wind howled, Nett was downstairs making chocolate chip cookies. The howl of the wind and the smell of the cookies made the children feel quite safe. No matter what was happening outside, there was always a cookie waiting inside.

The children slept heavily that night, the wind taking all of them on dreams of adventure set about the high seas. When they awoke, the storm had passed. As always, there was a still calm about the air.

Time for church, but this day all the talk was of damage from the wind and rain. Luke was most anxious to get back home to see what had washed up on the beach. The weather kept everyone away, and the beach stood deserted after the pummeling it took the night before.

He quickly ran upstairs and changed his clothes, with Blake two steps behind him. Both scampered down the stairs, taking them two at a time, letting out all that pent-up church energy. As they ran down the walkway, Ellie appeared on her steps to skip in front of them.

"Grandmom's cooking a big chocolate cake today, so don't forget," she said.

"Oh, we won't. Come on, we won't be long. Just wanted to check on stuff." Luke circled her and turned around to walk backward and beg her to join them. Blake was motioning over his head toward the beach. Ellie followed.

They all saw the dark lump of netting at the same time. It had rolled up on the beach out of the sea, collecting all manner of debris along the way. But something was curious. First, about half a dozen dolphins were close to shore in the newly calm waters, just clicking and whistling away as if to raise an alarm of a shark in the area. The dolphins were making the greatest chatter. The kids ran up to the mass, and Ellie held her hand over her mouth as they stared at what appeared to be an almost human face staring at them from the heavy trawler's net. The figure was gray and had very slick skin—not scales, but shiny. Maybe the wet was matting everything down. Its head was that of a man or something like it. He was either dead or asleep, because he was not moving around. He did have arms and hands, but his fingers were webbed. They gasped as they noticed that he did not have legs, but a fish's tail—a big one, kind of like the whale's tail they saw earlier. This creature had a wide mouth that was partially open to show short, sharp, pointed teeth.

Luke picked up a piece of driftwood and gently touched the side of the creature. It opened its eyes. They were glassy, like a fish's, and big and bulgy, but they were very sad. The creature said with his eyes that he was tired and dying, as he gasped for air. Ellie picked up a shell and began throwing water on the apparently dying mammal. Without thinking anything through, Luke reached down and grabbed the front of the net in his hand, winding a portion around his hand to get a good grip. He began dragging it toward the jetty. He received no argument from the other two, who moved up near him to help him pull the heavy net toward the water. Luke climbed up on the jetty while Blake and Ellie dragged the net to the edge of the wooden structure and handed the end to him. Again Luke got his grip right, but the net was so heavy that he had to sit down to get it. Meanwhile, Ellie climbed up behind him and grabbed a section to help pull. The two struggled to keep their charge from banging against the wooden pilings. It already showed cuts from the struggle.

Luke yelled for Blake to get back to the house and find a knife. Luke did not think he could free the creature unless he cut through some of the heavy rope that was restricting the strange body. The creature was beginning to make unfamiliar sounds as it continued to entangle itself further in the trap. The high-pitched sounds were in a different octave than a dolphin's, yet the sound appeared to excite the company of dolphin friends hanging around in the water near the jetty. They seemed to understand this sound, which was different from their own. The dolphins were waiting just beyond the breakers as they watched the children struggle to help their companion.

As he reached the house, Blake was careful to stay away from the adults while finding his grandpop's special fillet knife. He thought that telling them what was happening would cause them to kill the mammal from fear of what it looked like. This thing was trapped in a fisherman's net, and someone had to help it. Blake did not want to harm it, so he secured the knife, avoided any questions, and returned to the jetty where Luke and Ellie were struggling to pull the creature farther out to deep water. The dolphins were jumping and carrying on out in the ocean, making it even harder for the kids to communicate, even though they sat side by side. As they inched the netting farther and farther out to deeper water, Blake crawled up behind them and handed the knife to Ellie, who reached over and put it in Luke's hand. Luke began to cut away the part of the net he could reach without harming the injured naiad. The creature started to come alive. It did not look happy, opening its mouth and baring its sharp teeth. The children began to have second thoughts about trying to save it.

Maybe the squealing dolphins were saying, "Put it back," not, "Save it." The children hesitated for a moment but decided to continue to free the creature from the net. As they scooted down the jetty to deeper water on that narrow bridge, it was getting harder and harder to maintain balance, as the waves began to control the net. Luke started to pull the netting in one direction to unroll the sea creature from its trap. Meanwhile Blake was also inching his way down the narrow walkway made by the pilings to help Ellie, who was sitting and straddling the jetty trying to take up the excess net as Luke freed the creature. Luke cut, Ellie and Blake pulled away, and the creature—tired of the fight and weak from the unfamiliar conditions—flayed around so much that the tangling was getting worse. Finally it gave up. With this opportunity, Luke eventually cut the correct cord to let the naiad swim free.

At the same time the sea creature rolled free, Ellie heard a splash. At the sound, Ellie turned to see Blake head first in the ocean, going straight down. Ellie switched from her straddle position on the jetty and stretched to hold on to Luke, also looking down at Blake, knowing that this was not good. The sea creature being free while Blake was in the ocean caused the two older children to be anxious, and they began to focus on getting Blake away from the dangers of drowning and being eaten.

Luke reached out to help both Ellie and Blake. He held on to Ellie as she placed her body across the wooden fence and tried to stretch to grab hold of Blake. But Blake was gone. She could only see him at the bottom of the jetty, clawing frantically at the slippery boards that would not allow a proper foothold. In both their minds, they were afraid that the newly freed creature would find Blake and harm him. But it was already among the waiting dolphins, being led out to sea away from Blake. Luke thought about jumping in also, but then in a flash, a thought occurred. A second before he stood to jump over he yelled out, "Ellie! Send help!" and he poised himself to dive.

Luke could only think of those words, but they were enough. Ellie straightened up and closed her eyes, concentrating on sending a message to help Blake. She sent her thoughts to the dolphins: "Please help!"

As always she had learned to repeat, repeat, repeat, and think good thoughts. Holding hands, they both concentrated, not knowing on what. Just as Luke prepared to dive over, Blake's head appeared as his body was lifted up astride the back of a dolphin. The surprised look on his face told the other two he was all right. As he held tight, his arms wrapped around the dorsal fin, and his chest was up against the curved edge. The dolphin kept steady as he surfed in on a breaker close enough to shore for Blake to touch bottom.

Ellie blew a kiss at the dolphin pod, and she and Luke carefully made their way back to the beach on the slippery jetty. The dolphin watched them go, and while waiting for Ellie to find her way safely off the jetty, Luke turned once to see the sea creature lift almost waist up to wave at him in friendship. Luke finally took a minute to think about what had just happened. He had encountered a creature that he had only heard and had seen pictures of in old English maritime books that Grandpop had. But this creature was not even like those.

It did not have flowing hair, and maybe no hair at all. Maybe what he saw was a fur like hair, similar to a seal's. It did have long, bony arms free from its body—like a human's, not at all flipperlike—and with hands that attached to a translucent type of webbed fingers. Maybe claws, too? Something like that. The fur went down the raised spine to the waist, which was sort of like a shark's or a dolphin's skin. The head was round with an exposed bone sticking above the skull that had skin stretched over it, and maybe it had muscle on both sides. It looked like a vertebrate all the way down from the head down the neck to the back. There really was no neck, but a thickness like a dolphin's from nose to shoulder. The creature's sound was similar to a dolphin's but a much higher pitch. It did make a sound similar to the dolphins as they were panicking waiting for it to be freed. It was strange to think that the dolphin and the creature were friends. Inhabitants of the deep were like inhabitants on land. They existed together, and at times protected each other.

All these things were rushing through his mind as he was jolted back to the present.

"Luke, come on. The tide's coming in, and we have to go to dinner. Grandmom's blowing the conch!" Ellie was waving her arms, and Blake's back was all Luke could see as he ran toward the house, hoping to sneak up the unoccupied side of the assistant keeper's quarters and to his room for dry clothes. Luke turned around once more and looked one last time toward the water. The creature was still waving as he moved out into deep water, and the dolphins were jumping in tandem as they too headed out to sea. The children waved back. That was the second time they had communicated with sea creatures. Luke listened to his conch before dinner. No cries, only ocean sounds.

After eating as much chocolate cake as they were allowed, the children helped Grandmom clean the dishes while Nett and Uncle Bill discussed a serious change in things with Grandpop. The conversation was so serious that Grandmom told the children to go for a walk on the beach to see if they could find some unusual shell for her. This was an invitation for them to get lost—how wonderful. They were free to go adventure hunting. But they were so full of milk and cake, and so tired from their earlier escapade, that when they got to the beach they decided to stretch out on the soft, warm sand and take a nap. They were tired from their struggle. Another adventure could wait.

Yet the three saints had been waiting for this opportunity. They had watched twice as Ellie and the boys had used their special mind strength. Both times their efforts had connected to the mind of a sea creature—maybe three times if the mermanlike creature was counted. Travis, Micah, and Brendan, the saints, summoned a silver blue mist and directed it at the sleeping youngsters. The memory dust they ordered up settled over the children as they slept, while three billowy clouds dipped in silver threads floated above a mist that developed over the ocean. Within minutes, the mist and silver evaporated, settling in one long stretch of porous lacy clouds above. The three guardian saints waited and watched the sea foam begin to rise. *What a beautiful spray he was creating this afternoon*, they mused. A dream was in the making.

The three youngsters slowly became conscious of a very dark sky. The warm sun was gone. Was it night? Did they sleep through the afternoon? Ellie sat up and rubbed her eyes, careful not to get sand in them. Luke rose to his elbow, and Blake sluggishly opened his eyes. What Blake saw was the face of a giant, old, white-haired man looking down at him and dripping water from his beard into Blake's face. Blake reached up and shielded his eyes to see who this giant old man was. The looming figure straightened up and indeed did block out the sun. Luke leaned farther back on his arms to get the full view. Ellie lay back and cupped her head in her hands as a pillow and just stared. In front of them—half in and half out of the water—was Poseidon, the king of the sea. All the children knew exactly who he was. They had seen pictures and heard stories all their lives. And now he was looking at them. His crown was made of bone from walrus or seal tusks. He had seaweed all over him, hanging from his shoulders, the crook of his arm, and his trident, the huge, three-pronged spear he carried. The water splayed off of him from his crown to his waist. Across his chest was armor made from horseshoe crabs, and a spear sack full of reed was tipped with their spiked tails.

His trident was made from a whale's vertebrate with barbs of giant lobster leg casings slipped around the three prongs. He carried sharpened clam projectiles at his waist, his wrists sleeved in the thick skin of a whale. His blue-gray hair streamed past his shoulders onto his massive chest. He had a craggy face and huge bushy eyebrows that rivaled his long hair, mustache, and beard. His eyes were deep set and dark, but a glint of twinkle in his eyes gave the children a comfortable feeling that he would not harm them. He was standing beside a magnificent chariot pulled by six blue-winged horses, presently pawing at the waves in front of them and snorting foam from their noses. The chariot was an enormous clam with beautiful ruffled edges and a translucent pink pearl chair at the hinge.

Poseidon straightened up from leaning over the three surprised children. He had made sure they were not afraid as he sprinkled over them common jingles shell glitter.

"*You have saved my children more than once,*" he said in a booming voice. "*I have been made aware of you by those whom I protect. Come, I have things you need to see.*"

With that he threw up in the air three silver threads that were untied, but in the middle of each stretch of silver was a clear cylindrical crystal stone. Each child felt the silver thread land on either side of their neck, with the crystal hanging down and resting on their chest. Instantly, the thread wrapped itself into a knot, leaving the ends free again.

"*Do not take this stone off as long as you are in the ocean. This is how you will breathe. Keep it to your chest.*"

The children stood up and faced the old man, who had crawled back into his pearl chair on the chariot. He had on a silver cloth wrapped from his waist around his lower body and each leg, making both pants and leggings. He picked up a bow and a weathered bag sitting beside the throne and strapped it to his shoulder. In the bag was a quiver of arrows. The massive blue-winged horses were impatient at being held in place, but it looked as if they enjoyed the foam they kicked up as they pawed in place in the breakers.

The children reached for each other, as Blake was the first to step forward. He recognized then the dolphin who had given him a ride into the shore that morning. Blake felt like giving him a name. *Oh, how about James?* he thought, and on his own he accidentally connected with the first dolphin. He touched the carved ivory dolphin in his pocket and smiled.

The Neighborhood

oseidon set adrift three floating sargassum mats toward each of the trio. Blake climbed on, as did Luke and Ellie. Their respective carpets were made of the grass that dolphins like to play with, laced with tiny silver threads—similar or exactly like the ones that held their crystals. Blake's mat floated toward James, and as the dolphin hesitated in the water, the mat floated over his back, stopped, settled, and formed a saddle. The threads of the mat begin to create a harness under the dolphin's belly, attached to the already formed saddle on which Blake would sit. The threads from his necklace joined to sew a loose covering around him, like a skin of lace made of silver thread. It formed around his feet and ankles, giving him flippers, as it also created a hood complete with goggles, nose guard, and mouth guard. When the thread finished, Blake looked like a silverfish, holding on to the harness and rein that had been crafted with the saddle. All three were soon wrapped in suits of loosely woven silver netting. Luke touched his new suit. It was soft and did not feel wet. He looked over at Ellie and wondered how they would talk.

She thought back, "Just like this," and smiled.

Blake had the dolphin he recognized, and Poseidon indicated for Luke to take the second dolphin that surfaced. It proved to be faster than the others and full of tricks, as it flipped backward and landed with a splash in front of Luke.

When it was Ellie's turn to accept a ride, Poseidon gave her a wink, and out of the water—straight up and with a twirl—came the most beautiful dolphin Ellie had ever seen. It was not gray, not dark at all, but an albino with striking pink eyes. In her mind Ellie heard the master of the sea say that this was his most special girl, and he wanted this little maiden to have her. Ellie immediately named her Moira. Moira was talented, full of energy, and ready to communicate with Ellie. Moira was also quite capable of keeping up with the boys, as fast as she was agile. Their spirits matched, and Ellie could feel the heart of her new friend as she was molded to her saddle. They were a striking twosome: the little silver girl and her shiny white dolphin. The companionship they would eventually form would prove to be most helpful. Their minds met, and Ellie's power of speaking to the sea creature was matched by the connection the mammal made with her.

All three, safely atop their dolphins, began a journey across the sea, following the blue horses prancing across the swells of the ocean, kicking up foam, wings folded back, with their blue hair and tails standing out in the wind they created and the spray they threw. The dolphins followed with the children tightly grasping onto their backs as they dipped in and out, surveying the blue ocean.

"*Welcome to the neighborhood,*" Poseidon bellowed, and it truly was what lived just outside their yard.

It seemed like a long ride to the middle of the ocean before the great god of the sea dipped under the waves to survey the ocean floor. The dolphins followed, and the children were astonished at what they saw. As the dolphins twisted and turned toward the bottom of the greenish-blue underwater mountain, the colors became more alive—and the dolphins truly were alive also, as they swam by or swayed with the movement of the wave action miles down. Giant red, pink, and orange coral stretched and twisted its limbs outward, while tiny creatures hid behind the branches to escape the jaws of something larger than themselves. That's what this part of their neighborhood looked like, the children thought. When empty shells rolled up on the beach, now the three knew what had lived in them.

Poseidon stopped at a huge stone platform atop a wide stairway going thirty or so steps down to the dark below. This platform was the top of some other structure. It had thick, stumpy round columns around the edge. A huge throne sat in the middle of the stone, with giant pearls and gems surrounding a huge, deeply set crystal with a design crafted on the back of it. The throne had survived whatever quake had taken down this temple. Etched in the middle of the platform floor was an inlay of gold, depicting a sun with thin gold spikes radiating out from the center. Poseidon sat down on his throne, with his skin touching the crystal, splayed out his legs, and relaxed in a slump before his charges. He had one leg straightened out, arms stretched wide, and a restful look on his otherwise scowling face.

"*The dolphins will show you around and take you home. You need to know your neighbors in order to help them. They, in turn, will get to know you. This visit is at their request. You have been entrusted with higher powers and should experience how to use them. You are standing on the spot where they first originated. You are one of us.*"

With that, the dolphins whisked the children from the platform and began to play around with a giant octopus who sent out dark ink to enable him to get rid of them so that he could go back to sleep. The teams went about exploring caves and watching the flow of the colorful yellow, green, and red grasses that moved and swayed in the current created by the wanderers as they whooshed along. Schools of fish darted back and forth, scooping up specks floating in the water, and soon a larger fish would swim by and scoop up a meal of the smaller fish. It seemed to be okay for that to happen. One cave was off limits to the dolphins as it was home to an electric eel. It looked like a long navy-blue snake, big and fat, sort of striped, but with lightning sparks leaping from its body because it was so heavily charged with energy from the sea.

They passed one of the huge turtles—one with a tortoise shell so large that he made them all look small—who had also watched the kids try to save the young of his species. He hailed the dolphin to warn them that there were sharks ahead, and they appeared to be on the hunt for mischief. The other turtles were headed in the opposite direction. The dolphins and their riders turned. Sharks off Hatteras Island fed regularly two times a day, usually on the sandy shoals and reefs that dot the shoreline near the beaches. They ate around daybreak and around sunset. The dolphins were taking no chances. Even though it was mid-afternoon, they headed for deeper water and friendlier neighbors.

The dolphins went out where the Gulf Stream flowed past The Point. Here in the deepest of blue water, they met the blue marlin. He was magnificent, his grand beak glistening in the sun as he jumped and twirled in the air above the waves. When he rose to soar, he unfurled his colorful sail, and it caught the wind that sent him even higher. Soon, as if to really impress, the one blue was joined by a school, and as the sun hit their glistening backs they changed colors from deep navy blue to turquoise to yellow and green, in a perfectly executed arch. Not wanting to be outdone, soon the sailfish took to the air. A much more delicate fish, their sails were unfurled as they took off horizontally, skimming across the top of the water. Each wanted to make Poseidon proud. After all, he was clearly bragging about his children, showing them off to those who now fell under his protection. The barracuda slipped through the water, making a silver stream in a straight line, and the Portuguese man-of-war furled in their extremely long tentacles in order to display their richly colored crowns. With the man-of-wars' deadly sting, other sea creatures gave them a wide birth as they showed off their ribbons of death.

The children realized that the ocean held beautiful creatures as well as deadly inhabitants. As the dolphins surfaced for a gulp of air and a skim of the water, floating so close to the top, the children were startled when a stream of pelicans dove just beside them for the school of fish that came too close to the crest of the waves.

The ocean was crowded. Even the blue crabs were fighting over something that hit the floor of the reef. They would come at it in droves. Even though the piece was not large enough for all those crabs, they showed up anyway and proceeded to scuffle. Crabs seemed to be the greediest. The clams were the most solitary and unfriendly, closing whenever anything came their way. Most friendly were the baby octopi, which attached themselves to arms or legs and just sat there taking a ride. The mother octopus was always asleep.

Probably the most fascinating creature was the seahorse. It so proudly swam upright but never went very far. It proved to be a lazy fish, too slow to get anywhere, and it never wanted to let go when its tail wrapped around something. Its favorite was coral, sargassum, or just any kind of reed sticking up. The seahorse mated for life, brooding sorrowfully if it lost its mate, but when that happened, it would look and find another partner. Unusual about the seahorse was that the male carried the baby eggs and gave birth to fully formed seahorses by the thousands. They lived on sea trash. People said that Poseidon's chariot was drawn by seahorses, but that was not true as they were truly too small, too slow, and not very good swimmers—and they didn't seem to want to go anywhere.

One of the most grandiose of sea life was the giant ray. It glided through the water and cast a dark shadow wherever it went. It was so big, but it did not appear to have any enemies. Whenever it would saunter by, most creatures ducked or sought shelter. The dolphins did an abrupt turn and went the other way. Maybe they needed to protect the children who were riding them, or maybe the move was for their own safety. The children saw that the ray clearly had a quite a bit of power on his own.

When the ray passed, it looked like the roof of a house going by. Its disc shape was at least thirty feet across and had a life span of around twenty years, weighing close to 3,000 pounds. The ray had eighteen rows of teeth when seen from underneath. The huge, dark figure looked like night, riding overhead. The children could see that on the bottom side it had several white or light spots of varied shapes, sort of like a cluster of stars, making them most unique to each other. This was much like the distinctive markings of the right whale, which also had its individual characteristics, similar to the unique looks each human had to distinguish one from another.

For the giant ray, after the young pups were born—maybe when two to four feet in size—they were deposited near coastal waters to protect them from being food for sharks or other predators. This all made sense from what Grandpop had said to the children about "shuffling their feet" when they were walking in water where they could not clearly see the bottom. This was a warning that the small ray sat on the bottom near the sand and most times blended in. When someone accidentally stepped on it, the tail whipped up behind and was likely to strike the intruder in the leg, creating quite a poisonous sting. It was a protection device for the ray, but a devastating blow for the victim. Pop warned the children because that exact thing had happened to a man in the village. Not only did the poison affect his mind, but he walked with a very prominent limp for the rest of his life.

They found that riding their dolphins was fun, as these three appeared to be getting play time away from the rest of the pod. Maybe it was their version of getting out of school. It was especially fun when they all decided to jump at the same time. The suits made by Poseidon's thread were perfect replicas of what a fish would need. There was no worry about falling off. They learned to guide with their knees, motioning their rides to take them to unusual places.

At one point the children neglected to see the rock that had risen up in the ocean. The dolphins also appeared not to have noticed it either.

They did not realize how far south they had played, so they were surprised to see that they had caught up with the whales, but this was a leisurely bunch anyway. The dolphins, being part of the family of whales, were familiar with the huge creatures and always glad to be swimming with them. Blake recognized the spots on the top. He slowly realized he was one foot away from the whale who had passed the lighthouse not more than a week ago. The huge creature saluted the children with shots of water from the dual blowholes. They were happy that the dolphins reintroduced them.

Down the three dolphins went again—speeding past schools of fish, lace coral, and giant clams, through the forests of giant kelp stretching up high enough that the chartreuse color of the translucent leaves caught the shards of sunlight penetrating the surface of the water—and landed on their tips to make them look like gold as they were swaying and teeming with tiny sea life. The fast dives were the most exciting. This time they ended back at the platform where they had last seen Poseidon.

As the sea god leaned back against the giant crystal set in the back of the throne, he put on his undersea crown. Instead of the tusks that made him appear so menacing, this crown was made of sargassum roping, its green flowerlike leaves wound around colorful blue crystals. As he donned his crown, his body began its change from man to sea creature. Poseidon's legs morphed into the tail of a fish. As this was taking place, he picked up a huge horse conch, the largest of the family of snails living in the ocean and the most predatory. Horse conchs could be from two to twenty feet in length, and they feed on other conchs. This one was hollow, three feet in length, with several horny low nodules on its whorls. Poseidon was using this one for a trumpet. As he blew on one end of the huge conch, the sound vibrated and traveled underneath the water. Soon several of the sea creatures like the one Luke had saved swam into view and hovered, swimming upright, near their king. They were armed with bows and spears. There seemed to be a colony of them. Some were female, as their young swam silently just under the body of the adult, creating a shadow of the mother's body. Without a word and only the swish of a tail, the company of sea creatures, led by Poseidon, swam off in the direction of the shark sighting.

The old turtle floated by again and cautioned the dolphins not to follow. He indicated that the sea king and his legions were going to confront the sharks. The turtle appeared to be well respected among the underwater neighborhood. He had the greatest longevity. These turtles did not produce eggs until they were thirty years old. They could live past 100 years. Therefore, they knew everything about their domain. They were confidants to Poseidon, and he sought their counsel many times. They were watchers for him.

Poseidon was a strong ruler of the sea. He did not take well to some of his creatures bullying others. The sharks were expected to eat, but not to bully smaller fish. The militia caught up with the school of sharks, and it was not without some hesitation that the army of Poseidon faced the sharp-toothed opponents. The sea creatures reached around and took from their quiver a spear made with the tip of a horseshoe crab. As they were all armed, they moved toward the sharks with spears ahead, pointing at each shark's tender nose. One touch of the spear on that spot of the shark sent it reeling backward, causing it to turn tail and swim away, the shark's nose being the most sensitive part of its almost indestructible armor. Poseidon did not want to hurt any of his creatures, but he would not have them hurting each other without need. The waters cleared, and the dolphins, at Poseidon's insistence, took the kids on their final view of the neighborhood.

They were off to see the wrecks near Diamond Shoals. This trip was magical. They swam around sunken pirate ships and small sailing vessels, whatever was left of anything beaten apart by the wind and waves. As they went in and around, the dolphins headed down to the very depth in one strong, straight pitch dive, fast and deep, then leveled out to come straight back up. All six were playing, mammals and humans. As they made the U-turn at the bottom, they were amazed at the ocean floor—the mounds of beautiful rock, shiny stones, thickly bushed smaller trees, and the bottom feeder, the clam. He was accompanied by the conch, shrimps, scallops, and snails, plus all of the magnificent spiral and ornate shells with their homes on their backs. Their muscle inside looked like a slug, and they moved on their bellies along the surface by the gooey mass coming out of the beautiful house. Whatever caught on the bottom mouth of that fat mussel was their food. They also secreted a substance that colored and made the sturdy house they lived in. Their houses varied from type to type, each creating a different whorl.

Other fish and crabs fed on the conch or clam mussel when it came out to move or feed—and thus the beautiful shells of a sea creature were just as lovely in death as in life. Their empty shells washed up on the beach and became treasures to someone like Odessa Jennette. They also had a legacy of beauty to pass on.

The dolphins swam away from the shoals to show the children one more wreck. This did not look like a ship, and it was only partially made of wood. It was a huge structure made almost entirely of sturdy metal that encased all sides of the vessel. On the top deck was a round box without windows. There was an opening at one end, and inside, the children could see a huge cannon. Luke knew what it was. He had read a lot of books about the Civil War, and he recognized the iron-clad ship that was lost in a storm off Cape Hatteras. This was that ship. While they were swimming around and around the circular metal box, the dolphins suddenly bolted away, almost jerking the children from their saddles. *Shark!* No time to get another look. Poseidon's army was nowhere around, and they needed to get away.

The shark followed quickly, with the dolphins separating and going in different directions to get away from the monster. This was a great white shark about twenty feet in length. The children held tight to their mounts as they sped away, only glancing back in time to see the stretch of pink gums and huge teeth from an open mouth. The shark followed Luke and his dolphin. Luke leaned down almost flat against his ride as the two of them streaked across the wide ocean floor, looking for a place to hide. They presented a sleek projectile with both bodies connected and giving off no wake, and they soon were in the area where the coral and caves of the ocean allowed them some cover. As they streaked past one cave, the electric eel came to see what all the commotion was about. In his blind condition, the eel ran right into the oncoming shark. The shock of electricity was so great that the huge predator sank to the floor of the ocean, unconscious. Should he stay there long, he would drown, but Luke and his steed did not stay around to find out the beast's fate.

They had been down a long time and needed some air. So this time, they slowly ascended without being chased on the way up. Luke observed life along the rocks. Beautiful small snails and conchs attached their underneath mussels to the crags of a rocky wall. The conchs were born inside a gel that hardened. As it did, and they grew, they spiraled or whorled out, and the leftover formed a spiral or usual top. They were all sizes, and some could live for forty years. The giant scalloped clam was nestled between two rocky sides rising from the ocean floor. This one had bright blue on its great big lips, all wavy and scalloped. The inside looked like hair, fur, or fuzz. Also inside the middle was a fleshy part that stuck to both sides. At the center was an opening like a sucker mouth, but inside that was a huge pearl, just sitting there all blue and purple and pink, changing as the light hit it. Those big clam lips were like the giant clamshell Poseidon used as a throne. The one in the rock was blue on the lips and inside, and totally white on the outside. Poseidon's throne—the shell—was stark white. The shell on the inside was embedded with silver dust, and on outside was pearl dust. The seat appeared to be fur over sponge, but the fur was actually minute tentacles covering the inside of the clam, making it appear fuzzy. The arms were the curve of the clam.

Luke watched as the huge clams drifted down and away while Willi, as Luke had named his mount, thrust his muscular body upward.

They quickly found Blake riding James along with Ellie and Moira, her dolphin. In their minds, the children wished to go home. They had experienced enough excitement for one day.

The dolphins picked up the thought and swam toward shore. When the waves began to break on the beach, the dolphins surfed them in and let the three children dismount. As each touched a foot to the sandy bottom, the crystals around their necks fell away, the thread loosed them from their suits, and they awakened to the sun sinking behind them. Their clothes were dry, their hair was only damp, and they rubbed their eyes to get out the sleep that crusted on the lids. This adventure had come to a close, and what an exciting and educational adventure it had been.

Ellie was happy to see Luke. Her last thought was that Luke was gone, possibly eaten by a great white, but he was here, as was Blake. They all sat motionless and silent for a good long while.

"Did you see all those things that live out there?" Blake's innocent question brought the kids back to reality, and they began discussing the creatures they had met.

"There is a whole village in the ocean," said Luke, "and we met them all. I think they know us, too."

"Poseidon's crystals let us breathe, and him, too," said Ellie. "I wanted to keep mine, but maybe it wouldn't work if Poseidon were not around."

"Know something? Everything around us is alive. They look like they have as much fun as we do. But I wouldn't want to be running away from sharks all the time." Luke was thinking out loud, having been chased by a thing he had just learned to fear.

"I know I won't go swimming while they are eating. I know that!" He wanted to tell Grandpop about the ship at the bottom of the ocean, but there was no way to explain it. At this point, Luke—and maybe the other two— knew there were some things that they would not ever be able to express.

Luke began to think about Powwaw and how he knew the old shaman would understand. He wondered if he would ever see Powwaw again, or if he could talk to him in the future. Luke decided he would try, maybe just before going to sleep. Maybe Powwaw would visit him in a dream.

As the chill picked up in the air, the children realized how long they had been gone, so they stood up, brushed off the sand, and headed back home. This time there was no chatter. What they had experienced was just sinking in. Ellie's gifts were beginning to become comfortable. The gifts that Powwaw and Mingan had given to Luke and Blake were enhanced by Ellie's power, and all three were feeling the responsibility of such special knowledge.

They had been gone for a while, as indicated by the sun's position. They needed to get back for supper and homework. How could they ever concentrate?

Supper was quiet. The children thought that they were in trouble until Nett revealed the news that Bill had been called back to the navy, to be shipped overseas. This was what everybody was whispering about when the adults told the kids to go out and play. Nett explained that there was trouble in Europe, and the United States was building ships ready to help on the side of England. As a valued mechanic, Bill was to be reassigned his station.

When this happened, Nett and the two boys would move in with Grandpop and Grandmom. It had been decided that they would not try to follow their father. Chances were that he would not be at home for long. He would be shipping out soon. The boys cried and got up to hug their father, who was also crying, as was Nett. They decided that for the next ninety days they would spend as much time as they could with their father.

★ 5 ★

Portsmouth Island

The weather was getting colder. It was now the month of the full cold moon, which the Indians sometimes called the long nights' moon, and it was getting time for Christmas vacation. Since Bill had received his orders for shipping out, everyone was trying to make time count. Bill had some time off until March. Once in a while the service interviewed for a new keeper, but so far, one had not been hired. Bill was given the opportunity to settle his affairs on the island, the time for orientation on his new deployment, and the chance to find new living quarters. Of course, the navy would pay all expenses to settle Jeanette and the boys in town if they so desired. Normally, as service members, they would just stay where they were until the sailor came home. But Bill's situation was different. He was the assistant keeper of the lighthouse, and lived in the assistant keeper's quarters. As such, he no longer could occupy that particular lodge. But Nett and her pop wanted to keep the family together. If war was coming, the children would be better off together, as would Grandmom and Nett. They decided to move into the main keeper's quarters. It wasn't a big move, but it was a move nonetheless. It took away from the sadness that once in a while washed over one or the other of them, and their faces flushed at the thought of what was really happening. But it hit them only one at a time, and they were able to fight the sorrow with some new challenge as they moved.

On one particular morning their dad was organizing the Coast Guard boys to get the gym ready for action. With everything in a mess, this now was considered only a small eyesore.

Nett was next door, fiddling around in the new quarters upstairs at the main lodge, and Grandmom was measuring Ellie for some Christmas dresses. Luke and Blake thought, *Poor Ellie, but better her than us.* Luke and Blake decided to act on a plan they had been hatching for quite some time. They were going back to Jennette's sedge, where they had buried their Indian gear. Luke's bow and arrow, was most important. Blake had his flint, his knife, and his hatchet. Ellie had jewelry and girl stuff—mostly for her hair, and those boots. They had to get back those boots! Around back of the lighthouse they went and south along the beach until they were far enough along to start looking for landmarks.

They picked their way along the sea oats on the dune line, keeping an eye west to the stand of trees that began to appear at what was the beginning of Jennette's sedge. They got close enough from the top of the dune to spy what might be the marker of branches they had laid over "the grave." Slipping on their butts and heels, they scurried down the steep sand hill until they landed near the scrub oak. They began to push aside the pile they encountered just far enough in to determine that they were in the right place. They found it! All of it! It was a little damp, or maybe just cold, but it was all there. Now, they wondered how to get it to the barn without someone asking questions. They were going to need Grandmom for this one. But both boys were so excited that they took off their shoes and splashed in the cold December water all the way home.

Hiding the newest treasure was easy. There was nobody around. Grandmom and some other lady were pulling and poking at Ellie. Mom was still upstairs. Some of the Coast Guard boys were moving furniture around in the new apartment and bringing in other pieces. These guys were Bill's fighters, at this point doing his bidding. Bill had a method in his madness. Luke and Blake eased around back to the barn where they were all by themselves. The only person they couldn't account for was Grandpop. Being crafty, they temporarily hid the Indian treasure and set out to find him.

Grandpop was at the top of the tower, polishing the lens and singing church songs. There was so much to do on that structure. Besides all the brass that needed to be polished, the kerosene needed to be fed into the mantle lamps, the wicks trimmed for the evening, and the fragile chimney glass needed to be cleaned, as did the many prisms that formed the beehive-shaped lens. The light had to be projected just so for a ship to pick it up, and thousands of lives depended on Grandpop keeping those glass prisms sharp. The boys said hello and offered to help. This time Pop said, "No." He knew it was the beginning of vacation, and they surely would like some time away from all the work going on. Why did they think he was up there cleaning imaginary prints from the Fresnel lens? Grandpop was also pretty crafty.

Back at the barn the boys found the perfect place to pack away their treasures. They laid out the buckskin and smoothed it out to get rid of any creases that had formed when it was hastily stashed. They made piles for each person. All Ellie's stuff was together. Blake had the most. His pants must have been falling off the whole time with so much in his pockets and strapped to his body. He did not leave anything. Blake had the biggest grin when he pulled free the tiny deerskin patch that held his flints. Strange what makes people happy. Ellie was going to love those boots. Luke was on top of the world that his bow was not harmed. He felt like he could repeat how to make an arrow, but Manteo had made the bow just for him. It was fine. Even the long feathers at the top were bright and full. He turned an arrow over and over in his hand to see if he could make them all by himself. Luke remembered all that Manteo had taught him. Manteo even combed the area with him to get the correct feathers that would guide the missile. Luke could do this.

That night at the supper table, there was much to talk about. Of course, it started with Bill going away, but quickly went to the spectacle that was building up at the docks between Buxton and Frisco. Supply boats were crowding into the sound in anticipation of bad weather and wanting to unload everything by the holidays. The boats were filled with the anticipated needs for the winter, the list ordered by the local residents. Grandpop was going to have to hitch up Old Tony and Big Roy to pull the wagon for hauling large amounts of freight for the lighthouse, Coast Guard station, and the community.

The holidays were a busy time on the island. It was like a colony of animals storing up for the winter, but instead it was the natives who were preparing to hibernate during the cold months. Immediately all three children sat up straight and stiff with chests out, as if to say, "Ready for duty, Cap'n." They did everything but salute. They wanted to ride down to the docks and watch the unloading. They also wanted to help make all of the deliveries. Truth be known, Grandmom and Nett wanted them to do just that. Much remained to be done at home—not a time to be bothered with a trio of bored children. But if these three were ever bored, it would be news to Grandmom! She went along with the plan, though, seeing on their little soldier faces that this was a big deal.

The wagon pulled around. Grandpop and Bill motioned for the kids to board, and up they went to stand behind the bench and be in on all the day's business. They were going to the "backyard" of the lighthouse, to the canal, down to the Pamlico Sound. Out in the sound were vessels moored to stakes or their own anchors. Ships from the Merchant Marines, for the Coast Guard and navy stores, freighters hauling commercial orders, and side-paddle lighthouse tenders were delivering whatever goods had been ordered through them. The lighthouse tender was waiting for Grandpop, and lots of small "lighter" boats were about, anxious to help haul the cargo to shore and get paid for doing it. Everything came from boats. Uncle Baxter was there with the *Odessa W* and his boys Lindy and Cantwell Jr. He and Captain Charlie had a lot to do. They also joined up with the Coast Guard to lighten the load, allowing the freighters to leave in just hours.

Everything on the island was supplied by these tenders, which ferried goods from the merchants to the villages. They supplied the groceries, building supplies, coal for heating, and all the amenities that people might want. They even brought the church a new piano when the keys just gave out on the old one. But new sounds would be welcomed for this Christmas. What an exciting day! Along with the loaded wagons were pieces of paper saying where the crate or bundle was supposed to go. Everybody tried to organize the deliveries by area, but sometimes that plan went awry. Captain Charlie kept a Kinnakeet crate for two days before he had the time to go back and deliver it.

While the other men were working, Grandpop and Uncle Baxter worked up a trip across the sound to Morehead City, on the other side of the sound and down some. They needed to go fetch Uncle Jack from East Carolina Teachers' College, and it was quicker to go the back way by the water. Jack was scheduled to go to the coast of Morehead City, where lots of fishing boats came and went. Grandpop, Uncle Baxter, and his group, who fished out of there all the time, offered to pick him up and bring him home. When Luke spread that word to the others, they both gasped. That would be the best trip. They had never been that far in a boat. How in the world could they convince Grandpop to take them? For the rest of the day they were simply angels—helpful, quiet, and obedient. This was their biggest challenge yet, except convincing Mom and Grandmom that they wouldn't be in the men's way. They had to be more than just good. They had to be a help!

The next morning Grandpop was greeted at the bottom of the tower by three very eager helpers. With rags in hand they were there to polish the lens like never before, and this, they were hoping, would give them a chance to talk Grandpop into letting them go to Morehead City. A "city"!—they just had to go. They started in about fifteen minutes after getting their assignment. But Grandpop was ready. He had no intention of being badgered all day, or "mommicked" as most islanders said, by begging kids, and he knew what was up. He'd already talked with Grandmom and Bill. Lindy was in favor of the plan when Grandpop ran it by him before they parted the day before at the docks. It was pretty much a go from the start. Talk about a clean lens? Grandpop only had to put his old boots on at the top of the rail and stare out at the ocean all day. What a beautiful day. He didn't get to enjoy them all like this. What a lucky man. Now he knew why Jack and Lindy wanted them around. They really were no bother. As a matter of fact, they were a help. He thought, *This could get to be a regular thing.*

Baxter's boat was loaded off Ocracoke Inlet around breakfast time. The kids had been up for hours already. All the men were awake on lots of coffee, but it was still early. When the children crawled aboard the *Odessa W* they immediately went below to get some sleep. The men just laughed, pretty much glad to get them from underfoot. It was a calm morning, with pretty yellow-orange streaks coming up through the blue, where the sun was thinking of busting through. The water looked like oil had been poured on top, the colors of the sky just sitting on it like a mirror, picking up the dancing hues as the soft waves slapped the side of the boat. After all the supplies were loaded, Uncle Baxter revved up the engine and off they all went. The roar of the motor put the children immediately into a deep sleep. They slept all the way to Morehead City. Whatever boat ride they had anticipated, they slept through. Maybe they would see things on the way back. They were rested and ready to go when the boat docked.

Uncle Jack was waiting on the dock grinning, so glad to be coming home. He threw his duffle bag at Lindy and hopped aboard.

"Okay," he said. "Let's get 'er headed north and give 'er an eastern hitch." He was so ready to go home. "Oh, just a minute," he called, and he grabbed a big white bag of something and tossed that at Lindy also—this time gently, more like a swinging motion.

Lindy gingerly caught it and opened it up, and stuck his nose in it.

"Ahhhhhhh," he said. "Shrimp and hushpuppies! Just for *me?*" He laughed, as there was enough there to fill the huge bag.

"No way. For all of us. I figured you would want to stop for lunch, so I thought we would get home faster if I had it waiting. That way we could go home now!" Jack was not even trying to hide his eagerness to get under way.

"Okay, boys. Hop up there and fill up these tanks. Lindy, go pay the man. Jack, run over there and get another bag just like this. These men are hungry. Take the kids. They can help, and they probably need to go to the bathroom." Pop was doling out orders like he wanted to get back, too. Seems he saw something brewing in the clouds. So did Uncle Baxter.

The kids didn't realize there was any problem for a while. They were too busy going—here, there, anywhere anyone would let them, and stuffing shrimp and hushpuppies in their mouths all the while. They had never had shrimp, and these hushpuppies, from the dock restaurant, were the best they had ever had.

By the time everything was primed and ready for the trip back, it was early afternoon. The men were fresh, and all was stowed away. Pop had warned of a little squall coming up over the horizon to the east. Could be a small nor'easter, he said, so the boat got ready even for that. The kids were hanging over the side watching what went by. They were up front hanging onto the rails going up the bow, so they were safe from the spray beginning to kick up ahead of them. They saw two gigantic turtles and some floating grass with some fish under it, but that was about all. They were beginning to get a little wet from the spray, as the boat had encountered a large chop in the water heading toward them. It was actually more of a wave than a chop. The waters of the sound were beginning to form whitecaps. Lindy and Jack had moved from the stern where they were riding the boat, their arms crossed and their knees surfing the bottom of the swells that were lifting the boat and dropping it down. They decided to move forward on the deck because they were getting awfully wet.

"Okay, young-uns. Time to get inside. Looks like this thing is coming this way. From those clouds up ahead, looks like we're in for a blow. Luke, put everybody's life jacket on, and toss a couple out here," Jack said while looking up at the cabin tower to see how his dad and uncle were doing. Standing straight was getting more difficult, as there was a terrific pitch in the boat now. Out came the two life preservers. "Two more!" yelled back Jack. In a few minutes, out they came. Jack climbed the ladder to hand the two jackets to the men at the helm.

"She's a-comin' up! Settin' in now! Tighten down everything, and keep them children under the hatch! Hold on, she's getting bad, and it's gettin' dark heading into 'er!" Uncle Baxter was spitting out the information, and Charlie was white-knuckled holding on to the control box, taking each roll with his knees, trying to help Baxter see what was ahead. It was coming at them hard now. The rain was so heavy that judging anything was impossible. The sheets were washing down the cabin windows, but the wind was pushing the pellets into the glass and making it look like they were going through a waterfall.

"Charlie! Can't keep this up. Gonna burn the motor out or sink 'er, one!" yelled Baxter. By that time everyone was soaked, and water was beginning to collect in the cabin underneath.

"I think we're pert near Portsmouth, southern end," yelled Charlie. "Lots of marsh there before you get to any shelter, but you won't drown in it. It's so thick you can probably walk on top of it," he said. "Try to pull 'er to the right to catch that shoal off Portsmouth. We can anchor 'er there and come back to get 'er in the morning, but we can't do much now!"

Baxter began to edge the boat to the right, trying not to turn it into the wind and get flipped by one of those waves that had kicked up. He had to keep the bow heading into the gusts, as even a slight turn might catch just the wrong blast and dump them all in the water. Everybody was ready to go overboard just in case. The children were anxious but excited. They were quiet and listened. They had experience with danger in the swamps of Roanoke Island, so they were trying to also be prepared here. They always felt safe. Something took fear away from them. Everything was a lesson to be learned, and they were willing to study—and they had been wet before.

Finally, after another half hour or so of battling the raging whitecaps and the wind driving them back, they felt a sudden pull at the bottom of the boat. They were running aground! Cantwell Jr. was the tallest and jumped over first. Up to his waist on the deep side he began pushing the stern toward the reeds and the sandy bottom leading into them. Jack and Lindy went overboard on the front, chest-high and leaning all their weight against the front to ground it in the marshy shore. The wind was helping in this effort but beating mercy out of the boys. At last they had the anchor buried as well as possible in the weeds and sand to hold it firm. But where were they? They needed to find shelter and get out of this squall.

The soaked group crawled down from the boat and began to struggle toward dryer ground. It had to be around there somewhere. The sand that they had to go through was very soft mud, and it was hard to keep their boots from being sucked right off their feet. Blake walked out of his shoe twice, and it must have been so uncomfortable, as Ellie also found out. The sludge was between the weeds. It got so sticky that the only way to travel over it was to step up high to trap the grass underneath and to keep the shoes in place. All they had to do was go to the northeast. At last they hit the hard stuff, and at least they could unstick their feet from the sludge, hoping the continuous rain would wash the mud off. Walking while carrying around a cement shoe of mud was difficult. But the troop kept going until they saw a two-track road. Then they spotted the first house—without lights, but shelter nonetheless—and a second house with lights on. That was com-forting. Everybody went to the first house, and Charlie went to alert the folks at the second house that people were stranded nearby.

Near as Baxter and Charlie could figure from where they ended up, they had landed just north of Sheep's Island and had found Straight Road. It was called Straight Road because it was just that—running straight as a stick through the occupied part of the island. They say that old Stanley Woolard would dig ditches on either side of the road and throw the mud on it to keep it above ground. He did it all with a shovel. Luckily they had been pushed a little north, because just south of where they were, they would have encountered a rather large canal that they might not have been able to cross. They were located in Middle Community.

Finally they located a dry place to sleep. Pop and Uncle Baxter orga-nized a fire brigade to find dry kindling and paper, if they could, for getting a fire started, and also—most important—dry wood. Pop began the search for a match. Dry wood was pulled from the middle of a pile stacked under the front steps and all along under the porch. The top rows were wet, but the wood underneath was still dry. All of it was ready, but they had no match. Blake dug around in his overalls and touched the deerskin pouch he vowed to always have. He offered it to his grandpop. Captain Charlie's face dropped, astonished. "Where in the world?" he sputtered. Baxter laughed out loud, grabbing the flint from Charlie and making sparks for a fire.

Everyone in the cabin was standing around with their arms clutching their bodies, shivering, all waiting to get dry, surprised that the little kid saved the day. They all seemed frozen in amazement, and cold and shaking from the wet and the wind—who knew which? Whatever the reason, the discomfort was soon replaced by some good-natured ribbing as Lindy produced an only slightly damp bag of shrimp and hushpuppies.

Everybody settled down to the sound of torrents of rain beating down on the roof and equally strong gusts of wind. The wind lasted most of the night but died down before dawn. The rain lasted until the early morning, and then that also stopped. Meanwhile, the soaked group huddled around the fire, taking turns sleeping as a fire watch was set up to keep the heat of life going. They all awakened dry, and nobody seemed sick. The kids were allowed to sleep on through. They had been real troopers during the whole ordeal, no whining about anything.

Out came the sun, and the company stirred to survey their surroundings. In the old days, Portsmouth Island used to be a bustling town, full of men who captained the lightering boats and lived there with their families. There used to be two churches, a combined post office and general store, several houses—two of them rather large—a one-room schoolhouse, and the lifesaving station. There were about a dozen structures in all. Next door, the fisherman and his wife hailed them from the window as the group began down the road toward the buildings on the horizon. They needed to hurry. No telling what condition the boat was in.

They got to the old lifesaving station after about an hour of exploring the area, looking at what used to be a prosperous village. It was now populated with only a few fishermen and their families. The houses were run-down, and most were gray from the onslaught of weather. Only a few had ever seen a coat of paint. The group could see old outhouses still standing and the houses they serviced in a rubbled heap near them. The cement cisterns were left sticking up above the ground, no longer in use. There were three huge two-story houses that carried white paint on their clapboard sides. They actually looked livable, but they also were vacant. One could see where some of the houses had smaller houses in back that had been kitchens. They were not adjoining the main house, as people of the time were afraid of fire. As most fires started in the kitchen, the cooking area was separated from the main building.

There were several large canals poking into Middle Community, which was the main island. These people could make a good living fishing, clamming, oystering, and crabbing, with a navigable creek reaching right up to their back door. But Mother Nature had other ideas for Portsmouth Island. Because the creeks came up to the front door, the water from a storm could also visit. There were places where small peninsulas formerly attached to the main island had been overtaken by the water, and they became islands unto themselves. They were still used as haulovers, because a horse and carriage could pull up to the little spit of land at low tide and bring up merchandise—or anything that could be delivered in a barrel.

Hurricanes had begun to wash over the island regularly, so these inhabitants knew their time on this place was short-lived. At the lifesaving station, they used a shortwave radio to contact the Coast Guard at the Hatteras station. Within three hours the cutter from Hatteras arrived to pick up the wayward passengers. When everyone was stowed away, they left the docks at Portsmouth Island, and instead of going toward Hatteras the seamen gave in to Captain Charlie and Captain Miller and went in search of the wounded *Odessa W*, hoping she was still in one piece. They found her on her side—maybe turned around a little, but rolled over just enough that she could easily be floated at high tide. The cutter headed for home to get hooks and gear, deposit the unnecessary cargo—each having a name—and get back to right the *Odessa W*. She must have been built well to have avoided sustaining serious damage. Grandpop was proud, and so were all the boys. They all had a hand in building her, under the watchful eyes of Captains Charlie, Baxter, and their trusted carpenter and designer ol' man Calvin Burrus. Burrus was a boatbuilder, having built one of the most famous fishing vessels on the island, the *Jackie Fay*.

The kids had the run of the station while waiting at the Coast Guard complex at the tip of Hatteras Island. The sailors had already met the youngsters at baseball games and while hanging out with the Buxton boys. The Coast Guard boys had missed the company of children, and they looked forward to spoiling Luke, Ellie, and Blake. The galley put out a wonderful supper for the sailors and hungry crew. The kids got to go back to the kitchen and into the room where all the food was stored, and they were given homemade ice cream that the seamen had hand-churned. They had such a good time that they hardly noticed the number of hours their family had been gone.

The *Odessa W* came back with all on board, picked up the excited children, and headed back to Bernice's creek in Buxton. Bill would be there to pick them all up in the jalopy. All this planning happened with communication between one Coast Guard station and another. Sometimes it was quite convenient to have them as part of your network of friends.

Jack was more than excited to be home. He was happy to sleep in the assistant keeper's quarters as Jeanette had completely disrupted the furniture in the upstairs rooms at the main quarters in anticipation of moving in. Besides, he slept in the unoccupied side, and Lindy slept in the other bedroom of the unoccupied side. They were training for boxing, and with the ring being downstairs, this was like a gym. This holiday would prove to be exciting.

Hatteras Jack

Home! Nothing like it! Everybody slept late that next day. Bill took care of the light for Grandpop, and Odessa and Nett made sure there was plenty of food for the starving athletes. Pop slept until 8:00 a.m.—in itself something of a miracle. Mr. Quidley, who had formerly served as lighthouse keeper, was retired, and had volunteered to do an extra day, knowing that his friend would be tired from his trip. Also, knowing what had happened, he was also proud of the Buxton boys' efforts. Jack and Lindy were still asleep at noon, and the children made it until ten, a late sleep for them. Their beds were all in Ellie's room for the time being while Nett organized the big room that had formerly had lots of beds and dressers for her brothers, whom Mom referred to as "the boys." But now, things would change. Nett was making a living quarters out of the large space upstairs so that she could keep out of her parents' hair. She alone knew what a handful the boys could be. Adding Ellie to that, and maybe her parents didn't realize what they had signed up for.

Everybody went their separate ways, and the boys took Ellie to the barn to show her the Indian treasures they had recovered. Ellie was delighted! The first thing she did was take off her shoes and put the boots on over her leggings. They were beautiful, just as she remembered them. She decided she just had to show them to Grandmom, so she took them to her room for safekeeping. Maybe Grandmom had some, too?

She ran her hand along Luke's bow and thought, *I'd like to do that.* Then she lost the thought, because who would whittle a limb for such a thing—for her?

Luke heard her thought and shot back, "I'll make you one." Then out loud he said, "Maybe not a good one at first, but I could learn, and by next year, you will have one."

"Me, too?" said Blake, not knowing what he was asking for.

"You want a bow," said Luke matter-of-factly. He then added, "*You* want a *bow?*"

"Yes, I do!" said Blake. "I think it would be neat if we all knew how."

Luke thought about it for a minute. "You know? You might be right. That might be a good thing—for all of us to know something the same. And the bow is great to have. It's kind of a bridge to something, and we might just need a bridge one of these days." Luke had decided that each would have a bow and quiver of arrows.

"Well, what are you going to ask for for Christmas? From Santa?" Luke asked Blake.

"I think I'll ask for a whip," Blake replied.

"*What?* A whip? You don't know how to do that," Luke barked.

"But I could learn. You remember how Manteo taught Wematin? Well, you are my big brother, and I need someone to teach me, too. Whatsa matter? Scared I'll beat you like Wematin did Manteo?" Blake was really giving it to Luke now. Blake really wanted to be like Luke, but he needed his older brother's help.

"Well, if you get one, I'll teach you, but fat chance you will talk anyone into giving you one, so I'm pretty safe in the instruction area. What are you going to ask Santa for, Ellie?" Luke turned to the girl with her beautiful boots on.

"A bride doll," she said quickly and exactly, like she didn't even have to think about it.

Both Blake and Luke looked at each other and made a funny face. Guess they didn't know much about girls anyway. Why waste a wish on a bride doll? You couldn't even play with it!

Why couldn't *she* ask for a whip? It was for sure she was going to want to borrow one of theirs. Maybe they could change her mind. Ellie heard them but didn't care. Lots of luck. Let's see, maybe she would borrow Luke's. It had to be better, because Manteo made it.

The trio stored their treasures in some of the empty crates that Nett had used to transfer furniture and stuff to the big room. They were careful to pick the wooden ones that would not be thrown away. Then they wandered over to the assistant keeper's quarters to watch the sparring.

The boxers were breaking for lunch, so the three went back to the main quarters to share lunch with all the boys from Bill's training session. Some looked a little red-faced from being punched around, but they didn't seem to mind. Grandmom had made sandwiches and potato salad for everybody. She must have been practicing for Christmas, because she had pecan pie for dessert. But one smell was surely wafting through the house, coming from the kitchen: whiskey! Grandmom was making fruitcakes. After making the batter and putting in all the fruit she had marinating in whiskey and sugar for the last few days, she put a cloth over the whole thing. Every few days she would pour whiskey all over the cloth until it soaked in good. Then she would wet it again. It would get a treatment every few days until it had time to ferment. The children wondered if they would be getting any of that.

After lunch it was time to pester Grandpop, so up the lighthouse steps they went on a pretense of carrying him his lunch. He seemed to be ready to sit down. He probably had a worse day than anyone else yesterday, as he had the both the Portsmouth Island excitement plus the worry of these three.

The children sat down with Grandpop on the ledge near the railing, munching on cookies while Grandpop watched the sea and enjoyed his lunch. That, of course, did not last long.

"Grandpop," said Ellie. "Ever seen a white dolphin?" She still could not believe how beautiful her Moira was, and could she be real? James was real, and she thought Willi was real, but Moira was white. Could that be real?

"Matter of fact, no. Never seen a white one." Ellie looked disappointed. "But I heard tell of one," Grandpop said, and all three heads popped around in attention.

"Let's see. The tale is that ships were beginning to have trouble trying to navigate through the channel down at Hatteras. I think it was about the time when ships were larger, carried sail and lots of it to get across the ocean, with no engines at that time. So, when they had to sail through the inlet—with all those shifting tides, nor'easters like the one we just went through, hurricanes, and sudden squalls—the sand around the mouth of the inlet moved around, and sometimes, if the wind was right, the sand from the sound went out the opening into the ocean, blocking the entrance both ways. So, a ship possibly came upon a point they had passed through easily before, only to find it too shallow to pass through. The ships kept men on the bow at all times, with chains to lower and call out the depth of the water.

"Time was, say, around the Revolutionary War, when Aunt Sabra had her business. Anyway, it was important for the channel to be passable, for the good of everybody. They tell, it was about that time when Jack showed up. They called him 'Hatteras Jack.' He was a great, big, albino dolphin who made his habitat at the mouth of the Hatteras Inlet. He made it his business to guide boats safely through the inlet to deep water on the other side. It began when he jumped and played so hard in front of a vessel that they had to stop to keep from killing him. At that time, while waiting for that crazy dolphin to get out of the way, the ship took a sounding of the bottom to check the draft. The sailor's face was white as he approached the captain with the news. They were either on or about to board a huge sandbar. Jack had saved them from moving forward by distracting the ship. The ship kept watch on the incoming tide, and the captain kept watch over Jack. As the tide rose, the dolphin began frantically making figure eights in front of the bow, indicating the water was not high enough. Finally, the dolphin darted ahead and surfaced in a roll, motioning for the ship to come through. With the sail shortened and rolled tight, the ship slowly tacked in the same pattern of the white streak leading them. Eventually all made it safely through the channel.

"Jack was the one who celebrated the most. His barrel rolls, tail walking, flipping, and pattern swimming were unmatched by any show choreographed by a professional. Then it was off to the mouth of the inlet for more watchful opportunities to play his game. This went on for years.

"There were times when the captain would be in a hurry, and even though he knew the legend, he was impatient to cross through. Most of the time Jack would surface in front of a waiting ship—and for Jack, they all waited. He would give them a barrel roll ahead sign, or some gesture that would allow them to know it was not the correct time. But when a captain kept blowing his horn, even Jack knew the captain was anxious to proceed. At those times Jack put on a display of intelligence that astonished even the most seasoned sailor. He circled the ship slowly and deliberately, all around the edges, around under the bow, and come out the keel. He was measuring the ship. When he finished, he swam in front of the ship and proceeded to give either a go-ahead or a not-yet sign.

"Jack worked Hatteras Inlet until ships became equipped with horns, signals, and buoys in the channel, with motion detectors for ships. As Jack saw the new equipment and the ships going through, he did not come back anymore. They say that once in a while they saw him checking out the channel markers, but he did not come back to work."

"That's a good story, Pop. Bet it's true. What do you think?" Ellie was most anxious to believe in her newest friend.

"Of course it's true," Grandpop said. "You need to know just how smart a dolphin is. I do have another dolphin story, but not now. It's too long, and I got to get some work done."

He grinned at the kids. Such eager beavers. They loved to live in a fantasy world. But they had proven they could certainly take a dose of reality, he thought, remembering the storm and all that uncertainty. They had handled it well. Not one of them cried. Just did what they were told, and there was some telling going on. Everybody was shouting out orders the whole time, and the kids kept their eyes glued on Grandpop's mouth. When he spoke, they reacted—and not until. No matter what order they were given that day, if it didn't come from Grandpop, it went on deaf ears.

Uncle Jack and Lindy practiced in the ring every day. They went late into the night on the bags. It could be heard upstairs at the keeper's lodge. And during the day they worked out with Bill or some of the sailors who were also taking advantage of free boxing lessons. It soon came time for Jack and Lindy to go to Nags Head and visit the Casino arena where they would fight later on. The fights were scheduled for New Year's Eve. Bill and Grandpop volunteered to take them, because Grandpop had some business in Manteo. Of course, the three mosquitoes were allowed to go.

How could they miss getting into the sweaty old Casino at their age, without going with their grandpop, and it would be empty with only the clean-up crew on the floor. They would get to see everything. This was turning out to be a fine Christmas holiday.

The full moon of December was called the cold moon. Grandpop decided to go up the beach at low tide on the full moon. The boys were ready, as were the children as they slacked the tires of the old jalopy and took off across the dunes to the hard sand of the wash at low tide. Grandpop drove with Ellie and Bill in the front. The two boys sat in the back between Jack and Lindy, whose job it was to mommick the kids all the way up the beach. It was just a giggle fest back there, and Ellie spent most of her time hanging over the seat to participate with the fun going on in the back.

The moon on the water was like sheets of golden silk floating out to the big blue bright spot sneaking up through the night sky. Everybody was wide awake as they bounced along on the camelback ridges caused by the outgoing tide. As they watched the water, they at one point saw the tips of fins just outlined by the dawn in gold as the rising sun bounced off the slick bodies. A school of dolphins made its way down the beach, maybe going to play with the children. But they would be back another time. Now they were going to see the Casino. They would not get to see the boxing matches, but this was good enough.

Grandpop turned up just at Rodanthe, when he first saw the gravel pits or red sand. He saw ahead of him a straight two-track road, and it was empty. Maybe he would be lucky and catch the first ferry off the island. As he worked his way through the villages, he began to see cars ahead of him, probably being helped out of a soft spot or two. He saw no reason to hurry, so he allowed plenty of room between him and the car in front of him. As he got to the soft spot, boards were already covering the treacherous areas, and he went through with little trouble. A couple of times between Rodanthe and Toby's Ferry, Jack and Lindy had to get out and help the cars in front of them, but their work led to an easier crossing for Grandpop. As they reached the ferry, they saw only a few cars in front of them, allowing them to cross. It stayed that way until they could see the ferry coming their way from across the sound at Oregon Inlet. The sun was just beginning to show up and outline Toby's boat.

Just in time to catch this ferry, the big Blue Bus—the Hatteras bus line—showed up, which had first priority to be loaded ahead of everybody. This was an old school bus painted bright blue and serviced by the Midgett brothers. They were a couple of talented mechanics who saw a need and met it. These brothers started with an old government commando truck with canvas roll-up windows and the most uncomfortable seats known to man. The children always stood up when on that thing, no matter how far the trip. They had been known to stand from Buxton to Manteo and back. Now the boys had purchased an old school bus, painted it that distinctive blue, and it at least had windows. The Midgett brothers could work the gears of that old bus until it was as capable of pulling out of the sand as easily as the commando truck did. Here it was, first in line. Everyone else could get on or catch the next one, because the bus had arrived! Everybody knew the Blue Bus would catch low tide, and they had their suitcases on the dirt track in front of their houses, no matter what time it had to be. Nature ruled everything here.

As it turned out, Captain Charlie was waved on by Pam, Toby's assistant. "Come on, Cap'n Charlie. Give 'er some gas, git 'er o'er this hump. I got 'er." Pam coaxed Grandpop's jalopy across the ramp down on to the wooden ferry that he and Toby Tillett ran. In his island brogue, he would guide the cars to their proper places. Pam knew the island residents by name and was careful to space the cars correctly.

The trip over was a contest to see if you could survive the onslaught of the green flies trapped in the ferry's cabin. The kids thought that was where they could see best, but a couple of welps later they opted for the open spaces of the front bow of the barge. Some of the bus people were throwing bread at the seagulls, which were following the wake looking for fish to be churned up. But bread was just as welcomed—and not quite as hard to catch.

They spied the inlet store on the other side and hurried between cars back to their own vehicle, in plenty of time to load up. Getting off the ferry, they joined a caravan of cars making their way down the tracks to Nags Head. It took them a little over an hour to get to the first little store. They stopped for a sandwich at a familiar place, and the owner was extremely glad to see Grandpop. Seemed they had business together in the past and had somehow helped each other. The kids got free ice cream. *Oh yeah!*

These trips were great! They went a couple or three miles to this huge building, with some smaller buildings attached. This was the Casino. They went inside, and it was almost all empty. There was a big platform in the middle, and the ropes of the boxing ring glistened in the little bit of light coming in from the upper windows. There were no lower windows, so no one could look in. The Casino was used as a dance hall most of the time, and the platform in the middle was moved to one end of the hall to be used for a band. Most of the islanders were as familiar with the Casino as those who lived on the mainland. They were used to catching a ride on a Friday afternoon for a weekend in Nags Head, and dancing at the Casino was part of that.

Bill crawled into the ring and looked around. He wanted to make sure his fighters knew what to expect. It was a little bit bigger than the ring they had practiced in at home, and he was hoping that wouldn't present a problem. He did not want the boxers to depend on the ring at their back when they had at least a foot more to go. He made Jack and Lindy get in the ring also to check out how it felt to be in this arena. Everybody had their shoes off so as not to damage the cover, and Grandpop even hoisted up Luke and Blake to get inside and run around like they were boxing. After a bit, Bill and the two contestants were satisfied that they could work this ring, and they all knew Grandpop had a meeting, so they hurried up and got back in the car for their trip to Manteo.

This next journey was easy. There were paved roads on the mainland, and the children delighted in speeding down the blacktop like they were racing. It was their first trip into the world of what they called "the city." They did not make it all the way into Manteo, but stopped on the outskirts of town at a place called Meekins Motors. They pulled up to the business office, and Pop went in. Meanwhile Bill and the boys got out and were looking at all the cars on the lot. Luke and Blake were fascinated, and Ellie thought they were magnificent.

Pop came out of the office and threw a set of keys to Jack. "You boys want to follow me home to see I don't get stuck in this new thing?" he said.

Jack caught the keys, and he and Lindy hopped in the old jalopy and revved her up.

Grandpop walked over to a big black car that had a long sloping back and looked twice as big as the old jalopy. "Okay, boys! Who wants to ride with me?" he said with a grin. Bill crawled into the spacious front seat.

Blake pursed his mouth, opened his eyes wide, and rolled them from Luke to Ellie and back again. "Grandpop!" he stammered. "Is this ours?"

"Yup," said Grandpop and opened the back door for the kids to crawl in.

All three jumped in the new car and were like a bunch of dogs, fingering everything, smelling the seats, trying the ashtray, examining the floor. They were all over the place.

"Okay. Let's get going. We'll be lucky to catch the ferry. If not, we'd have to come back here to spend the night."

"Nooooo. Let's spend the night in the car!" said Luke.

Off they all went—Jack and Lindy happy to have the old jalopy, but sorry they had to follow Grandpop home. They wanted to stay and hang out at the Casino that night. All the young people had the greatest time there, and here they were, already in Nags Head. They wanted to stay some kinda bad, but with that new car, it wouldn't do to let that thing get stuck right off the bat. They followed Captain Charlie, Bill, and the kids to the ferry dock. The ferry was just coming in from Rodanthe for its last run of the evening. According to the number of cars plus the bus, Grandpop was going to be able to get on. There were so many local men in line for the ferry that Captain Charlie and Bill huddled to decide what to do about the caravan back home. Bill checked with some of the cars ahead and found that they were all going the same way—some dropping off at Kinnakeet, and some even going all the way to Hatteras. After a conference with his father-in-law, Bill walked back to the car where Jack and Lindy were waiting.

"Guess you boys don't have to take the ferry tonight if you don't want to. Seems there are enough men in line that if we get in trouble they can push us out." He hardly finished before a loud war whoop rose up from both young men, and they hurriedly shook hands with Bill before turning that old piece of junk around and taking off for the Casino.

The kids did not even see what was happening behind them. They were busy exploring in the new car, rolling the windows up and down, wiping imaginary dust off the seat. Never were there three more proud than the ones in the shiny new car. They did not even miss Jack and Lindy, so when they finally boarded the ferry, they never even got out of the car, not for the whole two hours. They sat, told stories, and played Comesey-Comesey with Bill.

"Comesey-Comesey."

"What do you come with?"

"A shiny object."

"What does it start with?"

"It starts with an *n*."

"An *n*?"

"Yep."

This was Blake's turn. They guessed and guessed and guessed until finally they all gave up.

"What is it?"

"It's a nob!"

"A knob? Like the handle of the door?" said Luke.

"Yep," said Blake, all satisfied.

"Blake, that starts with a *k*." Ellie laughed and laughed. "We wasted all that time and the letter was wrong!"

Blake looked a little embarrassed but then said, "I guess I won!" End of game.

Then they started playing I Spy. Whatever they had to do to stay in that car, they did.

The trip back was fun. The island roads were pretty packed from the day's travelers, and it was dark when the last car turned off the road to continue on its way home. All the vehicles had traveled the whole way on the two-track road, never once going over to the beach, but with all those cars in a line, they had little trouble with the soft sand.

Grandmom and Nett were waiting anxiously to see the new car. It was a surprise for the kids, but not to anyone else. They were all hoping it would get there before the floor of the old one completely rusted out. Bill had cut strips of wood to fit the floor area, so it was a little better, but this new car—what a difference. Even though it was not pretty like some of the others on the island—and it was black, like every other government car—it was still the nicest car anybody had ever seen, because it was *their* car.

★ 7 ★

Winter Vacation

The children were more than excited. They were going to the Coast Guard station to see their first movie. Movies were shown at the Austin Theater in Hatteras, but there were times when the children were not allowed to attend. The movies shown were also more of the adult variety and not suitable for a younger audience. On Sunday afternoon, the Austin Theater scheduled a matinee that was also usually an adult subject, but they didn't know much about movies anyway. The kids were such friends with the Coast Guard crew that the men ordered a movie for them to see.

Movies were usually passed around the various military bases for servicemen to watch, and this crew wanted to order one for the kids. Every man on the station was excited to view a film through the eyes of kids who had never been exposed to Hollywood. The kids were allowed to invite friends, making the parents equally excited. Since the venue was small, there was a restriction on how many people could be invited, so Luke asked Colby, Blake asked Thomas, and Ellie invited her friends Nancy and Agnes. The audience included the parents, children, and

Coast Guard, which pretty much filled up the room where the film was to be shown. The movie was *Treasure Island*, and everyone was excited. This was also a book they were familiar with, as Nett read it each year to her classes. It would be hard to tell who anticipated the movie more—the guardsmen or the kids.

Probably the most thrilled was Bill. He hailed from New York and had met and married Captain Charlie's oldest daughter, Jeanette—Nett—while stationed on the island. As a New Yorker he missed some of the perks of living in the city. He really wanted his boys to have some of the same experiences that he had. Truth be known, Bill was probably most influential in the idea of securing the film. He worked with the guardsmen to get a copy, one suitable for children, and get in the queue to be scheduled for a military base.

The seamen of the Coast Guard were as excited as the kids. They spent the day rearranging the room for the film to be projected on a sheet in the front of the hall. The galley was busy making treats for the audience, with special emphasis on what children would like. The cooks made cookies and brownies, and for those with healthier appetites, there were huge plates of sandwiches. The galley was even gearing up to have popcorn during the film.

The big night arrived, and there was no end to the children's chatter. However, Bill was the most animated. He loved the island so much, and it was very seldom that he missed his faster life on the streets of a bustling city. But Bill always wanted his boys to see a little more of life than what was available for them on the isolated island. Bringing in this movie was his gift to the children. He knew he would be going to war. It was a big war, a world war, and he did not know when or if he would back, so he was trying to see as much of his children's faces and reactions as he could before he left.

The night of the movie was busy. Nett and Grandmom were as excited as the kids. Everyone was scheduled to meet at the keeper's quarters before the film. Then they would all go over to the Coast Guard station for the showing of the picture. Since there was no chance of Bill not accompanying the children, Captain Charlie opted to stay behind. The lighthouse was his responsibility, and it was to be manned at all times on a regular basis. These days it would have been folly for the great tower to be left unattended. It had been sabotaged before, during the Civil War, so the level of importance was now heightened. Grandmom decided to stay with him. She was excited for Ellie and the boys. She had been to the cinema before and was more interested in keeping Charlie company than anything else. She also wanted to be the one the children rushed to so that they could tell their story.

As everybody gathered at the main keeper's quarters, the parents dropped off the children. Studying the looks on the parents' faces, Bill invited them to stay. Everybody liked the movies, and they all knew this to be a good one. It was in color! The movies they had seen before were shown from a projector near the road, on a sheet that had been hung in front of the post office building in Buxton, and the villagers brought their blankets and chairs to sit in the yard and watch whatever was on the screen.

On those nights, the hill leading up to the post office was full of people, and the projector, located near the bottom, displayed the movie on the screen. These films were shorter than regular movies, and sometimes more than one played on a given night. They were usually Abbott and Costello, a comedy team getting into all kinds of mischief. They were the most popular because they were funny, and the island was coming into a time when the country might be heading toward a war, with many of the local boys beginning to enlist in one of the branches of the armed services. The funny movies gave everybody a little laughter to take the place of whatever anticipation they might be experiencing. However, the island boys were a little excited to enlist and be shipped to sights and countries unknown. Joining the service was not viewed as a bad thing but rather as a chance to see the world.

Nett had had the part-time job of playing the piano for the silent movies at the Austin Theater, and now that theater was beginning to get more up-to-date films—ones with sound. These were still in Hatteras Village, though, and the children were too young to go that far. So this opportunity at the Coast Guard station was really a treat. Actually the kids in the other six villages envied their friends at school who lived in Hatteras because they could walk over to see a movie. This event at the Coast Guard station was going to even things out, as now these five children could also talk about having seen a film.

They all caravanned over to the Coast Guard station. The children were so excited, it was hard for even all those parents to control the noise and poking around. The girls were on their best behavior, but the boys were acting up enough for all of them. Agnes came with Nancy and her parents. Agnes was an orphan who also lived with her elderly grandparents, and she was one of Ellie's best school friends. Even if Grandpop had to go get her, Ellie was determined to have her there. As it was, she had a ride. As everyone loaded in their cars to make the short trip to the Coast Guard station less than a mile away, the children all opted to go in the new government car. Luke and Blake were so excited to show off a car with a decent floorboard. This left Bill with a carload of kids and the others following in their other cars.

There could not have been two happier boys than Luke and Blake. The girls crowded in the front seat with Bill, because there was complete bedlam going on in the backseat. Bill hoped they did not do any damage to Captain Charlie's new car. He had no reason to worry. There were not two better people for the clean patrol than Luke and Blake. This was their car, and it *would* be as clean coming home as it was on the trip over. But the noise was off the charts. Bill wondered if the movie could hold a candle to the trip over to the station in the car.

The film was the best Christmas present the children could have ever had. There were seven happy faces looking back at that screen—actually eight, because Bill was just as fascinated as the children were. All this island life, after growing up in a big city, was sometimes a little too quiet. Probably all the servicemen felt the same way, but it was something they had to get used to.

At the end of the film, the children were speechless. The sailors were as thrilled as everyone else to be a part of this little bit of the mainland. They were so far away from home—no family and not many conveniences. This lighthouse family was the best thing that ever happened to scores of homesick sailors.

In the movie there were sword fights, and *Aaaarrggh!* became the sound of the night. It was a growl that lasted quite a few days around the lighthouse compound, as everyone enjoyed talking to the kids about their new experience.

Of course, when Colby and Thomas were allowed to stay overnight after the movie, there was no desire for sleep. Grandmom did get some milk and cookies in them before they went to bed, but running back to the assistant keeper's quarters from the main building was a pirate scene playing out. The girls went home with their parents, so Ellie was free to play rough with the boys until bedtime. They were cautioned not to go to the beach, and encouraged to play near the houses. The night air was filled with *Aaaarrggh!* The problem was that everybody wanted to be a pirate, so Ellie was left to be the victim. She made a formidable one.

The next day, piracy took over the lighthouse compound. Luke was Long John Silver, and Blake was Ben Gun. Colby and Thomas were pirates, and poor Ellie was Jim and all the other characters who were not pirates. But she could hold her own, and she played all the English parts with flourish. Luke got himself a crutch for his wooden leg, and Blake tried to get as dirty as he could to be Ben Gun. Actually it was all Colby and Luke against Blake and Thomas, and Ellie had a hard time breaking into the story. But Ellie was a crafty little kid, and having grown up with boys, adding two more was no problem. She could outthink them at almost every turn. They decided to make a fort in the woods near the lighthouse.

While they were rummaging around in the woods, they found a bunker: a cement box with openings toward the sea. They could tell where people had been working on the site, which was unseen from any vantage point should a person step away and look toward the bushes. When picking around to get beyond the foliage, they could see the fading remnants of tracks that people and wheelbarrows had made about three months before. They looked around and played in and out of the structure. Jim Hawkins—Ellie—made this structure resemble the fort built in the film. They fought battles all over the compound. The small boat in the turtle pond back of the house was the pirate ship, and they kept running from one house to the other to find things to add to the reality of the activity. Finally Grandmom called dinner, and the kids came in for a midday sandwich of homemade bread and peanut butter from the store. In those days, peanut butter was the most delectable food on the planet.

Grandpop came in for a formidable dinner also, but peanut butter was not his choice. As he sat down with the kids and Odessa placed his hot meal in front of him, they excitedly confronted him about the cement room. The look on his face was one of total surprise. He stammered a little, trying to think of exactly how to tell them without revealing too much what the box was all about. He knew that he was no longer in the company of just his three young-uns. Two more little sets of ears would take whatever he said back to the village and discuss a secret among their family, and thus the information would spread across the village and then the island.

The captain decided to get out of it the best way he could, and then be sure to be on hand that evening when the parents came to pick up Colby and Thomas. He would confide in them as to the secrecy, and hopefully they would be patriotic enough to understand the need for not letting this information spread through the villages. It was a government project, and the fathers of both Colby and Thomas were former servicemen.

"Well," he began, "there have been some happenings around the lighthouse lately, and the Coast Guard thought they might need an extra person to watch the compound at night, so sometimes the sailors take shifts watching to see if the culprits would show up again. You are not to play around that area, ever! The Coast Guard might be planning to use it as a storage area, and they would not be happy if they found out that children were hanging around their workplace."

"But, Grandpop," said Luke. "It is a great fort. Can we use it when the Coast Guard catches the criminal?"

Charlie thought and answered, "I will ask them to tell me when they have finished with the little house and find out if they will let you play there. But they just started, so it might be a long time, and I don't want you young-uns pestering me every day about that structure. They must need it or they wouldn't be working back there. And I mean for you to stay away from it. You wouldn't want to have to move away from this little piece of federal land just because you couldn't follow orders, now, would you?"

The children all agreed that they could keep a secret, but among themselves they decided to find another place—kind of just like that one—and build their own fort. So after dinner, they set about finding old planks and logs they would use to build their stronghold. That activity kept them busy for the rest of the afternoon. Colby and Thomas declared that they would be back frequently over the Christmas holidays to finish the fort and to get back to playing pirate.

That evening, when Colby's dad came to pick up both boys, Captain Charlie called him aside to a place away from the children and out of earshot.

"The children found a bunker built by the navy about three months ago," he began. "You know, this country is headed for war with the Germans. Bill has even been called up, and I'm sure you know of others who have enlisted and ones who have been called back to service. Of course, I don't actually have any more information than others about when this will happen, but I think—and that's just me—that it will not be long. Because of the way the last world war turned out, they are expecting some activity off this coast. This will be the shipping lane used from one end of this country to the other, and it is expected to draw the enemy to our shores. To be aware of that, and to head it off before it happens, the navy has sent men here to man the coast. They built that bunker, and when the war starts they are going to put guns in there to keep the enemy off this island. If there is activity out to sea, we don't want any enemy survivors hanging out on this island. I told the children there had been some vandalism around the lighthouse, and the Coast Guard was trying to catch them. I am sure they will bring it up at some point, and it wouldn't do for the information to spread. This was to be a secret operation. Now we got these five kids holding some very top-secret information, and we have to put it to rest before we get our country in trouble."

Colby's dad agreed and felt the same way as Captain Charlie. He would squelch any talk about it with Colby and would tell Thomas's father to do the same. Then they spent the rest of the time talking about war. That Sunday, war was declared. The island was put on alert, and meetings began to take place in every village at every grocery store where the men gathered. There were lots of young boys planning a trip to Manteo to enlist, and talk of the toll that war would take on a place like this, separated from the rest of the country, became a concern that needed to be addressed. The island was always conscious of supplies. That might prove to be a problem, so each man went home to plan for the hard times to come. Meanwhile, life went on as usual.

This new war, World War II, would not present as much of a surprise to the islanders as World War I did. They had endured much during the first world war, and they realized that even though they were off the coast of the United States, they could possibly be in more danger than those who lived inland. Preparation was needed. Preparation. That was what the bunker was all about. The ships and activity offshore would surely end up here, and should it turn out to be true, this time the islanders would be prepared.

There was still much normal activity going on to occupy the children and keep them from worrying, even though the radio—when the static died down and the batteries were working—was always talking about war. Captain Charlie and Miss Odessa did their best to shield the children from the anxiety of their father leaving, not to mention the obvious difference with the Coast Guard and those navy men now always being around the lighthouse. Things were getting little crowded. But at night, Ellie sat around with Grandmom and held the string as she crocheted the beautiful figures that would go on the tree. She could not wait. Grandmom was always crocheting around Christmastime. She made bells, angels, Christmas trees, holly leaves, round balls, lighthouses, trumpets, other horns, drums, a little boat, and a special white dolphin that Ellie named Moira. Ellie asked for a wolf, but Grandmom said it was too difficult. All these little white beautiful ornaments would be starched stiffer than wood and left to dry so that they could hang on the tree. At this point, there were few commercial items to have, but most islanders had precious boxes of glass balls to hang on the tree, given to them from friends on the mainland or—like Grandmom—from a son or daughter sending them home.

The island ladies made their own decorations that were far prettier than anything that came from the store. Of course, there were probably newer things to buy on the mainland, but they were not on the mainland, so they had a style of their own. Uncle Fay had sent a package of some stuff called Angel Hair, and it looked like a great big sheet of spider web that could stretch over the whole tree. It made everything dreamy.

Activity around Christmastime that year, with all the uncertainty in the world, went on like normal. There was the church Nativity play, with children and adults participating. Uncle Fay was a wise man, and Grandmom had to make him a costume. The children ran around singing "We Three Kings," but the words might as well have been in another language. They only mimicked what they heard Uncle Fay sing, and they got it all wrong. They did not know what an "aurentaur" was, but they sang it anyway. They didn't know it was "Orient are"—"We three kings from Orient are"—so their versions of Christmas carols were always funny.

Nett and Miss Ormond were in charge of the pageant. Miss Ormond took all the ribbing from the adults about what happened when the school put on *Tom Sawyer*, but this was a church play. Such joking would not happen here, although the school play had begun to be a great source of amusement, one of those stories to tell. She even put Jack Peele in the play as a shepherd, but he had to promise to keep his mouth shut.

Nett was busy practicing Christmas carols on the piano at the keeper's quarters, while the men—Uncle Fay home on leave from the Merchant Marines, Uncle Jack from college, Lindy and his brothers, Bill, and any Coast Guard or navy guy that had any free time—were all at the assistant keeper's quarters helping to train Jack and Lindy for the upcoming boxing matches in Nags Head. Everybody was excited, because as huge as Lindy was and as skilled with a punch—as some of his sparring partners could relate to—they knew he would be going all the way to Dallas to fight for a Golden Glove. There was much to do around the lighthouse compound, and the bunker seemed to drift away from the children's mind.

With the boys over watching the boxing, Ellie got to hang out with her grandmom and help her with the decorations, the cooking, rumming up that fruit cake, and whatever else Grandmom asked of her. And then there was the game that all three participated in: looking for presents. Grandmom was always surprised when she would sweep under the bed and there was no dust. The kids had wiped it all away while shimmying under to check to see if anything was hidden that would make itself known on Christmas morning. They did find a big box of Whitman's Samplers chocolates, but they couldn't do anything about it because, if they did, it would be obvious that they were snooping. They just had to know it was there and anticipate the opening on Christmas Day.

Going to the church a couple of nights a week was fun. Actually, going anywhere at night was fun. The choir was practicing for the pageant as were all the players. Luke was a shepherd. Miss Tinker, the third part of the musketeers of Jack, Lindy, and Tinker, was the Virgin Mary. A nice man named Jamesy, who used to be sweet on Nett, was Joseph. Blake and Ellie were just spectators, which meant gofers, if they could be found. Most of the time, they were getting into mischief around and under the pews of the sanctuary. Ellie paid close attention to Miss Tinker. She was one of the most beautiful girls, with her long red hair. She was slim and had a horse that she rode everywhere, sometimes down to the beach to see the boys practice. She was a source of admiration to Ellie, and when Ellie grew up, she wanted to be just like Miss Tinker, horse and all.

During vacation, the turtles hatched and began their trek to the sea. The kids were there with old torn sheets Grandmom had given them, and they spent at least eighteen straight hours, stopping for food only, shooing away the gulls. Then, when night fell, it was getting rid of the ghost crabs, which came out of their holes by the thousands for this particularly tasty meal. It must have been like Thanksgiving turkey to them. But because of the efforts that the turtles' protectors put forth, the ghost crabs did not get as many hatchlings as they anticipated. Hundreds of little turtle things crawled or dragged themselves to the wash. Into the ocean with the next wave they went and were gone— hopefully to come back when the children were grown, to thank them. The old turtles watched the spectacle and remembered. They appreciated the fight put up by the lighthouse kids, especially when the raccoons would show up. This took great courage, but there was a lot of that among the three.

The day came for Grandpop and Bill to go into the woods for three Christmas trees. One huge one was for the church. It had to be the biggest and strongest in the woods. A slightly smaller one was for the keeper's quarters, and a table variety was for the assistant's quarters. Because of the boxing ring and Nett trying to move her things next door, there wasn't much room for a big tree, so the spirit of the tree was there, but no presents under it. Everything was at the main house. What the children did not know was that Uncle Tommy's store in the village was full of everybody's Christmas presents. It seemed like everyone in the village wanted to stash their gifts in the attic of the old store. The art of looking for presents was an old one, invented by the parents, and as they were wise to that game, the plan was hatched to keep them at the store or anyplace that did not involve "under the bed."

The best part of Christmas was upon them: *the Christmas tree!* The kids were tied together, meaning that they were bundled up from head to toe, with strings around their wrists and ankles. Going into the woods meant ticks, and Grandmom had taken the precaution to keep all avenues blocked off that a tick could crawl up or into. Ellie especially was a concern, because her blood disorder did not allow for the presence of bloodsucking ticks. So *if* she got to go, she had to be protected from the elements. Grandpop got his ax, he and Bill loaded the kids into the jalopy, and off they went into the woods for a Christmas tree—or two or three.

The first one they saw was a monster. It had to be twenty-five feet tall, and it was full and gorgeous. Grandpop said he had looked at that one several years before and was waiting for it to get taller. This was the year. They struggled chopping it down. Both men took turns with the ax, and then it took all they could do to drag it to the forest road, where they would come back with the horses and wagon to pick it up. They also figured that they would need to empty the boxing camp to help them, but those guys would welcome a break. Next was the tree for Grandpop, Grandmom, and the kids. They passed several small ones for the boxing complex, but that would be last. The tree for the keeper's quarters had to be the perfect size, with no holes, no sparse spots, and round and tall as the living room, which in those days was maybe eight feet. They foraged around in the woods, having a great time, until they came upon the tree they all agreed upon. Bill cut it down, and everybody helped getting it to the forest road.

They were full of themselves as they told Nett and Grandmom about the trees. There wasn't enough room for them to go with the fellows to get all the trees, but that was okay, because some lonely cookies needed their attention. In anticipation of decorating the tree the next day, Ellie and Grandmom got out the boxes of decorations that had been saved over the years. There were lots of things to go on the tree in those boxes, including childhood toys from all three children that were small enough to hang. It was truly a magical time. The most special of the ornaments that Grandmom had made were placed in a small box to be taken to the church for placing on the community tree. Here again was a competition. The ladies of the church were in a little bit of a rivalry to see who could produce the most special ornaments to be displayed in the church. There was usually no shortage of gorgeous angels, appropriate for the church, and every lady wanted her angel to be the most spectacular. The most beautiful angels would occupy the position near the top. There was room for four up there, under the star.

Mr. Johnny had made the star years before, and everyone decided there could not be a better one. Over the years, it had been fashioned with mirror pieces cut to fit the pattern, and it glistened and winked with the flickering light from the oil lamps hanging from the ceiling. He and others were also building the set for the Nativity scene. And each night the week before Christmas, villagers would take turns standing in place at the living scene on the church lawn. It was a much-anticipated job. The locals had a special treat in riding by and seeing two living Nativity scenes, one at the Buxton Methodist Church and one at the Buxton Pentecostal Church up the road. On specific nights there were carolers, with the two churches working together so that there would not be any competition.

Christmas was coming, and the days were just going to get better and better.

Welcome, Christmas

The air around the compound began to smell like Christmas. Bill, Jack, and Fatio put up the tree while six wide eyes looked on, crawling around the floor to help the men, spotting whether the tree was straight, which was quite indispensable to the process. Now that the tree was up, Grandmom and Ellie organized the decorating. As a bonus—and because of the disorder at the main house, with Nett trying to manage both homes, and doing so while her things were boxed up—Bill put a small tree in each of the boy's rooms at the assistant keeper's lodge, and of course there was one in the boxing ring. So the boxers were getting a full dose of Christmas. Nett and the boys got busy decorating the three small trees, while the older fellows were busy knocking the stuffing out of each other downstairs. What a wonderful time everyone was having—just the best Christmas, with never a dull moment.

Luke and Blake made sure Nett and Bill knew exactly what they wanted from Santa, both wanting a whip, and they wanted one for Ellie also, even though she did not ask for one. Grandmom and Ellie were busy decorating the main tree. Ellie took the opportunity to push hard for a bride doll, even as Grandmom tried to switch her to just a "doll." Ellie was having none of that. It was a bride doll or nothing. Santa would just have to understand. The seamstress had finished several dresses for Ellie, using the old treadle machine on the enclosed back porch, and they were laid out on her bed with her colony of dolls. Each night she would move them, and every morning she would put them back. Looking at the dresses was almost as good as wearing them.

She was so excited for the boys to move in that she made several trips upstairs to their rooms to check to see if Nett needed any help. Hanging around the sweaty competitors was fun for a while, but she was absolutely bored with just sitting there, so she was getting in some girl time next door. Being a tomboy was okay sometimes, but not all the time. She kept making little walks near the woods, hoping to see her wolf, Twylah, but the woods were quiet.

A couple of days before Christmas, Ellie had another one of her dreams. This time it was Twylah. It was like Twylah called to her. Ellie had been thinking so hard about the animal, it must have sensed her thoughts. In her dream, she met the wolf as it beckoned to her from the woods near the tower. She heard the howl and tiptoed downstairs and out the door in her nightgown. At the steps of the lighthouse she met the huge creature and walked straight up to her for the first time ever. When the wolf did not turn away, Ellie decided to pet her. When that did not spook the wild one, Ellie put her arms around the mighty creature and laid her head next to Twylah. The beast turned slightly and licked her on the cheek, similar to the time just days after her birth. When Ellie pulled away she saw what the wolf call meant. The wild creature had something to show.

In the background, behind Twylah, were four tiny wolf pups. They were just little puppies, all wiggly and wanting to cuddle. Twylah moved aside, and Ellie sat down on the ground and waited for the pups to come to her. They did. For what seemed like hours, Ellie and the puppies played. They crawled all over her, got her smell, and became at that moment her friends for life. In wolf lore, if a pup does not have contact with a human before it turns three months old, it can never be trusted to come to them—ever. Twylah must have wanted her pups to know her friend Ellie, so she brought them to her.

When awakening from the dream, it was just turning light. Dawnland was showing its winter colors. No wonder the Indians referred to it as Dawnland. Looking out over the ocean from her second-story window, she saw the sun rise out of the sea. It was fascinating. She didn't think she had ever before watched it sneak out of the water from behind the purple line that separated the sea from the sky, not just lying there propped up on her elbows and watching the beautiful sunrise come to life. She felt a chill and a slight shiver, and then she noticed the familiar silver and blue clouds that indicated to her that her spirit, Travis, was there. Everyone always said Christmas was a magical time, and Ellie found that to be true. Even Christo's crowing seemed more like a song.

Ellie had learned from Weroansqua that when the great land of legend slipped below the sea, only the edges were left. The Croatoan chief thought part of the edge referred to in the legend was this island, and the wolves that were here had survived that great implosion as they held a great deal of importance to the people of the civilization that disappeared. To the Indians, the outer edges of the coast were the ghosts of dead mountains.

Finally she dozed off, still in front of the window, and did not stir again until she smelled the fresh fire in the hearth and biscuits cooking in the woodstove. She put on her leggings and one of her new dresses and went downstairs to give her grandmom a kiss. Odessa also had on a pretty dress, maybe something she had ordered for herself, Ellie thought. It did appear that there had been a delivery from the seamstress, because over the new frock was a crisp new apron tied in the back with big pockets in the front, and a colorful kitchen kettle design crocheted at the neck.

Grandmom was an island woman, and like most, they were well aware that they lived on an island where being casual could take a turn toward being sloppy. They wanted to be considered proper, and as strangers noted whenever they visited the island, the women were unusually pretty. They also did not go out in the sun. Maybe they knew the dangers of overexposure, and maybe they protected their skin from blisters. At any rate, they had smooth, unblemished skin void of any makeup. All the island women were quite conscious of their appearance. They searched the catalogs for facial products, and the salesmen on the mainland did not realize was that this could be their biggest account. Odessa liked special creams, beautiful buttons, and nice frocks, and the ladies were quite particular about their hair.

Captain Charlie always invited salesmen to the lighthouse complex, and to his delight, Odessa ordered cosmetics, cologne, brushes and combs, good china, a full silver service for the table, mirrors, cloth, and kitchenwares. These things were not sold in the stores. Desirable products came to the island by way of the mail boat and the salesmen who rode in on it, hoping, on an outside chance, that the people who lived here wanted nice things.

This morning was spent in the kitchen, helping Grandmom gather together the things that would be available for Christmas snacks. Ellie could hardly wait for the boys to come over so that she could tell them about her dream. She wondered if there really were pups born to the wolfpack.

At last, the boys appeared loaded down with more things Nett was trying to move. They must have smelled the cookies from next door, because the boys arrived just as the cookies were coming out of the stove.

"Not yet, young man," said Grandmom as Blake reached for a fresh one. "Have you had your breakfast?"

"Yes, ma'am," replied Blake, and Luke stood just behind him ready to pounce on the batch and do damage.

"What we doin' today?" said Blake with a mouth full of cookie.

"Did you bring a jacket?" asked Ellie. " I was hoping we could go check out the beach. We haven't been for a while, and I was going to look for a special shell for Grandmom as one of her Christmas presents."

What she really wanted was for them to get away from everybody so that she could tell them about her dreams of the wolf pups. They all agreed. Ellie went upstairs to get a jacket, and to her surprise Luke and Blake followed her. As she curiously turned around, she saw the stupid grins on their faces. They had brought some winter clothes over in the boxes that morning, and all they had to do was retrieve them. *This is going to be fun*, thought Ellie. Having them around so much meant there would be more time to explore and talk and wonder at the world. However, she could not help but be sad at Uncle Bill having to go to war. He was like a second father, besides Grandpop. He never purchased something for the boys without having a present for her also. She knew how much it was going to affect everybody, but she would make sure they were not sad.

The morning was chilly, but it did not bother the kids. It was once again adventure time, but these three thought of every day as adventure time. They realized how lucky they were and tried to live up to all that pleasure. Ellie's friend Agnes also lived with her grandparents, and sometimes Ellie wondered if she had a life as wonderful as hers. Her thoughts were interrupted by Luke almost halfway walking into the ocean.

"What do you see?" Blake questioned.

"I thought I saw Willie. Maybe it was James, but I know it wasn't Moira, 'cause she's white. Keep looking, Blake. I think they are here. See? What was that? Is that a fin?" Luke was almost in the water staring out at the slightly choppy ocean.

All of a sudden three dolphins were jumping in unison, and the middle one was white.

"Look, look!" shouted Blake. "They are here. Look! There they go again! They are trying to say 'Merry Christmas'! I wish we could go for a ride." He stomped around the beach kicking up sand with his shoe.

Travis, Micah, and Brendan were lounging on a low-hanging slip of a cloud, in back of one that was made of such thin silver threads that it was transparent and changing colors every second: green, blue, purple, red, pink, on and on. As the sky turned a little dark, the clouds hung low in the horizon, and a silver stream of light pierced the center of an area and shot through to the ocean. Suddenly Blake kicked up something shiny. He reached over and picked it up—a crystal on a silver thread. He dug around in the sand again and found another. By this time all three were on their knees digging in the sand, even Ellie in her new dress. Finally they uncovered the other silver thread and pulled out the third crystal. All three quickly looped the string over their heads. Immediately the thread began its weaving, and soon there were three silver "fish" standing there looking at each other.

Then they heard the dolphins squeal, and as they stared out at the water, three huge sargassum clumps of vine laced with silver washed up on the shore, and the dolphins began riding in on the breakers. The children waded out to their friends, placed the mats on their backs, and watched as the saddle formed. Ellie gave a special hug to Moira, still the most beautiful creature the adventurous little girl had ever seen. She tried to compare her to the wolf pups, but by the time her mind wrapped around that, Moira was flying in the air. Ellie's attention shifted to the need to hang on and feel the freedom of a high dive back into the ocean. The wind, the sensation of speed, and the water spray were refreshing as Ellie put her head on the dolphin's back, making them enter the water as one smooth bullet.

At the same time, the boys and their mounts were separately doing the tricks that their particular dolphins had the most fun performing. It was exciting to do it with them. The kids were also learning to be a part of the trick. James proved to be daring. Blake was really glued to his back, and he surfaced with a big grin on his face when they breached the crest of the ocean. When James came up, he flew higher than the others. Because Blake was not heavy, the two youngest had quite a time. Once Blake came up holding a sand dollar, but he put it back in the ocean when he came down.

The sand dollar found at Christmastime was surely a lucky sign. The sand dollar had what looked like five angels at the center, in each one nestling the stars or doves. This shell was sometimes referred to as a mermaid coin. When the kids found sand dollars on the beach, they usually saved them. If they were broken, sometimes the doves would shake out. Pop's encyclopedia said those were the parts of the sand dollar's mouth.

Willi was fast. He and Luke liked the speed and the wake they could create. They also knew how to become one object, sliding effortless through the ocean. Once Willie did a barrel roll, and Luke seemed ready for it, because when the dolphin rolled over, Luke rolled up with him in the same position as when the roll was initiated. It was clear that the children were having no trouble communicating. The three saints sat on a cloud bank and watched as the six earthly creatures—human and mammal—frolicked in the ocean near the shore. They felt grateful and welcomed the responsibility to have received such charges. They knew that the plan was to have them learn and experience even more. But for now, their progress was satisfactory.

The six friends played close to shore until they heard the conch blow, and they realized that Grandmom was expecting them to go to church. It was dress rehearsal for the pageant on Christmas Eve, and Luke as a shepherd was supposed to be there. Quickly, they all kneed their steeds to shore and, as they hopped off, stepped on to the sand. The crystals dropped and buried themselves in the receding bubbles of the outgoing tide, the netting literally melting away.

As the three rubbed their clothes, they realized that they were not wet. Was this a dream? Or just a wish? Ellie looked over her shoulder to see if she could detect the blue and silver clouds. They were there. No time to tarry. Grandmom called, but Grandpop would be waiting, and that was not good. They raced back to the house.

This time it was Uncle Fay at the wheel of the government car, with Nett in the front. She was waiting for the kids to load up. They all crawled in and found a basket of sandwiches from Grandmom, and boy, did they dig in! Still a little shook up by the dream and the absolute fun of it—and with the mystery and anticipation of the play they were about to see in full costume—they sat quietly.

The day was a bit overwhelming, and their hearts were still racing with the dolphins. They ate silently—Luke, Blake, and Ellie in the backseat, each staring out a window and reflecting on the morning, the feeling, and their beating hearts that had just matched that of the dolphins they rode. They tried to calm down. There were things to process, and the sky seemed to understand. It was a great comfort to think private thoughts to something as available and as quietly listening as the sky.

There was so much to understand about the earth. Grandpop used all of it, and so did the Indians. They had seen how important their neighbors in the sea were, and it would be great to live in that world, too. But as they looked at the sky, with its comforting blanket of protection overhead—making silly cartoons on its canvas that made them laugh or wonder—they liked the cocoon they lived in. The earth, the ocean, and the heavens—and in the middle was them. The sky sometimes talked back, in the form of cloud formations. Today it would be silent questions, conversations, and thoughts to the fresh gray-blue air above.

The kids looked around in fascination at the beautiful decorations in the church. Every tall, arched windowsill had a green holly or yaupon branch, heavy with red berries, tied up with red ribbon and a big home-made candle sitting in the middle. This, too, was a point of pride throughout the villages: candles, with shells, with leaves, with things from the sea, a small starfish, a sand dollar embedded in the tallow; the candles in the church were beautiful. The ends of the pews had bunches of green leaves and red berries of holly and yaupon also tied with a red ribbon. Hanging down from the ceiling were the pull-down oil lamps used for lighting the church, and hanging from them were sprigs of mistletoe. Everyone in the village and half the Coast Guard station would be there on Christmas

Eve for the celebration of the arrival of the baby Jesus. Also lined up against the wall were decorated barrels filled with small bags that looked like lunch bags folded over.

The village's celebration of the birth of Christ included old and new together: the giving of gifts, the bounty of the harvest, the birth of the Christ child, the choir and congregation in an all-out songfest for the joy of the occasion.

At the front of the church, totally transformed to a stable as it must have looked behind the inn in Bethlehem, was a roughly made manger, and covering it was a lean-to structure that was built to look like it must have appeared all those centuries ago. The ground in front of the manger and shed was covered in small green bushes and pine straw. There were trees standing in the back, placed in pots that made the scene resemble the outside. The children were absolutely amazed. There was even a stage curtain attached to the far side on the wall, and the rope ran along one of the beams to the other side. How dramatic. Miss Ormond was getting better.

The new piano down on the floor in front of the first pew was covered in the greenery of magnolia branches and their huge open cream-colored flowers, next to red bows and candles. The whole place was converted to a wonderland of old Bethlehem. Covering the entire left corner of the fifty-foot cathedral-ceilinged church, with the intricate woodwork connecting the roof to support the rising arch of the ceiling, stood the biggest tree the forest had to offer.

The tree took up the whole side of the church. Not only was it huge, it was covered in the signs of Christmas: handmade ornaments of lace, ribbon, wood, shells, branches with blooming camellia flowers, holly branches loaded with berries, tree moss, carvings from bark—some painted (a fishing skiff with Santa aboard)—and ornaments painted from spools of thread. The tree was magnificent! Hanging all over the tree were new toys: dolls, air rifles, BB guns, wagons, watches, necklaces, beautifully wrapped boxes, a baseball and bat, an elaborate box of soldiers, locally carved sailboats, little stoves, a dollhouse handmade by somebody's grandpop, a couple of guitars and banjos, and one horn—whatever the children of the island had desired. Most everybody got a harmonica. What if they formed a band?

The local stores had also ordered toys from the various catalogs to be given to the underprivileged children in the village. They were labeled and hung on the tree. On the night of Christmas Eve, it was standing room only.

The rehearsal went almost until dark. Nett didn't trust the roads, so they got out as soon as rehearsal was over. The weary thespians finally got back to a warm fire, their own Christmas tree, and good food. The following day was Christmas Eve. A happy sleep awaited.

Breakfast was pancakes and honey and lots of laughter. Christmas Eve was finally here. Ellie and the boys were covered with flour, helping Grandmom prepare to serve the crowd. Her sons were here from school and service, as well as the ones who lived in the village. Everything was so lighthearted. Grandmom said the children could have sugar because it was Christmas. The children counted the numbers of wrapped presents under the tree that had miraculously appeared since the day before. There were lots for them, even ones from their uncles, and there were packages labeled for all of them from each other. The next morning might be the most important time of the year!

This day went by fast, with the kids checking on their ever growing fort. The fighters quit around lunch and disappeared. No telling what the young men and women had in mind. Theirs was a world of local parties at each others' houses, or pull candy with the old lady in the woods in the middle of Buxton—hanging around the porches of each others' houses or the grocery stores, a movie if one was playing in Hatteras, a dance at one of the community halls located in each of the villages, bonfires on the beach. There was much to do, and this day was just killing time waiting for that night. They helped Grandpop with the horses and Grandmom with the chickens, so they got to wish all their animal companions a merry Christmas.

Grandmom said that there were two Christmases—one on December 25, every year, and the other, the same event, the birth of Christ, but on a different old-timey calendar, and that date was January 6. It was called "Old Christmas." This island celebrated Old Christmas also. Most other people did not, but that made islanders different, and sometimes that made life better.

Grandmom said that on the night of Old Christmas, the universe celebrated the son of God and his creation of all the animals. The birds and creatures of the sea were given the ability to talk to each other. It was a night for all creatures of the universe to say what they wanted to say. Creature to creature, maybe creature to human, but the night was for the animals. The children decided they would stay up late and go out to see to Ol' Tony and Big Roy, and maybe the turtles wanted to say something to them, but in their minds and in private they talked about going into the woods to check out what the wolves were thinking.

In the afternoon the family dressed for church. Ellie put on one of the new dresses, the one that was for church, with leggings that matched. She stood ready to deal with her thick hair. This special occasion called for something unusual. To tame her thick, curly hair, Grandmom usually put it in braids that hung down in front of her shoulders. This afternoon, Grandmom weaved into the braids shiny satin ribbon the color of her dress. The shiny new ankle boots looked beautiful. Ellie always wore ankle-strengthening shoes. They were crafted of soft leather and made her stronger, as she played hard for a frail child. The sand made her strong also, as she and the boys were barefoot most of the time away from the house.

The ribbon caught the light and made a halo around Ellie's head. With her sandy hair, thick braids, and new dress and leggings, she looked like she stepped out of a picture. Even the boys took notice. They didn't look bad themselves, with their Christmas outfits and their hair watered down and slicked back. They all knew that hair would only last until they got to the car, but for a little while the boys looked sharp. Grandmom served an early supper, and they all piled in the car and headed to the church.

Jack and Lindy had the jalopy, and their plans for Christmas Eve promised to be more than just the pageant. As expected, the yard around the large white clapboard church, even early, had men dressed for evening, in their dark suits and fedoras, smoking and having pockets of conversation as people filed up the cement walkway to the covered stoop. Inside, it was beginning to fill up, but Luke, Blake, and Ellie took seats near the back, on the inside aisle. Blake and Ellie saved Luke's seat for later, shooing everybody away. He was in the play and would return as soon as it was over.

The service began with Christmas carols, mostly the religious ones because they were getting ready for the pageant. The congregation gave their loudest and best renditions of the favorites: "Hark, the Herald Angels Sing," "Joy to the World," and "O Little Town of Bethlehem." The choir sang some pretty songs. Miss Myrtle tried to ruin them, but nobody cared. Then the ushers pulled down the oil lamps and turned them low. The church was lit by candlelight. Mr. White was the narrator, and he read from the Bible the story of the birth of the Christ child. Each player came on stage as his part was read, and when the choir sang the appropriate song—"We Three Kings," "Away in a Manger," and "What Child Is This?"—the performers came from the back of the church down the aisles, middle and sides, so that the villagers were brought into the pageant happening around them. The participants moved to the manger area and took their places. Each of them held a candle. Uncle Fay looked like a real king, with his painted-cardboard gold crown, standing beside Luke, who had on a bathrobe and carried a stick for controlling his sheep. Miss Tinker looked absolutely angelic as Mary, and the newborn baby they borrowed from someone in the village slept through the whole thing. When it was over, the sheet was pulled as everyone sang "Silent Night," and when the sheet was removed there was only a pine-covered stage: no players, no props, just pretty pine straw, holly, and a stand of trees. Luke slipped silently in the end seat beside Blake. Now for the fun part.

The lamps were relit, Grandpop stepped to the front and wished everybody a merry Christmas, and the congregation sang "Jingle Bells." Suddenly a man dressed as Santa appeared beside the tree, kind of looking the part. But it was Mr. Luke, and he did have white hair and a beard. Since his wife took in sewing, his suit was perfect. He really did look like Santa Claus. Maybe some of the younger ones thought that. He carried a huge sack with wrapped presents and toys just like Santa. Grandpop invited Mr. Santa to read the names on the gifts. Each person called would raise a hand, and the elves would deliver, or the person would come up to get the present.

Blake, Luke, Ellie, and every child on the island had their eyes glued to that gigantic Christmas tree. Ellie saw maybe three bride dolls hanging, and several other pretty dolls she maybe had never seen before, and these were going to make a few of the girls in the church very happy. There were air rifles, probably one for Georgie Tolson, and BB guns strapped to the tree—but not many, as last year Freddy accidentally caused his little brother to lose an eye. There were hand-carved boats, two absolutely beautiful two-foot sailboats painted just right and fitted out as two-masters. Grandpop gave Grandmom an outrageous church hat, and when she held it up everybody laughed, but when she lifted it out, under it was a pretty one. This was such a happy night.

Santa called out one after another. Luke and Blake got the two sailboats with the idea of floating them around in the turtle pond, and if the wind was right, racing. They were perfect, made by Mr. Willie in Kinnakeet Village. The kids had visited his home and shop with Grandpop. He was a master boatbuilder and an equally good carver. They were each "a piece of work," as Grandpop would say.

Ellie's name was called, and as she walked to the front she saw the ladder placed near the back of the tree where the gifts were not easily seen. The man with the elf's hat climbed up and unhooked a box. Careful not to tip it over, he handed the open box to Ellie. The gift was a large baby doll in a pink satin, lace, and ribbon baby dress. The name on the box was "Sweetie Pie," and that became her name forever. This doll was so huggable it was warming. Ellie lifted her out of the box when she got back to her seat, and she fit just right against her chest. Sweetie Pie had short, curly brown hair and a bonnet with lace tied under her chin. Her eyes blinked shut, so she could be asleep, or open for listening. Her face was porcelain, as were her arms and legs. She had on shoes and lace socks, and everything was pink. What a happy night. The people were all smiling and laughing and showing things off, with lots of hugs and best wishes to go around.

If getting presents from the tree was not enough, Pop announced that before anybody left, they were to take home bags of candy for each one in their family. He began to call names and quantities, and while others were getting ready to leave, a member would go to the front of the church and pick up the number of bags of candy for each person in the family. Mr. Johnny, seven. Mr. Owens, thirteen. Mr. Fred, three, and on it went. Even members of the Coast Guard—every name was called, and one guy took a box loaded for the ones at the station who could not attend because of duty. If someone had a baby the day before, the child received a bag of candy. Even the members of the Pentecostal church did the same thing. The system left out no one. Everybody in the village got candy.

Each bag contained two cups of assorted hard candy, peppermint, wintergreen, peach blossoms, fruit, cherry, one or two wrapped Mary Janes, a handful of unshelled mixed nuts, one orange, and one apple. The kids were excited to get one and to see others get bags also. On previous afternoons before Christmas Eve, they had gone with Nett to Uncle Tommy's store to help work from the two rows of long planks that rested on sawhorses and served as a huge table. With bags opened on the table, around the edges were barrels of candy complete with scoop. The helpers put in a scoop of candy, then on to the nut guy, and on to the orange and apple guy, and the folding and putting in the barrel for the church guy.

Captain Charlie and his friends—Mr. White and Mr. Bernice, Uncle Baxter, all the store owners, various local men, fishing friends, hunting friends, men from both churches—all chipped in to buy the candy and fruit. It was just a labor of love from everybody. People began to depend on that candy and would even more later, as rationing of sugar got worse and those things were just not available. The church emptied out with neighbors and friends wishing everyone a merry Christmas as they went home to anticipate the next day and their feast of drum stew and fresh turkey, beginning with raw and steamed oysters on the porches.

For the lighthouse crew, there would be punch and a punchbowl with pretty cups—one of Grandmom's purchases—and plates and plates of goodies, both the vegetable kind and the sweet kind. Grandmom made every kind of fudge imaginable. She also made the softest mints ever. They melted away before the second one could be added. Cookies were oatmeal and chocolate, some lemon, fruit and nutty kinds—just a variety, and nobody told anyone not to indulge. But not to worry, because the kids were not really big sweets eaters. They had other things to do.

At almost the break of dawn the children bounded down the stairs in their pajamas. Ellie grabbed Sweetie Pie, vowing the night before to never sleep without her, and almost elbowed out Luke to get there second. Santa always came to the keeper's quarters, every year. Uncle Fay said he heard on the shortwave radio on Christmas Eve that the jolly old man was over New York, and the children raced to their bedrooms. The boys talked themselves to sleep, and Ellie talked to Sweetie Pie.

That morning the squealing was enough to wake the dead. Nett, Bill, Grandpop, Grandmom, and the boys from next door had to cover their ears. Santa ate and drank everything Grandmom left him. Exactly right in front of the tree stood the prettiest bride doll that had ever been left at the foot of a Christmas tree. Still clutching Sweetie Pie, Ellie dropped to her knees in front of it, and at that height, the doll was almost as tall. She was elegant! With real tears flowing, Ellie put her now wet nose up against the veil and just cried. Meanwhile, with not even a nod toward their weeping cousin, Blake and Luke unfurled their whips, and each got a pair of skates as there was a concrete walkway leading from the assistant's quarters to the keeper's quarters. Ellie was a little sad, but she knew the dangers of her falling, and it would be fun to watch the boys. She had to be content to get her bride doll and the whip, which she had yet to pick up. Blake was almost ready to try the snap when Bill bellowed out a navy order that would stand down the most unruly sailor.

"We're only gonna do that outside! No exceptions. Now is just for looking and feeling," he said as he descended the stairs.

Then everybody was there in their nightclothes and robes, with Grandmom and Nett getting coffee, milk, and sweet buns to the revelers on the floor. Paper was flying. Grandmom got the biggest box of candy, and lo and behold she opened it right there and passed it around. Candy in the morning: Christmas was magic. Everybody got clothes, toys, and a special treat. After passing around the various items for others to see, the recipients began to pick up and clean the floor. As was their custom, the presents were repacked on top of their boxes for viewing under the tree. Not Ellie, though: She was not going to let go of those two dolls all day. She was absolutely of no use to anybody.

Bill sat down in the pile of Christmas paper next to the boys. "What do you boys think about helping Grandpop this morning by feeding the horses?"

The kids stopped tearing at the packages, and almost as one they said, "Now? Daaa-aad! We haven't seen what everybody else has."

Then they hesitated and looked at their father's eyes. Instantly, they knew how much they would miss him, and because he asked, they both agreed. They still had on their pajamas and said, "Can we go like this?"

Bill thought about the chilly temperature and sent them upstairs for warmer clothes. "Just put something over your pajamas. We'll be right back."

They were only a minute, as they wanted to get it over with so that they could get back to messing up the room—legally.

"Can Ellie help?" Blake asked. If he was going to be inconvenienced, so was Ellie.

"Sure. Ellie, go put on your coat and boots. We'll be right back," said Bill.

As they waited for Ellie, they were so concerned with themselves that they did not look at the smiling eyes around them. Ellie returned, and the four went out to the barn. When they got to the barn and were loading up the buckets, Bill said, "You only have two buckets. What about him?" and he pointed down the dark barn to the far end where the Coast Guard surf horses sometimes stayed when they were anticipating a pull with the other two. It was usually where all Grandpop's boxes were stacked up, but now, it didn't appear to have any debris.

Luke squinted as he tried to see in the dim light. Grandpop had all the window shutters down, keeping out the light that usually streamed into the barn. As he looked he heard a strange noise. It was a whinny, but not the usual one. Ellie was ahead of all of them, fearless to run into the barn's dark edge. She let out the longest squeal, and Blake and Luke came running.

"Daddy! Daddy!" the boys shouted.

"Grandpop!" Ellie echoed.

In the very last stall, with two stalls empty in between, peered the beautiful, soft golden head of a horse. He was amazing. His mane was creamy, his coat a dark golden, and his tail was flaxen white. His eyes, even in the dim light, were different—not brown like Ol' Tony's and Big Roy's. By that time, everybody from the house was dressed in heavy coats and standing in the entrance of the double doors all clad in their pajamas. They began to open up the shutters and the barn doors so that the children could see that his eyes were blue. Luke was first to touch his muzzle. It was soft and warm, and the horse responded with a low woof-snort from his nose. Blake was reaching, and so was Ellie, and Grandpop handed them a cut-up apple. Luke held out his hand for the horse to nibble at the fruit with his lips, careful not to nibble hand as well as apple. Blake also held up a chunk, and the horse reacted the same. Ellie reached out her hand for some apple, and Grandpop put a piece in her hand.

"Please, Pop, two?" Ellie said with eyes a little teary.

She took the two pieces and ran around the astonished watchers to give one to Ol' Tony and one to Big Roy. Ellie had such a soft heart that Grandmom beamed with pride. It was the same way she treated her dolls. She always wanted to give the exact amount of attention to all of them so that they would not feel left out. As soon as Ellie had satisfied the desire to share, she was back like a flash to take another piece her grandfather handed her. She, too, fed the new resident.

"I just couldn't leave you boys without a friend to give you a ride. I am usually ferrying you guys around, and when I'm gone, I wanted to make sure you had a ride if you needed it. Sometimes Grandpop has to work, and Grandmom is busy, and we all know how much work your mom has to do, so I thought that since none of you can drive a car, you might get tired of walking."

Bill hardly finished before he was attacked by three little munch-kins—one at his knees, one his waist, and Luke, as he was getting taller, grabbed him around his neck and almost threw him to the ground. They hugged him so hard that they were crushing each other.

Grandmom smiled and thought, *I guess they will all be having their meals out here from now on.* She gave herself an inside giggle at the joke she made. She dared not say it out loud, lest it become a fact!

They had to drag themselves away from their prized possession. They still could not think of a suitable name. They had so many, to the point they got silly with them. Whitey, Creamy, Sam, Socks (he had white feet), Blue (for his eyes), and finally they asked the group.

"What is your favorite name for a horse?" Luke asked his dad.

"Admiral," answered Bill, thinking of the famous thoroughbred War Admiral.

"Seabiscuit," said Uncle Jack, this being the horse that was on everybody's mind.

"Seabiscuit. That's a good one. We live right on the sea, and Grandmom makes the bestest biscuits. That's it!" declared Luke.

"Pegasus," said Nett. "He was the winged horse who belonged to the mythical god Poseidon, king of the sea, and he was white with wings, making him fast as the wind."

The three looked at each other and knew that this would be the horse's name. No doubt.

"Pegasus," Luke repeated. "Pegasus. We'll call him Gus."

"Gus?" said Blake. "Why Gus?" He was wrinkling up his nose in disapproval.

"Because it is pronounced like that, and I like it, too, so that's two against one!" Ellie said as she took a don't-mess-with-me stance, putting her hands on her hips in defiance. One look at that face, and Blake stomped his foot and reluctantly agreed.

It was decided that the horse would belong to all of them equally, and they would all ride. Grandpop opened one of his boxes and pulled out a fancy horse blanket. The kids looked at each other as he did it, and they could have sworn it was the same box as their Indian treasures, but maybe not.

Luke put the bridle on Gus and led him to the fence, making it easy for the two youngest to get on. Bill decided he needed to build a box for them to stand on to mount, and also to get the blanket straight. Sometimes the blanket was so crooked it hardly was under anybody's butt at all.

The rest of the day it was hard to get the kids out of the barn. Bill was so happy to have finally given this wonderful animal to his kids. He had been thinking about it for at least a year, ever since Captain Charlie had seen the new foal at the corral in Hatteras. Charlie was friends with a man in Hatteras Village who raised horses, and he had the finest. He had seen the foal right after it was born and fell in love. He and Bill discussed the animal at length over the next two years as they watched the horse grow. Captain Charlie had purchased him on the spot, knowing that, in a couple of years, both horse and kids would be of the right age. He and Bill made regular trips to the corral and paid for all the care, training, and maintenance until the time came to gather it and bring it home. This was the day.

On that day—with all the sons and daughters and wives and such—Grandmom and Grandpop went out and sat on the porch swing with a cup of coffee. Grandmom hummed quietly, and Grandpop smoked one of those Camel cigarettes that turned his fingers brown. Soon, with the cleanup accomplished, everybody was sitting all over the porch and the porch steps, eating cinnamon buns, drinking coffee or milk, listening to the low roar of the ocean, and marveling at the beautiful, breezy Christmas Day. Gus was tied to the porch post.

Billy Mitchell

The war was coming to the Island. Bill had been reassigned to the destroyer tender USS *Melville* docked in Norfolk, Virginia, that would ship over during the second week of March. He was sorely needed as manpower on the island, but he was a quite a gifted mechanic, and the navy thought he would best serve on one of the huge fighting ships due to join the convoy in Europe. The United States remembered World War I and the havoc it played on the lighthouses and beacons located on the East Coast. They were sure that it would be repeated during this war, and probably in greater measure. A couple of days after Christmas, several U.S. admirals came across Toby's ferry to the Coast Guard station near The Point to survey the situation. This inspection was going to concentrate on defense of the area in case of clashes between submarines and ships off this piece of land. This was a gold mine for any enemy trying to disrupt supply ships moving up and down the coast.

In World War I, a sub had severely damaged the lightship off Diamond Shoals. It was the theory of this enemy, as it had been to the Confederate Army, that destroying merchant ships delivering supplies would weaken the enemy, and a way to do that was to darken the lights that allowed ships to know where they were. So the admirals were inspecting the readiness of the Coast Guard and their navy partners to spot the subs, warn the allied ships, and keep the Germans on the other side of the ocean—or send them to the bottom.

The admirals were well informed about the island. They knew it to be some of the best duck and geese hunting grounds in the world. The numbers of wild fowl hunted from lodges on the reefs of the Pamlico Sound were legendary.

Billy Mitchell, a most famous World War I participant, had fallen in love with the place and chosen the waters off Hatteras Island to prove the new power of airplanes. They also knew that Chief Bill Finnegan was probably one of the best hunting guides in the area—plus he was navy, had access to the local knowledge of places to go, and connections to good trained dogs for retrieval. When the admirals finished their inspections, they began planning for their hunting excursion.

Grandpop and Uncle Baxter had between them over 100 decoys. They had canvas-backed geese, brants, snow geese, Canadian geese, black ducks, mallards, canvasbacks, teals, redhead ducks, and pintails. Each decoy was painted, and its neck arched into an exact replica of the bird it was representing. The feathers were carved out and the wings perfect, as was the color. They were considered masterpieces by some of the men, and they sought decoys of birds from special locals who were talented. Men took great pride in their depiction of the intricacies of the fowl. They tied them out near their blinds and waited for the flyover of birds that would want to stop and chat. The fake birds just sat there, waiting to fool other birds into flying near the blind, sink box, or boat where the hunters were waiting. Locals also had live decoys to lure in flocks of geese and ducks.

The hunters used the lodges to get warm and for meals and sleeping. The shelters were in the middle of the sound, on stilts, and were owned by those who had a permit from the state. Hunters came to the reef house by boat and had small skiffs tied to the pilings supporting the building. There were only two lodges at that time: one owned privately and one owned by a hunt club. Bill took the admirals to the privately owned structure. Mr. White, Grandpop, and two other avid hunters owned the lodge.

The boats were camouflaged with twigs, limbs, and foliage to hide the occupants inside. From the lodge they went to a blind, which was a loosely constructed box whose walls were not solid, but lashed together with plenty of air holes stuffed with foliage to make the structure appear natural. Blinds were also used by those who did not intend to stay over-night but just go out for a day of hunting. Had the box been solid, the brisk wind on the Pamlico Sound would have blown it down. There-fore, the blind was constructed to let the wind blow through. If it was in the sound—there were two kinds: on the water or in the marsh, where hunters could walk through the reeds to access it—there was an open end to drive the boat into it and keep the hunter's feet dry. As there was a need for obscurity, the fourth side was leaned up against another wall to be put in place when the boat was secure. As the birds flew over the decoys, the hunter rose out of the blind and shot as many as he could.

The birds were retrieved by a couple of breeds of dogs, called retriev-ers. There were the Chesapeake Bay retrievers—a stocky, dark brown, curly haired, burly swimmer—and also the slimmer and sleeker Labrador retriever, usually black or yellow. Seasoned hunters were particular about their dogs. They even had shoes made for them, to protect their feet from ice or slicing marsh grass. The dogs were workers, either trained by their masters or by a trainer, usually ones who were skilled dog handlers, mostly local men known to have a talent for training dogs. It was important also for the dog not to be gun shy, meaning not to react to the loud crack of a rifle going off near its ears. Male and female dogs were both desirable.

On command, the dog's job was to retrieve the fallen bird, swim back to the blind with the treasure in its mouth, and drop the bird in the hand of its master. Then they patiently awaited the command to do it again. They had been trained to have a soft mouth, which meant not to bite down, but just to hold the bird until it was delivered to the hunter. This task was not easy, as bringing in a large goose was difficult. Sometimes the dog would lose the bird, but he always went back to retrieve—as many times as it took to bring it in. This breed has a natural desire to retrieve, like a shepherd possesses the same nature to herd. They all do what they do because it comes naturally to them. Coon dogs go after and tree their prey, but on this island, the retriever was the desired dog to own.

The women of the island sometimes were jealous of the attention paid to a good hunting dog. The animals were pampered and the pride of their owners. In every way possible, they were royalty in their own world.

The hunters took turns shooting, as in all hunting. Never would more than one hunter stand up to shoot out of turn. There were strict safety rules. If a hunter missed, he waited his turn to come around again. But it was hard to miss. The geese and ducks flew over in such a tight V formation—honking and honking and so compact—that even a wild shot would bring down a bird. Their tight formation allowed their mighty wings to draft off the birds in front.

Of course, some hunters had duck calls, used when decoys were not practical or available. The wooden callers were unique to the type of duck the hunter wanted to attract. Most hunters had several hung around their neck, in anticipation of the types of birds that were known to be in the area. For instance, the drake (male) mallard had a nasal call and a high-pitched whistle, while the female had a deeper quack, similar to the common sound a duck makes. These sounds of the duck did draw in a flock, as waterfowl seem to be quite social and look forward to company. Some duck calls were purchased, and some were fashioned by locals who thought they could make a wooden reed with tone boards inside that, when a hunter blew into one end and the pieces flapped together, simulated the particular sound of a certain bird. Mostly they were made of wood, because when metal ones were attempted, they froze on the lips of the caller and created a problem. Duck calls, like hunting dogs, had to be just so in order to work correctly. It was an art.

At that time there were no limits on how many birds a hunter could kill, and some just killed and killed but did not advertise the fact. Usually on the island, waterfowl was never wasted. It was not unusual for a person to awaken to find a mess of ducks or a goose left on the doorstep, when a friend had been hunting and got more than he could eat—or if the person needed it. The islanders were so conscious of the delicacies of the island that, in the old Indian spirit, hunters only killed what they could eat. All over the island, those who hunted shared with those who did not. Those who fished also shared with those who did not. People with gardens traded with those without. Most skills were available to the neighbors, and the barter system kept everyone's life complete.

After their inspections were complete and reports ready, the admirals contacted Bill to take them hunting. They came with their own shotgun, Winchester 12-gauge, and Remington pump. They appeared to be seasoned sportsmen. Bill and Captain Charlie picked them up in the wagon, in order to carry all the decoys in the back, and off the party went for a two-day hunting trip. Captain Charlie was disappointed not to go, but the lighthouse needed twenty-four-hour surveillance, and this was Bill's trip. The children were also sorely disappointed at being left behind, but they were not allowed to be around serious guns. They were allowed to practice with an air rifle or a BB or pellet gun, using a target, but bullets were another matter. They waited anxiously for the hunters to return, as did Grandmom, who was looking forward to a mess of fowl. Boy, could she flavor a goose! She stuck an apple in the cavity, which soaked away most of the fowl taste and made the goose more flavorful. These visitors knew that they were cutting into the time the kids had left with their father. Only a few weeks remained.

The children almost rode poor Gus to death those first days, until Bill told them to give him a rest. It was a good suggestion, as they were beginning to run out of places to show him. He did not seem to mind the weight on his back, and when Luke led him by the bridle to the fence for the three to climb on top, the horse began to leave the barn and go straight to the fence post and wait. Bill built them a box, and life became easier for Gus and his riders.

In order to take away the fidgetiness the children displayed, and to keep their minds off the horse, Nett promised them a trip to Mr. Hollivey's store. Mr. Hollivey had a grocery store near the church at the far end of the village close to the edge of town, so it was not a place the kids went often. They could only hope to get a ride down there for the special cargo Mr. Hollivey sold.

That special cargo was comic books. The kids did not have many, but they were stingy with the few they had. Blake could not just go into Luke's room and get a comic book. He had to ask, and then Luke had to exact a life-or-death promise from him in order to loan it out. Nobody cared about Ellie's comic books. She was all into *Mickey Mouse* and *Donald Duck*, while Luke and Blake bought *Superman* and *Batman*. They were excited about going, and it did relieve some of the waiting for the men to return. The afternoon went by fast as a comic book exchange took place in the newly decorated boys' room at the keeper's quarters.

Late in the afternoon after the second day, the men returned. Grandpop hitched up the horses and went down to Bernice's creek to pick up the hunters and their prize. The children bundled up and hopped on the wagon, letting the backboard down and dangling their feet off the back as they passed through the village. It was already beginning to get dark, and the kids thought it a treat to be out that late. Down at the dock, the boat pulled up loaded with men and birds. They threw the catch of geese and ducks into the wagon, along with the decoys, and all crawled on to the front bench—some kneeling behind it—with the kids dangling off the end trying to keep Grandpop informed when a goose began to fall off.

Ellie picked up a mallard. She had never seen such vibrant plumage.

His head was totally a glossy bottle-green with a distinctive white collar separating the color of the head from the purple-tinged body. When she lifted a wing, she gasped at the iridescent purple-blue reflective feathers edged with white that could only be seen in flight. The under feathers reflected light like a mirror. It reminded her of the feathers the Croatoans collected for headdresses, decoration on clothes, and ornamentation for hair. She had learned that the under plumage was the most beautiful in all birds. Man could not match these colors.

They made their way carefully to the Coast Guard station, where the admirals and their bounty got off, and the rest went back to the lighthouse compound. Given time to clean up and eat, the men planned to get together one more time at the keeper's quarters to discuss the day's adventure and what those who lived in the area thought about the plans for their protection as the war began to escalate. They especially needed to talk about the wireless station, manned at this time by Captain Charlie's son Wallace. This was a new concept, whose experiments proved that a signal could be bounced off an object to determine the distance away. The navy was worried about enemy ships. All these devices were planned to keep safe the people of the protruding island as well as the entire United States.

After supper, the guests returned with two huge Canadian geese, ready for hanging. It was important to hang the fowl for a few hours or a day, because they were too tough when eaten right away. Grandmom went straight to the kitchen to plan a meal around them. The men gathered on the porch of the keeper's quarters to discuss the adventure, eat some of Odessa's potent fruitcake, drink a cup of coffee, and spend some time with their hosts. Both boys took their place on the swing with their father in between. He had his arm around Blake as the youngster rested his head on his dad's chest. Luke was also leaning in, with his arm looped underneath his father's. It was a comforting feeling that Bill would later recall often. Grandpop chose a rocking chair, and Ellie chose Grandpop's lap. The men all sat around in the porch rocking chairs. They began talking about the previous days.

Bill inquired how the three naval dignitaries knew to bring their shotguns. Did they know about the wealth of fowl located in the sound off the island? The officers said they had heard of this island and its struggle in World War I, and they were aware of the uniqueness that this island afforded from the tales told by U.S. Army Air Service General Billy Mitchell, who spent time waterfowl hunting in the area in the years around World War I.

Mitchell received praise for his theory—and later proof—that bombers could sink ships. This knowledge in World War I was not accepted, so Mitchell staged several demonstrations of his theory, which was to advance the acceptance of air power used in war. One of the demonstrations took place off the coast of Cape Hatteras. When Mitchell, an avid sportsman, was stationed in Virginia, he became aware of the bounty of fowl and frequently visited the island for excursions. The islanders grew accustomed to seeing his small plane, a de Havilland, on the hard-packed sands of the Hatteras beach, near Durant's Station between the villages of Trent (Frisco) and Hatteras. These trips were designed solely for waterfowl shooting and fishing. He befriended the islanders—staying in Hatteras Village, hunting, playing cards and dining with the locals—and generally had a warm feeling for the people, and they for him.

Mitchell had the idea of using the island two years after staging a moderately successful trial off the Virginia coast. He learned much from that experiment and then had to battle his detractors, who claimed it was not conclusive. They said he was just lucky. This time, he was completely successful in sinking two decommissioned battleships—the *New Jersey* and the *Virginia*—six miles off Cape Hatteras. This added two more ships to the collection in the area around Diamond Shoals, but these two were not accidents. Throughout his remaining career, even though he never returned to the island after advancing in both rank and importance, he bragged about the lucrative waterfowl hunting on Hatteras. The admirals, realizing they would be in the area of such noted sporting grounds, were determined to extend the time of their inspections to include the hunt.

By the time the Mitchell story was recounted, the naval officers were ready to get down to the business of securing the island. Bill and Captain Charlie sent the children to bed. Blake was actually already asleep, as was Ellie, so they carried them upstairs, along with Luke, who was persistent about wanting to stay, but to no avail. The men went back out on the porch to discuss the art of war. The subject turned to the bunker and the wireless station. They had previously checked with Captain Charlie's son Wallace on his thoughts concerning the wireless, which was located in the marshy land between the beach and the main Coast Guard station. It was a tall, solitary building that housed only one operator, who searched the screen to see if the sound bounced off any solid object that was not supposed to be in those waters. What an important part the island would play in keeping the country safe. Bill and Captain Charlie were both pleased to be of such service. They felt that it also ensured the safety of the residence on the island, should there be as big a war engagement as the last time.

In recognizing the respect the admirals had for the island, Captain Charlie decided to add to the awe they already expressed by telling them about another remarkable event that had taken place years before the Mitchell experiment. Reginald Fessenden, a former chief chemist for Thomas Edison, had set up a tower on this island and one on Roanoke Island, where he successfully transmitted the first sounds leading to the first radio broadcast. As Fessenden and his superiors at the U.S. Weather Bureau argued over patents, his work was stalled until his resignation in 1902 to do private research, which resulted in the first musical notes being sent over the airwaves from Massachusetts to the tower in Buxton.

The navy men left with an exalted opinion of the sandy stretch of land that had fostered such a courageous and patriotic people. As they stared at the sky on this December night, whose full moon was referred to as the cold moon, the beauty of the heavens made each think of the holiday season, the reason for it, and how absolutely breathtaking the night looked. The moon was waning, but it enhanced the deep blue of the heavens. There were silver streaks ambling across the night, drifts of cloud runs, and a thick blanket of stars. The islanders had always enjoyed starry nights. There was no ambient light on land to obscure the stars as they shone. The stars had no competition. The men began to point out the constellations. They compared their experience this night with being on a ship in the middle of the ocean, where everything was so clear. No lights from land to drown out the beauty of the stars, and it was remarkable how close the heavens looked here, just like at sea.

All three children were placed in the same room. The boys' room was newly painted, and Nett worried about them sleeping in the fumes, so the two single beds were put side by side with Ellie's bed in the front room, over the porch. As the three slept, conversation disturbed their dreams, and with the sprinkling of stardust that came through a crack in the window, they began to dream of airplanes and stars and adventures with the radio . . . and all the other suggestions that came in their minds from the conversation downstairs.

When the kids awakened, life had returned to normal. Christmas was still all over the house, with Grandmom almost making the house look like it was outdoors. She had the boughs of red-berried holly bushes, yaupon twigs loaded with red berries, magnolia flowers, clusters of candles with ribbon, special tea towels embroidered with figures of the season, great smells coming from the kitchen, and the smell of wood burning in the fireplace and the stove in the kitchen. It would stay that way until Old Christmas—everything, including the tree.

Grandmom was slaving over the goose, and Nett asked the boys if they wanted to visit some of their friends in the village. She took them into Buxton and dropped them off at Colby's house, promising to return in a couple of hours. She wanted them to play with their friends. School seemed to have been out so long, and she was worried that they were already getting bored. Of course, Ellie went also. Nett wanted Ellie to go with her, but she stayed with the boys. The talk that afternoon was all about a haunted house that Colby had heard about, located in the woods between Buxton and Trent. Several of the boys in the village had been around the place in an effort to gather up the courage to go in but had been scared away by wolves and strange noises. The kids shot each other a glance, thinking in unison, *Our wolves?* while Colby kept talking.

When they got home and were on the swing with Grandpop, Luke asked him innocently about the house.

"Grandpop, is there a haunted house in the woods near Trent?" Luke didn't expect the answer he heard.

"I don't know what you mean, 'haunted house,'" Grandpop replied. "Do you mean the old mansion at the top of the hill near the ridge?"

Luke, Blake, and Ellie were shocked that Grandpop seemed to know clearly what they were talking about.

"Maybe," Luke said. "Is there a huge house in the woods?'

"Yes," said Grandpop, "and it belongs to us."

The children almost fell off their chairs. *What does that mean, "It belongs to us"? Is Grandpop crazy?*

"Pop, what do you mean there is, and it belongs to us. Who is 'us'?" Ellie questioned.

"My heavens, child. Where are you getting all these questions?" the captain responded.

"My friend Colby says there is a haunted house in the woods, and some of the kids have been playing around there, and they saw ghosts!" said Luke. He did not want to say they saw wolves, because he was not wanting Rafe, Theo, or Twylah to get in trouble.

"Well, son, there's no such things as ghosts, and the house is just old, not haunted. It belongs to your grandmother and has been in her family for over 200 years. Yes, it probably is a little run-down, and maybe it looks haunted. But your grandmom and I have been trying to keep it up little by little over the years. Maybe we should go back there and take a look to see if anyone has done any damage to it. It used to be a beautiful old mansion, but being so old, it is hard to keep it in tip-top shape." Grandpop was thinking out loud.

Too late. They were on it like a snake.

"Go take a look at it? With you?" Blake was too excited for words. "Can we go with you. We can help you rake the yard or fix the chimney."

"What chimney?" Grandpop had to laugh. Mention one thing and these three had the imagination of a story writer. *Where in the world do they get all their crazy thinking,* he thought.

"Well, all old houses have a chimney, don't they? Places where bats hang out?" Blake was in full fantasy mode now, and his mind was racing. He had read too many *Batman* stories.

"I can't remember if there is a chimney. But let's go see. What say we go tomorrow, right after I tend the light? Your dad can take over one more time."

Captain Charlie might not have known what he was starting.

★ 10 ★

Trent Woods

first thing in the morning, every morning, the kids fed Gus. They would feed him again in the afternoon. It actually became a chore they shared with their grandfather, as he was taking care of the other two horses at the same time. All the duties associated with owning a horse seemed not to be a chore but a pleasure. They almost rubbed his skin raw brushing him until Grandpop made them stop, tacking a schedule for grooming and other responsibilities on the barn wall. They rode him every afternoon. Actually they rode him all the time, until Bill thought his sons would lose the use of their legs. If the three were tight before, they were surely connected now. Ellie complained to Grandmom about a sore butt about the third day, and Odessa suggested she take a break until she got used to riding. The horse was not going anywhere, so she might as well relax.

They ate the hearty breakfast Grandmom put on their plates. They anticipated not wanting to be hungry as they toured the old house. For this day they didn't want to argue over not wanting this or that. If she said more, they all held up their plates. They did not want anyone getting mad at them. This day was too important. The night before, they slept once again in the room with Ellie, and they talked almost all night long about what they might see. They also decided that they would be braver than the other kids. They were on the ultimate adventure in their minds—one they would get to brag about when they got back to school after the holidays.

Grandpop blew the raspy horn of the old jalopy, and the kids flew out of the house and scrambled in—Luke in the front seat, Ellie and Blake in the back. They bounced around with so much energy in the back that Grandpop couldn't tell if it was the road, the kids, or the old jalopy that was causing such a rough ride through all the ruts and puddles in the road. He guessed he might be a little spoiled at having the new car, or maybe he was just getting old. No matter. He never even considered taking the new car, not into those woods with limbs sticking out to scratch the paint. He would endure the rough ride, and the kids certainly didn't mind. Luke was actually having fun watching the track go by through the floorboards, and he decided on the spot he liked this car the best.

New cars were fine for a while, but everyone was so particular about them that it was hard to keep from messing up everything. So since nobody cared what happened to the jalopy, it became the ride of choice for the kids, other than Pegasus.

Luke studied the paths and trails that Grandpop took in order to find his way to the mansion. Sleeping had been hard on the night before the children were to visit the old house. *How come they never knew about it? How come other kids know about it?* The answer to those questions, for Luke, was that other kids explored the woods like the lighthouse kids explored the beaches. He decided they would have to be just a little more adventurous. In his mind, the house was his, and it would not be considered an intrusion if they visited it sometimes. Now that they were going with Grandpop, there would be no ghosts, and he knew the wolves were familiar with this group. They were part of Luke's pack, and Luke was a part of theirs. Luke had every intention of introducing the wolves to Gus. He just didn't know how.

The single two-track trail was not as clear a path as regular roads, because it was seldom traveled and had become overgrown with small bushes and fallen limbs. Fortunately there were no downed trees. Grandpop kept a good handle on that. He and Bill checked the site after every hurricane and also looked around to make sure the mansion was fairly intact at the same time. Charlie had often thought that, when he retired from the lightkeeper's job, he would move the family there. Knowing his plan, Bill and Jack were quite ready to see to it that the property was well maintained. So Charlie was not worried that there would be tremendous damage, because he and Bill had been there only a month before to check on keeping the road clear. He made sure the roof was always in good repair and that none of the windows were broken or cracked. He had, over the years, replaced windows and any part of the house that looked damaged on the outside. But the rumor of wolves and ghosts was never dispelled because it helped to keep vandals away. Uncle Jabez, and later Sabra, had constructed the most sound structure anyone on the island had ever seen. It looked like it belonged on Millionaire's Row in some fancy city instead of the middle of the Trent Woods. Captain Charlie also knew that it was going to take a lot of explaining to the kids as to why they had not been informed before about this piece of property and its contents.

Captain Charlie was not blind to the draw of curiosity, and he found it easier to not tell them than to have to listen to them wanting to go there all the time. Now that their school friends had spilled the beans, he felt he had to tell them. As a result, maybe they could, in their own way, discourage curious children from snooping around. He was carrying in the boot of the jalopy several pieces of glass in case new owners of BB guns and pellet guns might have gotten close enough for target practice. He doubted that also, as he was quite confident in the power of the wolves to discourage anyone who would come on the property, and there were many security preventions in case the wolves failed in their guardianship.

One of the things Bill had installed was a huge generator in one of the outbuildings, and he had linked the engine together with the pipe organ. The wires spread all over the yard connecting the two, so anyone who stepped on one of those wires would activate the pipe organ to play. Charlie thought that was ingenious. He and Bill had a great laugh about that. Bill had obtained a large ship's generator from the trash heap in the Portsmouth Navy Yard and brought it home for the family to use at the keeper's quarters to have electricity. On second thought, they realized it would save them a lot of trouble in their frequent inspections if they placed the piece of machinery at the mansion's site.

They were in line for another generator for the house, as the navy was upgrading all the ships in preparation for what might be a lengthy war, and there would be several generators replaced with newer and more modern ones. Bill was due to pick up two after the New Year in time to wire the keeper's quarters with electricity before he shipped overseas.

The path through the woods was close. The branches of untrimmed bushes brushed the side of the car as it moved in and around the puddles and deep trenches in the narrow road. This was probably a good time to be making this visit since the trees had lost most of their growth in the frosts and freezes of early winter. Grandpop always said a frost was not a bad thing, as it covered the plant and kept it warm. Freeze was a killer.

Going back into the Trent Woods was exciting. The kids kept a sharp eye out for a fleeting shadow that might indicate a wolf in pursuit. The forest was so thick that it created a canopy over the road and almost blocked out the sky. Shards of sunlight shot through the trees, making golden stripes along the paths. Everything was still so green. This area was protected from the wind where the trees were dense, and mostly were of the evergreen variety: cedar, juniper, yaupon, holly, and live oak trees with thick branches that in some places were six to nine inches thick, the trunks being three feet around or more. In the spring the dogwood, mimosa, and wax myrtle bloomed, adding to the already dense forest.

There were so many tall pine trees that the wooded road was protected by the winter loss of needles, which covered the tracks and allowed the jalopy to rumble through. Huge grapevines wound around the tops of trees looking for the sun, as was the case on the entire island.

Finally the curious group reached some type of clearing. There were only small-leafed bushes, lush low-growing greenery, and broken fallen branches from trees covered with the brightest green moss, both on the ground and growing up the spindly trees. Some trees had blown into each other, creating crosses and a jumbling of twigs. The trail ended at a fence of sorts. It was in disrepair, but it was obviously a fence. Grandpop got out of the car and walked along until he found the section he was looking for. He moved a few branches and drove the car into an opening that allowed him to get to the yard in front of the house.

The four visitors stepped out of the car and stared at the huge stone house in front of them. There were vines covering everything. Most was just ivy and Virginia creeper. Some was poison ivy, but it stood out with the obvious three-leaf cluster, each on individual stems, branched out along the vine. This was a familiar sight on the island, and the children were cautious. They had gotten a case of blisters from that vine before and were very careful not to repeat the uncomfortable condition. The plant was on the island as a shrub, ground cover, and vine. Poison ivy was not shade tolerant, requiring some sun to prosper, so it was not as prevalent here in the canopied forest as it was in the village. Anyway, the children were prepared, and as it was a chilly December day, they were covered with clothing. If they accidentally rubbed up against it, they possibly would not get the rash it offered. The vine was there, growing up the trees, but it was almost leafless because of the cold.

Aside from the dreaded poison ivy, the ground was covered in various varieties of fern and palm. Grandpop found a narrow path and motioned the children to follow in a straight line behind him. As they picked their way along, the sight was familiar, as this was the forest they occupied when they were with the Croatoans. Luke also began to point out plants to the others as being good ones or not so good —much to Grandpop's shocked look. Luke was remembering his time in the woods with Powwaw, and it made him very happy to remember the old shaman.

The mansion loomed large in front of them. Standing in the middle of their view was a huge stone-and-shingled multisectioned house. There were several styles of roofs—some parts pitched, some rounded as they topped spires. Most had dormers built into the roof, with windows for viewing out into the forest. The peaks, three of them, were on a third level, and one could see how they could view the water of the Atlantic because they were now on top of a hill. The kids had not really been aware of the climb as they were so interested in remembering their previous forest adventure. They might have been here before. It looked like it might be on top of the stream and grotto in the Indian village, but they saw no stream. As they stared at the sky, the house looked like it was at the same level as the surrounding forest.

Luke stepped away from behind Grandpop and obviously stepped on one of the connections to the generator. The ominous sound of the pipe organ caused all of them to jump, including Grandpop, who turned around and gave his grandson a look.

"Grandpop!" screamed Ellie. "They are here!"

"Sweetheart, calm down. Luke stepped on a wire that started a sound on the inside of the house. I put it there. Just be careful and follow right where I step," he said.

Meanwhile, the pipe organ was still pumping out a tune. It *was* scary. Grandpop could see why someone would say this place was haunted. He might even be thinking the same thing, the sound was so spine-tingling. Finally it stopped, and everybody breathed again. They reached the wide, moss-covered steps to the porch, and Grandpop warned them that it was slick and to walk carefully to the top, because moss on a stone was slippery and a fall would hurt. The wide porch stretched across the entire front and wrapped around the circular tower at the end. The tower was large, three stories high, and made a half circle around the right edge of the house. There, railing extended along the entirety of the porch. Reaching from the roof of the verandah to the railing of the porch were decaying wooden shuttered screens. They protected the first-floor windows, obscuring them from the yard.

Looking at the house from the front, left to right, there was a tall brick chimney reaching past the second level. Next was a pitched roof that was three stories high, with several windows on the second and third floors. It was over the entrance to the house. Behind that roof loomed a second roof higher than the first, which had an even higher-pitched roof and windows on possibly the second and third floors. This rooftop looked like the third-story room might have a very tall ceiling, as the dormer with windows was much lower than the pitch. Next and in front—like the first area was in front of the tallest part—was a rounded section that went around the corner of the house at the same height as the left group of rooms. This part had windows wrapping around both the second and third floors, with only shutters between the six or so openings in a row along the half-circled tower. An entire section of house ran all across the back like a second building, but it was built on. No wonder everybody called it a mansion. Neither the school building nor the church was even this big. The children were flabbergasted.

"Grandpop, can we pull up the shutters on the porch so we can see better?" Blake already had his hand on the dusty rope, ready to pull up the long shutter.

"No, son, don't do that. It is so old and rotten that it will break off right in your hand, and probably fall from the roof on top of you. Just let everything be. This house is over 200 years old, and everybody in the family has been taking care of it over the years. But it is all about to fall apart, so don't let it fall apart on you." Grandpop was trying to get the children to keep their hands to themselves, which was an impossible task.

"Just don't touch anything, not on the outside or the inside. Don't make me sorry I brought you here." He was trying to be stern, but he understood their curiosity and their little fingers.

Captain Charlie and the kids walked around on the porch, checking all the windows. They looked in good repair. *Thanks to the wolves,* he thought. Going back to the front double doors, he tried the locks and bolts, and the squeaky door creaked. What an eerie sound the doors made as they slowly and noisily screeched open. With just enough room to get inside, the group slipped sideways into the massive building.

The smell was overwhelming, but the scene was magnificent. Everything was covered with big sheets or pieces of cloth—maybe even sailcloth, but covered. They could not tell about the condition of the chairs or tables, or even the piano. They could tell what everything was by the shape, but it was all hidden behind those drapes of cloth. Ellie covered her nose with her jacket and just looked around. In the middle of the massive room was the most amazing staircase she had ever seen. Maybe six people could climb it side by side, almost all the way to the second story. She had never seen anything so grand. It started broad and narrowed near the top where there was a landing, then there were two sets of stairs, one going right, one going left that went up both sides to the second floor. The banisters were of thick carved oak, with ornate iron and wooden designs from the steps to the tops of the banisters. Blake's first thought was what fun it would be to slide down, but he kept it to himself, knowing Grandpop would have a heart attack should he try. The stairs were so wide that there had to be a banister going down the middle, and the edges flared out on each side.

On the wall at the top of the first set of stairs and at the back of the landing—where the stairs branched into a set right and a set left—was a huge carved wooden piece that looked for all the world like a framed door with a big carved circle in the middle. On the center rail posts were lamps on top of iron shaped figures of water nymphs holding them up.

These could be lit to light the way. On all the rail posts going up were also carved figures of more Greek nymphs. How strange, but how beautiful. All the wood was so thick, and the walls were of natural wood in big panels, not boards like at their house.

They did not go upstairs, but there was so much to see on the first floor that they began exploring. Meanwhile, Captain Charlie was checking everything out. The three children stayed right together. Actually the two younger ones stayed as close to Luke as they could get. The first floor was open. To the right and past the stair edge was a room—an obvious sitting room, judging from the covered chairs, sofas, and piano—having a stone fireplace on the far wall. Obscured from view was a circular room at the end, which looked out over the porch and to the front lawn. To the left there was another room, which appeared to be a huge dining room that could have been a banquet area. This room also had a grand fireplace on the far wall.

Straight ahead, the stairs dominated the middle of the double-story ceiling, and on either side of the stairs were sets of double French doors. Seen through the glass was another entire house. On further inspection, there were small doors at the back, on both sides of the stairs, which led to the space under the stairs.

The kids pushed open a set of doors to the left of the stairs on the first floor and found themselves in the middle of a kitchen that went across the entire house. It was the largest one they had ever seen. Across the brick wall in the back were several brick ovens. A huge, thick wooden table stretched most of the length in front of the ovens. At the left going toward the barn was the area where water was drawn and ice was stored. There were tubs for washing dishes and clothes. On the right from the door was storage for food and kitchen items. At the left of the kitchen, where the door led to the outside and the barn, was a small room called a mud room. There was also a big tub in that room for soiled items. Here, someone from outside could remove dirty boots before entering the house. Across from the mud room was a room with a door: an indoor toilet. Inside was a deep, six-foot-by-six-foot anteroom set back from the wall. It was about four feet deep, and on the back wall a bench stretched across the four feet from wall to wall. In the middle of the bench was a round hole. It looked like the outhouse at the keeper's quarters. And that is exactly what it was: an indoor outhouse.

The back door, though hard to open, led to a porch on the back of the house. The kids went out and looked around the yard. There were several outbuildings, a small cottage away from the house in the woods, and a huge barn. One of the outbuildings was apparently a boathouse. The barn looked bigger than the one at the lighthouse compound, but the double Dutch-style doors were closed, and they did not feel like bothering Grandpop over the barn. There was so much else to see. Off the porch was a long cistern and shelters for a possible chicken house. Someone could go out the back of the kitchen to the chickens. As they walked around the house—Grandpop having turned off the generator from a switch near the barn—they examined the outbuildings and the paths through the woods. Luke tried to see if he could figure how to get from here to the ocean from this part of the property. It was like the path they had taken into Jennette's sedge when they met the Indians for the first time. But here there was no sedge—just forest and a possible path to be forged in the future.

Grandpop blew the horn to the jalopy, and the kids came running. They were full of questions, and of course the first one was, When would they be back? Grandpop knew he was going to have to enlist some help keeping this group in check. He was a little concerned and a little enthused at maybe having some help getting this place under control. If the war turned the way he thought it would, they might have to make this place livable. The Coast Guard and the navy were going to be all over the lighthouse properties, and it might not be considered safe with a full family living in harm's way. He listened to the chatter—the ghost thoughts, the indoor toilet. Of course they wanted one. Grandpop smiled at the thought of tearing out a wall of the government's house to build a privy. He would have to tell Grandmom that one.

Once again Luke paid extremely close attention to the road and its twists and turns as they made their way back to the lighthouse. He also paid close attention to the sound of the surf, if he heard it, allowing him to know how far away from the beach the road was. He knew for sure he was coming back. He also knew he felt more comfortable if the three of them went. He never had any fear when they were all together. Luke also felt sure that the wolves would meet them there if they were to return.

★11★

The Lost Wolf

New Year's Eve had arrived, with the first of the fights taking place at the Casino in Nags Head. Everybody was going except Grandpop and Grandmom. Captain Charlie did not leave his duty, and Grandmom did not fancy watching her baby boy get the stuffing knocked out of him. She had heard all the talk around the table about how Lindy was so big and had such a strong punch—and poor skinny Jack was just going to get his clock cleaned. Jack was a good boxer, but he was so thin and not very muscular, and even though the matches were paired by weight, Jack really didn't look like much of a challenge. Lindy, on the other hand, was strong, tall, and muscular—all the things that Jack was not. The kids did not mind not being able to go. They had watched so much boxing in the last month that they felt like they had already seen whatever was going to happen.

The energy around the compound was charged. The seamen who had been training the two boxers were on hand to do whatever Bill asked of them. It seemed that Bill was the calmest of the bunch. He was sure of his training techniques, and without letting on to anyone else, he had his heart set on Jack. In his training sessions he had seen the clever way Jack handled himself. Jack was aware of himself at all times, and he seemed to be able to avoid the punches thrown at him. He covered himself well and waited for his chance to strike. Apparently the others had not noticed that Jack was a smart fighter, and he had a solid punch.

Dr. Folb showed up early. He was a navy pharmacist assigned to the radio station located at the right turn of the beach from Kinnakeet at the entrance of Buxton between the ocean and the sound, about a mile from the lighthouse, where Fessenden had placed his island headquarters. Dr. Folb married a local girl and was Captain Charlie's friend. The pharmacist treated many of the locals when they were in need of medical attention, as they did not have another doctor on the island. When he heard that a couple of the boys were trying for the Golden Gloves, he volunteered to be the team trainer. Bill thought he had never seen a better one, and he had been around boxing rings since he was a young boy growing up on the tough streets of Brooklyn, where the only recreation was the boxing gym on the corner.

What was funny was that Doc was always stitching up Lindy, not Jack. He turned out to be a good cut man, and he needed that skill for Lindy. Jack made it his business not to get hit. Lindy could take a punch but maybe should not have depended on that, as his strategy was to take the punch, then land a better one. Bill worried that the first punch one time might be a hard one, and Lindy wouldn't be able to punch back. So he was always cautioning Lindy to duck, cover up, side step, dance! Lindy continued to depend on his strong right hand and his knockout specialty, the three-punch combination.

The seamen were all over the compound, helping with the gear, calming down the fighters, doing whatever Bill told them to do. Anyone who did not have duty was going. It seemed to the kids that there were so many leaving from the island—Hatteras boys, Kinnakeet boys, and Chicamacomicers, all waiting down the line—that maybe there would not be enough seats for the mainland observers. Before noon, they began their trek up the beach with a caravan of cars. Jack and Lindy had plenty of supporters in their corner. Being from the island, someone might think they were underdogs, but with this crowd, the Nags Head boys might end up the ones without proper support. There must have been a dozen vehicles in the caravan making its way to the mainland. There were jalopies, side-railed trucks loaded down with equipment and luggage, a few decent automobiles, and a four-wheel-drive military vehicle that carried the seamen. All were packed with fans of the boys from Buxton.

This was one united group of island boys. They were all friends. The boys had reservations at a Nags Head motel, as the fights would not end until after the last ferry left for the island. Bill and Dr. Folb were the only ones who really wanted to go home after the fights. The rest of the boys were looking forward to New Year's Eve at the Casino. When the boxing was over, the ring would become a stage for the several bands that were booked for the late-night affair. The chairs were moved to the walls, and the whole room turned into a dance floor. Besides Jack and Lindy, the other boys had been looking forward to this trip for quite a while. The boxing matches, with two island contenders, made for quite a stir among the locals. Throw in a dance and mainland girls—what could be better? Hopefully Jack and Lindy survived in order to party with the others after the matches.

These were the qualifying matches. Whoever won in his weight class would advance to Norfolk for other rounds. After that, the last man standing in each category would have a chance to fight for the Golden Gloves in Dallas, Texas. There were a lot of gray areas in boxing. Some bigger guys lost a lot of weight before the fights so that they could fight a smaller opponent, but this was not a good idea if the larger boxer was so weakened by the weight loss that he became powerless and tired early. Also in that regard, Bill had studied the opposing fighters, and he knew which ones had dropped weight to fight a smaller man. Jack would face one of those. Bill had trained him heavily in body punches to take the energy out of his opponent, knowing the other man would already be drained of strength from losing weight. Another action Jack was to avoid was the larger fighter leaning on him, keeping him from punching, all the while resting on his smaller challenger and tiring him out. Jack learned all sorts of evasive moves to get away from his adversary.

Lindy's training was different. A big man, he did not lose weight to meet a smaller opponent. His challengers were men of his size, so he was comfortable in that area. He had sparred enough with the boys at the Coast Guard station to know that they could not bring him down. Lindy was confident, but Bill was worried. There was just no match for Lindy on the island, and that could be a problem. Lindy was strong as an ox and seemingly could not be hurt. Plus Dr. Folb was an expert at stopping a cut from getting worse, and with Lindy's willingness to get punched in order to find his knockout punch, he was planning on taking a hit or two, so the doc had his hands full.

Amateur fights were not so much about weight, but reach and speed. Lindy had a long reach but was not fast. Jack had speed and hoped he could avoid an extended reach. This was an exercise in bragging rights: the island boys against the mainland boys. In those days, being a good fighter was a plus. It was how Bill met Jeanette. There were fights at the local bar every Saturday night, and the Buxton boys knew they had a proven fighter in their midst. Bill Finnegan came on the island with a reputation for being hot-tempered and able to back it up. He was known as "the fighting Irishman."

One Saturday night, the Buxton boys brought Bill to the fights in Hatteras, and he wiped the floor with all his opponents. As the local hero, of course he caught the eye of the girls, but he only wanted to meet the pretty girl who played the piano for the silent movies at the Austin movie house. He courted and romanced Jeanette and finally won her over. Bill, a Catholic boy from Brooklyn, married Jeanette in a Methodist church on the island in a huge church wedding. He was a welcome addition to the Gray clan. He could fix anything, and he was handsome, funny, and an excellent shot—therefore a good hunter. His skill as a mechanic resulted in Captain Charlie requesting that he be assigned to the Lighthouse Service. Over the years, Bill had become as salty as any other islander, a better hunting guide even than most locals, and a perfect right-hand man for Charlie.

Charlie and Odessa took this opportunity to visit family in Kinnakeet, so they left at the same time as the Casino group. Again, Mr. Quidley volunteered to be the lighthouse keeper. The whole island had suddenly become boxing fans, and Mr. Quidley wanted to be on the inside, with first-hand information, so he took over Bill's duties in order to be there when the boys returned. Nett was all involved in creating a tiny apartment for herself upstairs in the main keeper's lodge and sent the kids out to play. This was a good time for Blake to confront Luke and Ellie about his problem. He had been preoccupied all morning, and nobody paid any attention to him. There was just too much going on.

"Luke, I have to tell you something, and I don't want you to get mad, but this is important," Blake began. "I left my lucky wolf at the old house yesterday. I remember playing with it on the back porch, and then you called me to look at something, and I think I dropped it. Please, please take me back there. I know if I wait 'til Grandpop can take me, it'll be too late. I can't lose it! Please, pleeeeze take me there. We could ride Gus, and I know exactly where to look."

The pleading look on Blake's face was hard to resist. What he didn't know was that this was exactly the excuse to return to the old house that Luke was waiting for. This way, he could say he was doing a favor for Blake, but he was really curious as to how to get there by way of the beach. He knew the way through the village, but he wanted to go by the shore route.

"Ellie," said Luke, "want to go?"

"What do you think Grandpop would say?" Ellie did not want to ask the question—she wanted to go on this adventure with Pegasus—but she felt guilty if she did not protest . . . just a little.

"Oh, please, Ellie, say yes." Blake was so afraid she would say no.

The carved wolf was his favorite companion, besides his flints. When he realized he did not have it the night before, he began to stress over the loss. It was his first gift from Mingan, and he would never get another one. He could not stand to lose it.

Luke yelled up the stairs to Nett to tell her they were taking Gus for a ride. Unknowingly, she granted permission.

Ellie knew how she would feel if it was her, so she agreed, and they hurried back to the barn to ready Gus. Grandmom had made a big roll out of an old patchwork quilt, which had strings and could be tied to the back of the horse blanket where she had also crafted holes to hold the rope. It made a back piece for Blake to lean on when riding behind Ellie. They filled the saddlebag with some cookies and things they might want, climbed on the horse's back, and headed over toward the beach to make their journey down the ocean path—around The Point and south to the area of the Trent Woods.

This trip was interesting. They rode beside the wash, looking around on the ground for shells and with an eye toward the ocean for some of their mammal friends. They scattered the little shorebirds and marveled as the sky turned black for a moment from so many cormorants flying overhead in a tight V-shaped flock, skimming the ocean near the shore for fish. These birds were large, and they flew in a pattern, carefully position-ing their wingtips in sync so that their flapping would catch the preceding bird's updraft, saving energy during the flight. It was similar to a race car catching the draft of the car in front, thus saving fuel. They could be heard coming as their rapid wing beat was loud and their wingspan was so long.

They passed the carcass of a shark, maybe fifteen feet long—longer than Gus—that had obviously been there quite a while. It could have been a small great white, as they did come around once in a while, or a more common bull shark, tiger shark, or hammerhead. All swam in these waters. The animals had gotten to it, but they did not disturb its teeth.

Luke and Blake both climbed down, and to Luke's surprise, Blake went to the saddlebag and got a knife. *This kid needed to be in the supply business*, Luke thought. He was always pulling out something obscure that nobody knew he had. They picked the largest two, and because of the decay that had already set in, the teeth were easy to extract.

Shark's teeth dropped out often, as the shark had several sets growing behind each other, and when one fell out, the other moved forward to take its place. The shape of a shark's tooth indicated what they ate. Those feeding on larger victims had pointed teeth with jagged edges. After they chose the two largest, they offered to pull one for Ellie. She shuddered and refused, not really understanding why they wanted one. They took two more—one for Colby and one for Thomas. This would be the talk of school, as they had decided to keep quiet about the "haunted" mansion. They washed their hands in the ocean. Luke helped Blake up, and the two riders moved the horse to a high enough sand hill for Luke to be hauled back to his position in the front.

They were approaching their destination from the back side of the house, so they all kept out a sharp eye when they knew they were near the desired area for a place where the dune looked to back up to a heavily wooded area. When they were with Grandpop, Luke had seen several paths through the woods from the backyard that looked like they might lead to the ocean. Surely the people who had lived there before went back and forth to the beach. At least he hoped they did.

The dunes were in several rows in this area, and they were not so close together. The group had to cross over all the sets to get to the wooded area. They walked Gus over the tough parts because they did not want to tire him by making him climb the hills with them on his back. Gus could have easily accomplished the task, but the children did not know it. After the second dune line, Luke spied a slight opening between the trees and decided to try it. It ended only a short distance from where it started, so they circled back and began looking again. The next time he chose the right path. As they ambled through the thick forest, they could tell by the stumpy bushes that it had been cleared once, a while ago. He decided they would return again to better clear the way. As they kept going up and up, they realized they were nearing the top of the hill, and they were rewarded when they could see the shingles of the roof.

When they arrived at the clearing, they dismounted and tied Gus to a tree limb nearby.

"Let me go first," Luke said. "I saw where Grandpop switched off the generator, and I need to do that so we don't set off the organ. Boy, I hope there isn't anyone here." He was thinking out loud.

Just at that moment, he saw a sight he had been searching for almost every day. Standing at the edge of the woods were the three wolves. He had seen them before, but he didn't know which one was his. Only Ellie had experienced a connection. They were out of sight of Pegasus, so the horse was not spooked, but Luke was glad to see them. He gained courage just by the sight of them, and he picked his way across the yard to the barn to turn off the generator. As he walked slowly toward the barn, one of the wolves caught up to him and trotted along beside him, like it was something he was supposed to do. Luke wanted to reach down and pet him, but he hesitated. He stuck out his closed hand, and the wolf walked under it, slightly touching as he went by. They had finally bonded. From that time until the time they mounted Gus to go back home, the wolf, Rafe, walked silently beside Luke. After he switched off the generator, he hurried back for his companions.

"Look, Luke found the wolf. How'd you get him to follow you?" Blake asked.

"I didn't. He just came over and started following me. The other two are over there at the edge of the woods. I was a little scared at first, but not now. They are all here."

Still Pegasus stood quietly.

The three made their way to the back of the house. Blake got close and couldn't wait any longer. He took off in a sprint to the porch, and about that time he was matched in stride by the big gray wolf he had named Theo. Theo was the largest, maybe the youngest, and had kind eyes. His hair was gray, tipped with white. His muzzle was totally white, a contrast to his very black nose. He had a thick mane of hair around his neck and chest, with white underneath, and one white paw. His short ears were fuzzy, with white hair on the inside, and stood erect. They turned independently of one another as they picked up a sound. Theo was almost as tall as Blake—truly a magnificent animal. There would never be any worry about Blake's safety.

Ellie's wolf, Twylah, was a light brown. She had a light brown muzzle with black circles around her eyes and strips of white just above the eye and just below. All over her body she displayed beautiful cream, white, and tan fur. She had white stripes down her cheeks that ended in a white stripe across her nose. She was thicker than Theo but not as tall. Hers were the kindest eyes of all. They almost looked sorrowful, as her eyes were outlined in black and shone bright gold out from under the furry hood of her forehead.

The wolves walked closely with their companions but did not engage. The children instinctively did not reach out to cuddle either. They were smart enough to know where the boundaries of a wild friendship should be.

Blake and Theo reached the back porch, and there was the carved wooden wolf, casually on the step, ready to blow away. Blake scooped it up and flashed the largest grin. He looked like he could either break out in a laugh or tears, he was so happy. He shoved it in his pocket and went to find his brother. Luke was looking around in the barn. It was a huge structure, smaller than the house, but a two-story barn that could hold maybe several horses and other things that Grandpop collected. The second story was just a loft, but tall enough for a man to stand up. It had double doors at one end for the delivery of hay. There was a pulley at the top over the doors, with a rotted rope that was probably used at one time to hoist hay for storage off the wet ground. When hay got wet, it mildewed and rotted, so people made a flooring under the storage to keep out the moisture.

The Dutch-style barn door could be pushed open, so the children went inside. It had been closed up for so long, it smelled musty, and Ellie covered her nose with her jacket. There were several stalls on one side, but no stalls on the other—probably a place for a wagon. If tools had once been there, they were now long gone. They shut the doors tightly as they left.

Next they explored the other outbuildings. An outhouse, similar to the one they had at the compound, was located next to the barn. Another smaller building held a rotten shove boat for the sound and fishing nets—also so old they fell apart when touched. There were oars, shove poles, and some other stuff they were not familiar with. A short way from the house, and in the overbrush that had grown for years and years, was a small bungalow, like a cabin in the woods, but located on the compound. Maybe a guest house? They tried to look in the windows, but the bushes would not let them get close. Ellie thought it would be a good playhouse and decided that she would convince the boys to come back and start working on that very project. Since they were not allowed in the big house, they could play around this one.

Behind the house, between the house and the trees that blocked off the ocean, was what looked like it could be a fenced-in chicken coop. The fence had long ago fallen apart in disarray, but it was obvious what it was.

Blake ran over to a huge live oak tree, with its thick twisted limbs, and was obviously thinking about climbing it when he heard Luke yelling at him.

"Come on, Blake! We've got to get going. We don't want Mom to worry, and we can come back."

He was already heading toward the horse. Luke reached out his fist once again—for Rafe to sniff, because he wanted to begin a friendship with the handsome critter—and Rafe gave it a lick this time. Luke was ecstatic! Finally, after all this time of seeing him in the shadows or at a distance, they were now friends, and he knew it.

Ellie put her arms around Twylah's neck and laid her cheek on her head. Twylah pulled away and licked her on the cheek. Wow! It was just like in the dream, except there were no pups. Just then, she spied them— four little furry things, a little larger than before, but still so shy. It made her smile inside, and also wonder if even this was a dream.

Blake literally strutted back to the group beside his large companion. Theo was right at his shoulder.

"Let's introduce them to Gus," Blake said. "I'll bet they like each other."

Luke told his brother, "No. Now is not the time. They will be near the lighthouse like before, and we will do that on Old Christmas. Remember, Grandmom said animals could talk to each other on that night. We will go try to find them, and maybe they will follow us so we can show them Gus. Anyway, they know him. They followed us here, didn't they?" Luke's head was so full of plans, he couldn't keep them all straight. But he did remember to turn the generator back on before they left.

This mansion on the hill, with all the stuff around, was spinning into an interesting scenario that he could see developing into a lifelong adventure.

As they neared the place where Gus was tied, the wolves dropped away and suddenly disappeared into the surrounding woods. The children mounted Gus and started through the path back to the beach and home. As Gus walked along, the kids were all talking at the same time. Ellie wanted to talk about the little house, and how great it would be for a playhouse or even a clubhouse. Blake wanted to climb the trees to see what was in the second story of the mansion. Luke, well, Luke had plans—so many plans that he had to sort them out before he ran them by the group. He wanted to go inside the big mansion. He wanted to go into every room and open every door. He even thought about asking his mother to teach him how to play the piano, so that he could play the big one in the living room that was covered up.

They passed the shark and half-walked, half-rode Gus as high tide made them walk in the soft sand near the dune. It was chilly, but the waves were not rough. The shorebirds were gone. The kids hoped they had not driven them away forever. Ellie got a conch for Grandmom, and they crossed over the dune to home, around the same time Grandpop and Grandmom were coming back from their visit.

As Grandpop saw his precious three riding Pegasus toward the lodge, he realized that they were growing, and before long they would need another horse. He did not know which kid would get it. He felt probably Ellie, because Luke seemed so connected to Gus. Captain Charlie thought he needed to take another trip down to Hatteras to see if Mr. Burrus had, or could get, another horse one that was just as distinctive as the beautiful cream-colored one walking toward him.

Grandmom had planned a small New Year's Eve party for the kids, and she and Charlie would be telling stories as they waited to ring in the New Year. She had decided to entertain them and teach them how to make pull candy.

Pull candy parties were frequent on the island. It was a social event for teens to get together. Young people would gather at a house and cook candy. It was mostly a situation that allowed the boys and girls to interact. The ingredients were boiled in a big pot until ready to pour on a marble slab. When the syrup cooled enough, the kids could begin to pull on it with oiled fingers and work the mass of goo into a ball. That ball was then pulled and stretched out until it could be folded over and pulled again, adding the desired flavor at the same time. The pulling of the candy was the most fun. The boys stood at one end, the girls at the other, and they pulled and pulled as the candy cooled to a taffy consistency. When the girl was collecting the mass to pass to the boy and had both her hands busy, the boy could steal a kiss. The kids had heard Jack and Lindy talk about going to a pull candy party and watched as they got dressed up to go, so it was curious to the kids why they had to get so dressed up to pull candy. Grandmom knew all of this but left out the social part, and only watched as they got all sticky and gooey pulling and pulling on that string of taffy.

As it cooled in a final strip, it was cut into bite-size pieces and eaten. The children and Grandmom and Grandpop had a wonderful time, as did Nett, who kept the pulling going by being the sixth person. What started out to be fun for the kids ended up by being fun for Grandpop and Grandmom, as Grandmom found herself holding the mass of candy and Charlie reached over for a peck on the cheek. That sent everybody in giggle fits of *oooohhs* and *aaaahhhs*. It turned out to be a great party.

Meanwhile, the local fighters were getting the mess punched out of them in Nags Head and hopefully were getting in some licks of their own.

RECIPE FOR PULL CANDY

PREP TIME: 30 MINUTES | COOK TIME: 20 MINUTES | TOTAL TIME: 50 MINUTES

Ingredients
3 cups sugar
1 cup boiling water
⅛ teaspoon baking soda
½ teaspoon salt
1 cup cream
¼ cup butter, cut into small bits

Preparation
Combine sugar, boiling water, baking soda, and salt in heavy saucepan and stir over low heat until dissolved and boiling.

Cover about 3 minutes until steam has washed crystals from sides of the pan. Uncover and cook without stirring to 236 degrees F. Reduce heat, but not below 225 degrees F, while gradually adding cream and butter.

Cook over moderate heat without stirring, to 257 degrees F, and pour syrup at once over buttered marble slab. Holding the pouring edge away from you, and a few inches above the slab, allow syrup to spread over the slab. Do not scrape pot.

General Taffy Pulling Instructions
Allow the syrup to cool briefly. This is the time to flavor the taffy. Because of the great heat, use flavoring essences based on essential oils. Sprinkle these over the surface of the hot syrup. Go easy as they are very strong. If using chocolate, grate it on the buttered slab before pulling.

Work the syrup up into a central mass, turning it and working it with a candy scraper until it is cool enough to handle with your oiled fingertips. Take care in picking up the mass. It may have cooled on the surface and still be hot enough to burn as you press down into it. When you can gather it up, start pulling it with your fingertips, allowing a spread of about 18 inches between your hands. Then fold back on itself. Repeat this motion rhythmically. As the mass changes from a somewhat sticky, side-whiskered affair to a glistening crystal ribbon, start twisting, while folding and pulling. Pull until ridges on the twist begin to hold their shape.

The candy will have become opaque, firm, and elastic but will still retain its satiny finish. Depending on proper cooking, the weather, and your skill, this pulling process may last from 5 to 20 minutes.

⋆ 12 ⋆

Old Christmas

r. Folb dropped Bill off at the compound. The boys were still in Nags Head. Everyone rushed out when they heard the car turning into the compound. They could not wait to hear the results of the fights. Bill gave Nett a kiss, hugged the kids, and turned to Grandpop and Grandmom, whose faces were a mix of anxiety and worry.

"Jack won. Lindy lost." That said it all. Bill continued, "Let's go inside. I'm hungry. Miss Odessa, got any of that New Year's goose left?"

"For you, my son, anything." Odessa was relieved and didn't really care about the details. She heard what she wanted to hear. She hurried into the back of the house to the kitchen and began to ready a huge plate for Bill.

"What happened, Bill? And don't leave out a single thing. I wanted to be there more than anything, so don't let me miss the details." Captain Charlie pulled up a dining room chair at the table and was staring at Bill, whose mouth was already full of the delicious goose.

"Okay. Pretty much everything happened that I thought, except I didn't count on that huge guy from Currituck getting into the mix. Lindy did great in the first fight, knocked the guy out. But then, in the next fight, he drew the biggest guy in the arena. Lindy crawled into the ring and took that flatfooted stance, the one I had warned him not to take. That guy punched him so hard, my boy hit the canvas and never got back up. Knocked out colder than a cucumber. First punch. I had thought about that, but I really didn't think it could happen." Bill sat there eating and shaking his head back and forth. "Just didn't think it would happen."

Lindy was a puncher, and a puncher stands flatfooted to get more solid mass behind his fist. Some boxers fight flatfooted— not many, it is a recipe for disaster—and others fight on their toes, making sure they can get away and move around. Bill had warned Lindy, but after all, he had won the first match using his own method, so he was overconfident that he could do it again. Maybe if he had gotten further into the fight, he might have remembered his training and gotten back to it, but as it was, that was not to be.

Jack, on the other hand, was light on his feet and danced around, almost confusing his opponent, and did his best to never take a punch.

"Jack did everything he was taught. He won his first fight, but it was hard on him, then he got into the rhythm for the second one. You know that guy, Jimmy from the Coast Guard station, who gave him such a fit during training? Well, his guy fought just like Jimmy. He did Jack the biggest favor. You could see it in his face. He recognized what he should do and did it. He kept saying, when Doc was working on him in the corner, 'He's just like Jimmy, just like Jimmy.'

"He got hit a couple of times, and Mom, he does have a black eye, but it looks much worse than it is. So next week we'll be going to Norfolk, to Little Creek Navy Base, and he fights there for the opportunity to go to Dallas to compete in the Golden Gloves. Tell you what a man Lindy is: He is more excited about Jack than himself. He is determined to toughen him up and is going to travel everywhere with us, sparring with Jack the whole time. Never sulked, never complained, just shook it off like a man and got into Jack's corner, and for all I know he carried him around the

Casino on his shoulders during the dance. Wouldn't be surprised. It gave me immense respect for Lindy. He's a man I'd want in my corner or at my back in a fight. Good man, yessir, good man."

Captain Charlie was beaming. He was proud of both boys, Jack for winning and Lindy for his strength of character. Buxton boys were the best! He and Bill sat at the table for an hour talking about the fights and what to do in preparation for Norfolk. They decided that they would get a substitute keeper as soon as possible to take over the duties of the lighthouse for a couple of days so that Captain Charlie could go to Norfolk and watch Jack fight. At least two men in the village had formerly held the position, and they knew they could get the go-ahead to allow one of them to take over Charlie's duties for those days.

Odessa sat quietly at the end of the table, listening to the two men talk, and when they finished, she said what she had been thinking all along. Charlie had to go into the village to Mr. Eph's cold storage or the icehouse past the church to get a piece of meat. Charlie agreed, just to make her feel better, but Bill had already asked Dr. Folb about steak on the damaged eye, and the doc told him it was the worst idea. He said if there was any broken skin, the raw meat was liable to cause an infection. He said ice or something cold. Most people knew cold, and they thought meat was a good remedy, but it was just the cold that was the remedy, not the meat. Doc had said just to keep ice on it for twenty minutes at a time, and after that let it heal on its own. Bill assured Odessa that Jack was well taken care of. Ice had already been applied.

Ice and cold on an island without electricity were a tricky deal. On this island, in the beginning, the islanders built storage sheds with thick walls and small doors so that the cool would stay inside. Then iceboxes for the insides of houses were invented. An icebox consisted of a thick wooden chest with an upper area that was heavily insulated for putting in a block of ice. Some were even large enough for two blocks. The top part kept the bottom part cool. By this time, ice was delivered in a huge insulated truck from the icehouse in either Hatteras—Frazier Peele also ran an icehouse—or Manteo. On Toby's ferry, the iceman went to the front of the line, and he delivered to Chicamacomico one day, Kinnakeet (or Avon) another day, Buxton and Trent another day, and Hatteras the last before the cycle started again. Everybody knew when the iceman was coming. His name was Mr. Basnight from Manteo, and he was a muscular man who lifted those ice blocks with tongs and hoisted them to the top of people's iceboxes. Sometimes he would chip off a piece or two for the kids, as they made sure the big heavy blanket was covering the rest of the ice while he delivered.

Food storage was an art. The villagers were not used to eating much meat. One did not kill a cow. It was used for milk. Bulls were also protected as they were needed to mate with the cows for more cows. All roamed free on the island with marks on their ears to indicate ownership. The Gray mark was a G with a little curl, as there were several Gray families in the area. Meat, if anyone had any, could be smoked, salted and saved, or dried. Vegetables were canned, pickled, or otherwise preserved. Odessa had a porch full of jars of all kinds of things: beans, figs, strawberry jam, pickled beets, tomatoes, okra, and more. Meat was mostly fresh when a pig was slaughtered. There were two hams, ribs, bacon, pork chops, and the underbelly of pork. Captain Charlie kept his meat at Mr. Eph's cold storage room, but the islanders ate mostly from the sea. Meat was usually chicken. So Christo, the rooster, was a valued member of the family. He made sure the hens were happy enough to lay eggs and that they ate the grain that made them fat.

Charlie, while he had all of Bill's attention and while Odessa was sitting there, discussed with Bill what he had thought while watching the children riding Gus into the compound from the beach. It looked like they were uncomfortable. Two on a horse was fine, but three was pushing it, and as they grew larger, it would be impossible. They both decided another trip to Mr. Burrus's corral was necessary to pick out another horse—this one for Ellie. She and Blake could share for a while. By that time Luke would be driving, and the problem of transportation would be solved.

The children went back to school after the holidays, just as excited as they could be to see their friends again. Luke and Blake had shark's teeth for Colby and Thomas, and Ellie was all excited about Gus. School went great that first day back, and as they all sat in assembly before breaking up to go to their classes, they were informed about two things. Nurse Draper, from the health department in Manteo, was coming the following day to give everybody an immunization shot, and the bookmobile from the Manteo schools would be there also. The children would be in line for shots, then go out to the bookmobile to look for a book or two, which they were able to check out for three weeks.

They laughed and laughed on the way home about Nurse Draper. Every year she came to take care of the island kids, and every year the entire teaching staff had to chase down Judy B to give her the shot. She was a feared child, because she could beat up all the boys, but when it came to that little needle, she went under the seats. She actually crawled under the auditorium seats, ran around the rows, and literally had to be corralled and held down to get that shot. Everybody in school was looking forward to the spectacle. Georgie Tolson even said that he preferred to watch Judy B over going to the bookmobile.

On the ride back home, Luke began his quest of getting his grandfather to take them back to the old house. They were all dying to go inside again. Blake wanted to climb that tree, and Ellie wanted to check out the little house on the property. Grandpop looked like he might go for it, but they knew it wouldn't happen until they gave a good reason. Grandpop was just too busy to think about it in any urgent manner. They would have to get their heads together and make a good case for at least one more visit.

The shots were over, the teachers were busy chasing down Judy B, and the lower grades went out to the bookmobile. The bookmobile was a huge green-paneled truck with the letters "BOOKMOBILE" written large on the side. Inside, the entire space was lined with shelves filled with books. It was a school library on wheels. Bookcases lined both sides and across the back. Down the middle were two rows of bookcases whose shelves were also filled with books. Kids could walk along the rows, looking at the names of the books housed on the shelves. Sometimes there were two of the same book, in case two people wanted the same one. Children were allowed inside in shifts so as not to make the space overcrowded, and they were given a certain time limit to choose. It usually took the entire day for all in the school who wanted to do so to walk through.

Luke went with the older kids, but Ellie and Blake were in there at the same time, so they helped each other. Blake got a book on Blackbeard the pirate. He knew Ellie and Luke would read it to him. Plus he chose another one on pirates in general that was an easy-reader book. He was excited about doing that one by himself. Ellie got three books—*National Velvet*; a newly published book titled *The Black Stallion*, which they both picked and decided they would read together; and *Heidi*, about a little girl in Switzerland who lived with her grandfather.

On that day riding home from school, Grandpop and Nett were amazed as they heard no chatter from the children in the backseat. They all had their heads in their new books. The grown-ups did not want to disturb the silence, so they also kept quiet, proud that the kids loved reading so much. Luke got a book on mythology, because he wanted to read about Poseidon and his temple. He also brought home *Captain Horatio Hornblower*, a book about a military man and the sea. He was thinking he could understand what his father was going to be doing. For a moment they were content, but all roads would eventually lead to the mansion on the hill.

Finally at supper, they all had a laugh at Nett telling about the trials of Judy B. The teachers had not allowed the other children in the school to stay around and watch, because they knew how traumatized she must be and they did not want to add to it. But around the table, Luke was snorting food through his nose he laughed so hard, and Blake was beyond eating. He almost had his head in his plate he was laughing so much. Ellie was laughing at Luke and Blake.

That night when Grandmom was listening to Ellie's prayers, when they got to the "and God bless" part—which for Ellie was long—Grandmom almost nodded off as the little girl went through the family, the animals in her life, her dolls, the chickens, somebody named Moira and another called Twylah, and then a new one: Judy B. Grandmom was not surprised. Poor Judy B, she was last on the list. Even Gus was mentioned before Judy B.

Grandpop was extremely pleased when he saw the books Ellie had checked out. *Black!* Both horses in the books were black. That was encouraging to him. He had really wanted the cream-colored horse for Ellie, but the horse had taken a shine to Luke, and Luke to him. It wasn't planned that way, but seeing that she liked the black horses of the books, he felt like maybe God really had come to his aid, because now he would not feel bad about asking Ellie to give up Gus. After the kids went to bed, and while Nett and Grandmom were upstairs hearing the children's prayers, he and Bill sat down on the porch and continued their conversation about the new horse. They began to plot out a plan to convince the women that another horse was needed. They felt like they might not see the horse on the first visit, but Mr. Burrus was always breeding with excellent stock from off-island, and they knew he would find the perfect riding horse for Ellie.

January was the full moon of the wolf. The Indians named the moon for the howling of the wolf, as hunger set in and food was hard to find. January 6 was also Old Christmas, the time when animals could talk to each other. The island paid respect to Old Christmas, especially in Chicamacomico—the three villages of Rodanthe, Waves, and Salvo. The community center was in Rodanthe, and the festival was always there. This was one party the kids were allowed to attend. The celebration was a custom held over from when the calendar was changed in 1752 from the Julian calendar to the Gregorian calendar, causing eleven days to be dropped and putting the date for the birth of Christ at December 25 instead of January 6. The original calendar was the one followed by the first English settlers, so the Islanders, honoring their Indian heritage and their connection to the first settlers, celebrated on that day also.

Finally, something they could all attend at the same time. All the villages, especially the young people, traveled to Rodanthe to participate in the festivities. There was an oyster shoot—the best shot at a prescribed target receiving a bushel of oysters as a prize. Music was supplied by groups of islanders either in a band or a single performance. More food was prepared than anyone could eat; oysters were roasting on several large oil barrels filled with wood for the fire and fitted out with a mesh wire on the top, on which oysters were placed for roasting. There were homemade cakes and desserts of all descriptions, lots of homemade candy, soft drinks and beer, fried chicken, the dreaded pone bread, fish being fried all over the area, and people waiting in line, plates in hand, ready to pile it on. On other metal barrels were clams and even trays of baked drum, a large fish that hit the island in droves during the cold months.

The biggest draw of them all was the appearance of Old Buck, the big mythical bull that supposedly roamed the forests of Chicamacomico. There were several stories as to the bull's origin. Some said he was on a ship bound for South Carolina when it was wrecked on the shores of Rodanthe. The men purchased him from the captain, and he was the stud who mated with the female cattle on the island, thus increasing everyone's herd. Other stories indicated he was a rogue bull that terrified the people of the villages and had to be put down. Thus, he returned every year at the festival to terrorize the people again. Men dressed a form made from two-by-fours or two-by-sixes, draped a blanket over the wood, fitted it out with horns—from some real bull that lived and had been harvested for being too old or a nuisance—and Buck was moved along by two men who were under the blanket. He faked a run at the children, sending them screaming in delight, and he danced with all the pretty ladies and generally was the center of attention.

It was a lucky night if the tide was low when everyone was ready to leave. It made for a lot fewer people getting stuck in the dark. But there were so many people from the southern villages that even digging out was fun. This night it was low tide, and as the cars traveled the hard sand of the wash, the moon danced across the blue-black water in rippling strips of silver and gold, like wide ribbons of satin resting on the top of the ocean. It made the stars shine even brighter than ever. The foam of the breakers looked like silver washing up on the shore. Then it slid back to make more mounds of fluffy silver.

Nett and Bill were in the backseat with the boys, and Nett had her head resting on Bill's shoulder. Grandmom was in the front between Ellie and Charlie, also nestled against her husband. Ellie stared out at the night, knowing she would be talking to the animals—or maybe they just talked to each other. Either way, what happened when they got home was going to be important. She dozed off, dropping her head down into Grandmom's lap, and Odessa stroked her head lightly, knowing she had been hoping to be able to stay awake to observe the animals. It was a magical night, one that the kids were happy to see, as this was the night they planned to introduce the wolves to Pegasus.

All of the children had fallen asleep on the ride home. The rhythm of riding over the camelbacks formed by the ocean waves as they receded was mesmerizing, lulling them to sleep. When the car stopped at the compound, they came alive. The first thing they did was hop out and inform the grown-ups that they were going to talk to the horses and chickens. Captain Charlie just shook his head and headed toward the house, followed by Grandmom. Bill and Nett told the kids not to be long as they headed to Nett's new apartment at the keeper's quarters.

Once the adults were out of sight, the kids struck out in the direction of the woods near the lighthouse. They fully expected to find the wolves. They were getting comfortable around the wild animals, and they were learning the rules. There was a difference between a domestic animal—like a dog or horse—and a wild animal. The affection for a wild animal was up to the animal, not the human. They never tried to touch their wolves, instead waiting for the wolf to initiate the affection. If the wolf wanted to get close, they waited. Otherwise, they were content to just be in their company. The kids were glad to have them around. They were beautiful, but like anything precious, one had to be careful about touching. Captain Charlie had taught them about interacting with a wild thing. He knew about the wolves but had never seen them near the children. He had only witnessed them standing guard in the woods nearby, and even then he was not sure. He saw only shadows. The children were disappointed that night, because the wolves were not there.

Next they went to the barn and sat there on the hay rise talking to the horses. Luke was down the line with Pegasus, Ellie was trying to communicate with Old Tony, and Blake was rubbing Big Roy. Twinkle, in the first stall, was just chewing her cud. They must have thought the animals would break out in English, but what they experienced was a bunch of neighing and whinnying.

As they were getting ready to leave to visit the chickens and turtles, they encountered the three wolves, side by side, standing at the entrance of the barn door. They immediately backed up and sat down on the hay rise to watch. By that time they knew there would be no English spoken, so they waited to see how this would play out. The wolves came into the barn. The horses stood quiet, not spooking or looking afraid. Theo, the largest, went to stand parallel to the stall where Old Tony stood. He just stood there, didn't look up or make a move to advance to the big horse. They just sort of acknowledged each other. Then he went to Big Roy— same story. The others mimicked Theo, and the same thing happened. As they moved down the line toward Pegasus, they gathered in front of his stall. He snorted, pawed the ground, whinnied, and shook his beautiful golden mane, and the wolves sent out a single howl in unison, as if to the moon. After all, it was their moon. Then silence. The wolves bowed to the ground and put their head on the scattered hay in front of the stall. Everybody was motionless, especially the children.

Ellie reached out and took Luke's hand, and he in turn held on to Blake's. Together they began trying to connect to the animals in front of them. Ellie closed her eyes and suspended her breath as she sent love and appreciation to the creatures that always seemed to have her best interest at heart. The three had discussed what message they would send when the time came. They wanted to let the animals know that their friendship and loyalty were needed in their lives. The kids had decided that Grandpop was correct in telling them that they should not try to physically interact with the wild creatures, so they did not attempt to pet or hug the wolves. They sat quietly as they felt the connection among all three: horse, wolf, and human. A wave of acceptance washed over the children as they experienced the bond. It made Ellie shiver. Luke put his arm around Blake and drew him near. He was proud of his exuberant little brother and the restraint of voice and movement he was displaying. After a short while, the wolves stood up. Single file, with Twylah in front, they started for the open doors.

At the moment the wolves passed in front of the children, each was close enough to touch their respective charges, but instead of any physical contact they locked eyes with the child each was destined to protect. The look that the wolves gave made the children's heartbeat quicken as they realized the strength of the bond that had formed. The wolves stopped just for a moment and then left the barn. When the children felt it safe to follow, the wolves had disappeared.

It was not quite what they had expected, but in their hearts they knew that a trust had been established, and they were satisfied. Blake took Ellie's hand and pulled her toward the turtles in the pond. They were not there, so the children blessed them and went to the chicken coop. All the chickens were asleep, but they seemed to be sleeping closer together than normal, so the children decided maybe they had already talked. They then blessed the chickens, Ellie sent a special message to Christo, thanking him for waking her in the morning with his unusual song and wearily followed the others to the house, where Grandmom was waiting up for them. She ushered them upstairs to listen to their prayers, then came downstairs with a glow inside for the love of her grandchildren.

The next morning the kids bounded downstairs full of energy. They had experienced Old Christmas and had the best time. Everybody, wild and tame, was friends. On to the next project. Today they would convince Grandpop to take them to the house. When they approached him at breakfast, they were shocked at his response.

"Your dad and I need to go down to Mr. Burrus's corral to check on something. We can stop by on the way home. How about that? Now don't mention it again. I will tell you when we are going. All you have to do is wait. Deal?" The captain was not sure what the fascination was, but he wanted to take Bill over there anyway as he needed some advice about the upkeep since Bill would not be around much longer.

"Deal!" they all chimed in, and Blake gave his silly look to both Luke and Ellie, like, "Wow, that was easy." And he flashed a big grin to Grandpop.

Inside, Captain Charlie laughed. Something was up, he just didn't know what.

Bill, the captain, Jack, and Lindy began planning their trip to Norfolk for the continuation of the trials for the Golden Gloves in Texas. Mr. Quidley had once again agreed to man the tower so that Charlie could accompany them. Lindy planned to take his father's side-railed truck so that Bill could bring back diesel generators from the navy yard in Portsmouth. He was to bring back three instead of the two he planned. One would be for Baxter Miller, Lindy's dad. Having won the Congressional Medal of Honor for Lifesaving, Baxter was definitely on the good side of the military, and since all the diesel generators were being traded out for new ones, he had no trouble being granted one.

Bill had plans to wire up both houses for electricity—one for Baxter and one for Charlie. The one they had hoped to do for the assistant keeper's quarters was no longer in the works, as there was nobody living there. Bill and Charlie planned to take it to the mansion, thinking the big house would need two. As a matter of fact, several trips to the old house were planned. If the kids knew that, boy, would their brains be working overtime.

The trip to Mr. Burrus's corral was this weekend, before they left to go to Norfolk. Meanwhile, the seamen from the Coast Guard station, Bill, and especially Lindy were hard at work training Jack for any condition he might meet. Jack and Lindy ran on the beach for miles. Sometimes after school the kids took Gus out to run along with them. The weather was cooperating. January was only cold for a couple of days at a time, usually when a nor'easter hit, then it warmed up again. Steady cold weather came in February, the month of the snow moon. One night in January during a particularly strong winter storm, it brought with it heavy lightning.

Grandpop said that, on the island, "if lightning struck in January, there would be snow in ten days."

The kids began the countdown.

★13★

Blue

arly Saturday morning the kids crawled into the back of the government car with Bill and Grandpop for a trip to Mr. Burrus's ranch in Hatteras. They were excited to go all the way down to the last village on the island. They seldom ever went past the church in Buxton. The two-track road to Hatteras Village was solid all the way through Trent— which was renamed Frisco in 1898, but referred to as Trent by the locals who had grown up with that name. Leaving Buxton to get to Trent, there was a canopy of trees of various types covering the road for most of the way, nearly blocking out the sky in areas before the first houses of Trent appeared. It caused the tracks to be totally covered in pine straw with only the rise in the middle showing green grass.

The only time the ride was a little tricky was when there was a puddle to go around or they encountered a car or truck coming the other way. At this point somebody had to pull over and let the other guy pass. If they were in an area where there was no obvious pull-off, each car moved as far to the right as possible, leaving the left two wheels in a track with the right running along the rough ground of the shoulder as they passed each other. Usually, whoever had the better solid ground near the right side of their track was the one who gave the right-of-way. Since everybody knew everybody else in the villages, they each gave a greeting and motioned for the other guy to go ahead, while someone relinquished the road.

There were more cars on the island now, and such a variety—ranging from large flatbed and side-railed trucks; Model As, which could be purchased for less than $400; to the top-of-the-line Town Car, for $1,400; plus the much desired, on this island, Model AA heavy-duty truck, which was a flatbed. As ingenious as the islanders were, they could take a flatbed and modify it to be whatever kind of truck they required for the job they had in mind. So the styles of trucks on the island fit the situation they would have to fill. Some were altered to carry boats, nets, or wood, whatever the need.

Even with more and more cars on the island, it was unusual to pass a car or truck that was occupied by only one person. Most did not have cars, so everybody gave a ride to anyone on the side of the road going in their direction. Most of the time, a vehicle slowed down—not completely stopping so as not to get stuck—and the rider jumped on the running board, hooked his hand under the roof, and talked to the driver until it was time to jump off. All cars and trucks had running boards. Grandpop's car was a 1940 Ford Black Tudor Sedan, but during this time General Motors also had cars on the market, thus giving a variety of styles to choose from.

After passing Trent, the trees thinned out. The two-track became more sandier and travel more difficult. In places where the road was not packed down hard enough to go through, the driver slacked the tires and went over to the beach, where at low tide the sand was as hard as a highway. Between Buxton and Trent and in at least one place between Trent and Hatteras, there were several ten-foot to twenty-foot wooden bridges, one named Peter's Bridge, allowing passage over the creeks running through the woods. Also in soft sandy areas, boards were left on the side of the road for placing under a buried wheel in order to supply traction to get out of the sand. One did not travel in the car without a shovel.

The kids were even looking forward to getting stuck—Luke especially. He knew that his father and grandfather both would have to get out to push, leaving him to be the driver. His dad was always letting him sit in his lap and steer. As he got taller, he was allowed to work the pedals. He was still a little rough on the clutch, but he could do it. He only begged to "drive" when they were alone in the car. Neither Luke nor his dad wanted the younger ones to get the bright idea that the privilege of driving was available until they got older.

The trip was interesting and took quite a while, sometimes two hours. On the way, they passed everybody's house who lived on the main road. There were two roads in Buxton: the main road and the back road. In Trent, where fewer than 200 people lived—mostly carpenters, pound net fishermen, and hunters—there were also two roads, front and back, but their back road did not go through. It stopped where the woods got thick.

Between the villages of Trent and Hatteras on that desolate road were two attractions: Tandy's, a dance hall and bar where all the young people congregated, and Durant's Station, a famous lifesaving station built in 1878 by the U.S. Lifesaving Service as one of twenty-six similar types on the coastal beaches. It was decommissioned in 1937 and used as the base of operations for Billy Mitchell's bombing experiments.

In Hatteras, considered the most cosmopolitan area, there was only one road, which split into left and right at the sound. Here was the Austin Theater; the Girls Club, a community center; the first motel, the Atlantic View Hotel at the entrance of the village; a huge dance hall across the road called the Beacon; several stores; the Weather Bureau; a Methodist church; and the docks, where much commerce and commercial fishing came and went. To the left at the fork, the Hatteras docks were active and important to the rest of the island. Also located near the end of the island in Hatteras Village was the ferry going to Ocracoke, the next island, and a Coast Guard station. Since the inlet was cut and deepened by the 1846 hurricane, this village became the hub of commerce on the island.

Also, in 1938, the Midgett brothers—Harold, Anderson, and Stockton, ages twenty, seventeen, and Stocky only thirteen when he drove—took over the franchise their father began, running a bus line from Hatteras to Manteo. First it was a commando truck, with canvas windows that rolled up. Later they purchased an old school bus that they painted blue, and the talented Midgett brothers tinkered with the engine to modify it and make it worthy of the trials that going through sand demanded. These boys were excellent drivers who took the best route available on a particular day and time—either the two-track or inside road, or the wash, which was the locals' name for the hard sand next to the ocean at low tide—whichever was the better situation to avoid getting stuck. When and if that happened, the passengers got out and helped push the vehicle out of the sand. The Midgett brothers were such talented drivers and good mechanics that they did not get stuck often. The Blue Bus carried mail, laundry, people, packages, the *Virginian Pilot* newspaper, and whatever needed to be delivered to the Coast Guard station or the lighthouse compound. People put their suitcase on the side of the road, and the bus stopped, blew the horn, and waited for the traveler. Sometimes people just stood by the side of the road and flagged down the bus. There were no official driver's licenses on the island. The fare was about two dollars. The bus ran once a day from Hatteras Village to the town of Manteo on the mainland, where it connected with the Greyhound Bus Line going to Norfolk.

At the fork in the road at Hatteras, to the right and located on the sound, were fish houses, a porpoise factory, boatbuilding sheds, and Mr. Burrus's ranch. There was a big grocery store, the Red and White, at the end where the fork split from left to right. Captain Charlie stopped there to talk to a man he knew, as the kids surveyed what Hatteras Village had to offer. They purchased two Royal Crown colas, an Orange Crush drink, a pack of nabs, and some peanuts in a package. Luke did what he had seen Uncle Jack do: put his peanuts into the cola and drink and eat at the same time. Bill took them over to the glass-topped counter, and they were allowed to pick out some penny candy of various flavors to have on the drive back home. The day was fun, and it had hardly started.

The trip continued down by the fish houses to the end of the road. Here they saw a corral with lots of horses, and they stopped. The kids jumped out and stood on the rail of the fence and watched the horses as they grazed. When Mr. Burrus came out to greet Bill and the captain, they were taken by surprise as Grandpop introduced everybody and told Mr. Burrus the point of this visit. He wanted a young black horse. *What?* Grandpop motioned for both Ellie and Blake to step forward.

"These kids need a horse, and it must be black, and it must be of your finest stock. Got anything we can look at?" Grandpop was all smiles, knowing how shocked they both must be.

Several emotions were running rampant. First, Luke realized Pegasus was going to be his very own horse. Second, Blake and Ellie knew they would get their own ride. Third, Ellie knew it would be her color. Blake's face said it all. His smirk and the rolling of his eyes to his brother and cousin were the funniest picture. He, for once, was speechless.

"Grandpop, am I getting a black horse?" said Ellie with her hand over her heart.

"You are," Grandpop answered, "but you and Blake will share until Blake gets old enough for his own."

At that, Blake fell down on the ground, acting like he had fainted. Everybody broke into the biggest laugh as Bill reached down and picked him up under his arms. The little fella heard the words, "until Blake gets old enough," and just could not contain himself. Probably at that moment, there were no happier kids on the island in all seven villages than these three.

"Just so happens, I have one you can look at. He's old enough even though he is young. He could leave his mother now, but I would need to start breaking him in for a child. He ain't never been ridden. Let's go have a look-see," Mr. Burrus said. "If you don't fancy this one, I can start looking when I go for more stock, but this little feller is 'bout as purdy as any one I've ever seen. Solid black, not a white spot on him, still a colt, almost ready to leave his mamma, good stock—the best, like all my steeds. If you want an older one, I'll look for that. But this here is one of the best, just young, almost two year old."

The group went over to the barn and through the back to the pasture in the rear of the building. Ellie saw him first, and this time it was her turn to faint, but instead she grabbed her pop's hand and squeezed. As Charlie looked down, he could see the pleading look on her face, indicating approval, and he smiled, motioning for her to be silent. He didn't want her eagerness to drive up the price, so he cautioned her to be calm. They walked over to the mare and her colt. The young horse stood quietly by his mother, almost touching her he was so close, and Mr. Burrus reached in his pocket and gave the mare a piece of apple and one to the colt. This friendly gesture allowed the rest of the group to get nearer. The colt was as tall as the mother, skinny and obviously young, but boy, was he magnificent. He was as pretty a black horse as Gus was a Palomino.

"Grandpop, he is just like National Velvet," said Ellie.

"Daddy, he is so black, he's blue," said Blake as the sun bounced off the slick black hair of the animal. "Ellie, let's name him Blue."

Well, if Captain Charlie thought he was going to get away with making Mr. Burrus think he might want to haggle over price, Blake just fixed that! It was obvious this was a sale.

It was Mr. Burrus's turn to grin. He was captivated by the three kids. The older boy had character, poise, and restraint, while life played out on the faces of the two younger ones. Yes, he knew he had a sale, but it might have been the happiest sale he had made in quite a while.

"What do you think, Charlie? This the one, or do you want to look some more?" The rancher knew the answer, but he and Charlie were friends, so a little kidding was in order.

"Now, Willis, you know the answer to that one. All I can say now is, How much?" Grandpop and Bill were stroking the beautiful steed and waiting for the answer.

"Tell you what, Charlie, same price as the last one, and I'll throw in an old saddle somebody left here with the deal." Jerry Stowe had purchased a new saddle at Christmastime and given his old one to the Burrus ranch for just such an occasion.

"Deal!" said the captain.

Blake was holding his pants like he had to go to the bathroom, and Ellie was bouncing around. Grandpop and Bill were both grinning, as was Mr. Burrus, as the two youngest were about to wet their pants.

Mr. Burrus took the excited children over to the outhouse and waited for both of them to go, then brought them back to the corral. The deal was set. Mr. Burrus would keep Blue until the spring and get him trained, saddle broken, and ready for the kids. He gave the saddle to Captain Charlie, along with some oil for use in softening it up, and there was a handshake to seal the deal.

"Okay if I bring them around some Saturdays to help you with your chores?" Grandpop said. "They are going to want to hang around him a little, so he can get used to them."

"Love to have them," Mr. Burrus replied. "Love to have them. Got some things I need to discuss with you anyway. Looks like we're gonna have another war."

"Bill ships out at the end of next month. One reason we need to get things straight with the kids," Captain Charlie said. He and Mr. Burrus shook hands again, and Bill extended his.

"Nice meeting you, Mr. Burrus. Thanks for helping me out with the kids." Bill couldn't have been more pleased.

"No problem, Bill. Nice meeting you, too. I think I've heard about you before. Everybody calls you 'Finnegan,' I believe. Charlie and I go way back. Nice to meet the man who married the prettiest girl on the island. She was always more of a reason to go to the movies than the picture show. Good luck overseas, son. Give them Germans what-for!"

The group got back in the car, and the captain and Bill prepared themselves for the chatter that was going to make the trip back shorter than the journey had been to get there. They decided to show the kids the docks and the ferry while they were in Hatteras. They struck out on the sandy two-track road that ran past the stores and docks that made up the Hatteras business district. The road ran parallel to the sound, and most businesses were rather far apart on the sound side. The garage that housed the Blue Bus, busy with men working on cars, was on the land side of the sandy tracks, and there was a public lodging house next to the garage. First they stopped at the area where the Hatteras-to-Ocracoke ferry was docked, waiting for someone who wanted to cross. This home-made ferry was a little smaller than the one Mr. Toby ran across Oregon Inlet and was operated by a Hatteras man, Frazier Peele.

The ferry was a wooden boat with planks nailed across the gunwales to provide a deck on which to put a vehicle. In the beginning, this ferry did not even have a ramp but two wide, thick planks placed strategically apart to accommodate the space between the front wheels of the vehicle to board, and the traveler carefully drive up for the ride across. Later, a proper ramp was provided, and the modified barge was fitted for cars. Frazier was an innovative local who was an important part of hauling freight across the sound to the mainland, mostly Englehard and Stumpy Point. He, along with the Midgett Brothers, was instrumental in the growth that Hatteras Village enjoyed. Both families were from multigenerational ancestry on Hatteras Island. They saw needs and creatively decided to fill them.

The Hatteras Coast Guard station was located beyond the ferry docks, so Captain Charlie and Bill went into the station to visit with the ranking officer, thanking him again for helping them when they were stranded on Portsmouth Island.

As Grandpop had promised Luke, they would stop by the mansion on the way back home. He needed to consult with Bill about the property and discuss the new diesel generator. Charlie wanted to know if they could use the extra generator, and if so, how. There was conversation going on in the front between the two men, and in the back there was wiggling, giggling, and whispering, as both the house and the horse were being discussed. It was to be Ellie's horse, but Blake was the most excited. Evidently being the third person on a horse had not been such a treat after all.

The car slowly worked its way up the road to the house. When it was in sight, Luke nudged Blake as if to say, "Here we go!" Blake spied the big tree first off, leaped out of the car when it stopped, and raced toward it.

"Blake! There will be no climbing today!" Bill said. "We don't want any broken arms on this day, that's for sure."

Blake gave his disgruntled scowl and immediately switched faces as he ran to catch up with Luke and Ellie. Ellie was heading to the little cottage, led by Luke who knew his way through the security wires. She had in her mind a playhouse. Luke watched as Grandpop and his dad also picked their way around back to turn off the engine connected to the wires. Grandpop let himself in the back door, and the three kids appeared miraculously at his side, almost beating him inside.

"Now, you young-uns be careful. This is old stuff, and we don't know how sturdy things are. Don't want anybody gettin' hurt. Don't touch anything. Just look around," said Grandpop.

"Can we go upstairs?" Luke asked.

"I reckon it will be all right. Just be careful." Grandpop and Bill began their inspection and left the children alone.

Luke, Blake, and Ellie started up the wide staircase to the landing leading to the second floor. When they got to the platform, they had to decide which side to look at first. Then they realized that it had a connecting hallway at the top of the stairs and they could walk the whole floor. The left wing had a huge heavy door, beautifully carved. When they opened it there was a huge sitting room on the left of the door, with huge double windows. It was kind of dark, because the curtains were drawn most of the way, but the sliver of light the crack let through allowed them to see that this was sort of an apartment. There was a large stone fireplace on the north wall and a big bedroom to the right, next to the windows that looked out over the ocean. This whole side of the second floor was made up of that one living area.

It was too dark to move around much and smelled of musk, so the children just peeked in and closed the door, not really looking around. They headed down the hall, passing the split stairs below them, and went to the other side. In the middle, there were two other doors. They opened one, and it was a large bedroom with sort of a sitting area. Here again, the closed heavy curtains obscured the dark room, so they just looked in. They went to the far end of the hall. As they opened the door to the room in front of them, a blast of wind rushed passed them, even blowing Ellie's hair. She shivered and wrapped her arms across her chest and glanced around. As they peered in to the right, they gazed at the most magnificent round room they had ever seen. This also looked like an apartment. The sitting area was totally furnished and had six tall-paned windows overlooking the front yard. To the left was an equally large bedroom area. Still there was not enough light to really get a look. Ellie was a little anxious to step back, as this room gave her a weird feeling inside. They started back to the stairs and encountered another door, and beside it a huge chest. When they opened this door, there was another rather wide staircase leading up to the third floor. About that time they heard their father calling.

"Luke, Blake, Ellie. Let's go. We can come back. Come on down!"

The three looked at each other, grinned at their discoveries, and raced down the huge main staircase. Blake squelched the urge to ride the stair rail down. At the bottom, they joined their father and grandfather and went out the back with them. Blake stopped to point out the indoor bathroom to his dad. When they got outside, Bill went to turn on the generator for security.

Ellie talked her grandfather into walking with her over to the cottage at the edge of the property. They could hardly get to the door, it was so over-grown, but Pop pulled out his keys, unlocked the door, and let her look around. It was a small cottage, with a combination living and kitchen area and maybe two bedrooms, both small. It was too big for either a playhouse or a clubhouse, but Ellie figured she could overcome that. She smiled and nudged Luke, who had followed them, and almost tripped over Blake, who somehow appeared ahead of his dad and was taking it all in.

"Pop, can we come back again?" Ellie asked. She needed a better look.

"Not anytime soon. We'll all be getting ready to take your uncle Jack to Norfolk, so maybe when we get back. Uncle Bill is bringing back another generator for the barn, and you can come back while we are putting that in. That will take a while to accomplish, so you young-uns can look around then. Let's get along. We've been gone all day, and your grandmother will be stressing over supper, so we better get back before it gets too dark in the woods that we can't see the road." Charlie was getting more relaxed with the kids being on the property, and he was glad he had shown it to them. He kept thinking, *They will be the ones to have to take care of it when Odessa and I are gone, so they might as well get the lay of the land.*

These last few days had been exciting, and Ellie wanted to hurry home to begin reading her book, *Black Beauty*. She had finished *National Velvet* and was anxious to read about the other black horse. This book she would read to Blake, who would now listen. *Blue, what a wonderful name,* she thought, and she put her head on Blake's shoulder and whispered, "We got us a horse."

★14★

Legacy

The children were so tired from their day that they almost fell asleep eating their supper. Finally, Nett and Grandmom decided it was useless to keep them up any longer, so they led them upstairs to tuck them into bed. As the next day was Sunday, they could sleep a little later than if it was a school day, and what food they did not get tonight they could make up by eating a big breakfast in the morning. It was a cold January night, and Ellie snuggled deep in her quilts and hugged Sweetie Pie tightly. She cut her "God blesses" short and fell asleep almost in the middle of them. Grandmom kissed her on what part of her head she could find under the covers, and before she got to the door, Ellie was dreaming.

As Ellie nestled in the bed, she began dreaming of the big round room she had seen at the mansion. Travis, her saint, sat on the bed next to her tousled head and stroked the little girl's hair as he blew shiny memory dust around the room to send her into her deepest dream state yet. This journey Ellie would take on her own. As the dream unfolded, Ellie found herself in her nightclothes standing in the middle of the room where she had felt the cold, shivering feeling earlier. The tall windows that faced the front of the mansion had velvet curtains from floor to ceiling. They were a rich burnt-orange color. On the far wall was a wide stone fire-place, with a gold fan–type screen cover, in front of a glowing hearth. Stretching across the top of the fireplace was a mirror framed in thick dark wood that had been ornately carved. The wood extended down both sides, also framing the fireplace. There were large, plush chairs and sofas upholstered in richly colored fabrics of orange, green, and gold. The floor was highly polished wood, with a large Oriental rug in the middle. There were unusual chests throughout, and fancy oil lamps on the walls. The fire had been stoked, the oil lamps lit, and in the largest of the chairs sat an elegantly clad Weroansqua. Her crown with the enormous pearl was prominent on her brow, and her hair hung loosely down her back. She stood and held out her arms for Ellie to come closer.

Ellie ran to her and unceremoniously gave her a grand hug. She rested her head on Weroansqua's chest and held on like she never wanted to let go. She was so happy to see her, because she thought she might never see her again.

"I have thought about you for such a long time, my child," started Weroansqua. "I have seen you in my dreams and watched over you every day since you left."

"Oh, Weroansqua," Ellie's muffled voice said into the queen's robes where she had buried her face and continued to hold tightly. The comfort of the great chief was welcoming to the little girl. At that moment in her mind, she had been transported back to memories of the many days she spent in the matriarch's company.

"Sit, child." Weroansqua led Ellie to one of the small love seats scattered around the room.

The sofa was covered in soft ombre pillows. They settled down, with Ellie feeling like she would never let this special person out of her sight again.

"We have much to talk about, my dear. I know you have questions, but you must remember, you can reach me in your dreams, should you so desire." The great chief was as pleased to be in Ellie's company as the child was to be in hers.

"But, Weroansqua, I have tried, and I think I don't know how. Can you show me again? I have missed you, and I have tried to remember all the things you taught me, but sometimes I get confused. I have talked to Grandmom, and she understands, but I don't tell her everything, 'cause I'm trying to learn on my own. Please tell me how to talk to you." Ellie was almost pleading.

"All you have to do is think, call my name in your mind, and I will come to you. I have seen how you have succeeded in practicing the things you know, but there is more, and this is the night I will teach you. There are three spirits of women who have demonstrated the same talents as you. I have invited them here tonight to help you to develop your gifts. They are female relatives of yours who lived a long time ago, like me. So far, you have done an excellent job. Do you mind if I bring in someone you have been wanting to meet? When you see these spirits, do not be afraid."

Weroansqua put her arm around Ellie to steady her for the part she was getting ready to experience, because she knew this was going to be quite a shock for the little girl. She tightened her support of the child and laid her head on the side of Ellie's head, whispering, "Do not be afraid. I am with you. I will not let anything happen to you."

Weroansqua motioned her hand above her head and signaled toward the door. Appearing in the entry to the room, sort of drifting through the doorway, was a young woman. She looked like Nett, was wearing white robes, had lighter hair, and appeared to be much younger. The figure began to look more real as she got closer to Ellie, and when she spoke, Ellie got such a warm feeling that she was unable to explain it.

"Ellie, this is your mother, Annie." Weroansqua whispered in Ellie's ear.

The look on the child's face was one of disbelief. She inched even closer to Weroansqua, speechless. Her emotions and thoughts were indescribable. She did not know what to say or what to do, or even if she should do or say anything. She stared at Annie, then at Weroansqua, then back to Annie. Still she could not speak. She was not scared, just confused, and maybe in a little bit of disbelief. She began to tear up but did not cry. The tears just started slowly down her cheeks. She clutched Weroansqua tightly and made no move toward the mother she had longed to see. All the teasing, all the stories, all the emptiness she had tried to hide came tumbling down her cheeks in the form of tears. By this time she was so close to the protecting chief that there was room on the sofa for all three, but Annie did not sit with them. Instead, a chair that Ellie had not noticed before was in front of them. Annie sat down and held out her arms. It was a gesture that child and mother had both longed for, and now it was here.

Ellie's spirit, Travis, floated overhead, sending the child strength. At last, Ellie stood and, kneeling in front of her mother, put her head in Annie's lap. Annie collapsed over her and gathered the child in her arms. It was a necessary ending to Annie's demise, and for her, it was the action that could now allow her to quietly pass over to the heavenly side. For Ellie, it was closure.

Both heaved a sigh of relief. Ellie actually felt clean, fresh, and stronger than she had ever felt before.

"Your mother loved you very much. She just wanted to hold you in her arms once before she went away forever. You, my sweet, also needed for her to do that, and now both of you can feel complete. Ellie, this will allow you to move forward with confidence that you are whole. You have a mother and a wonderful grandmother, and both love you very much. This was a wish I needed to grant to you before you could move on to a fuller life." Weroansqua watched as Annie lifted her child to her feet and stood in front of her, reached down, and kissed Ellie on the cheek, the top of the head, and on both teary eyes. Then Annie disappeared.

Ellie turned, resumed her place next to Weroansqua, and collapsed, burying her head in Weroansqua's lap and sobbing. The tears she shed were tears of joy, relief, and completion. Never again would Ellie bristle at the barbs others threw at her. There was nothing they could say about "ghosts" that would ever bother her again. It actually made her love her grandmother even more. Grandmother Odessa had felt so much love for Annie that Ellie finally realized how much her grandmother had lost, and in her little heart she was determined to show her all the love she could. She wanted to fill the void left in her grandmother's life by the loss of her daughter.

When she lifted her head, Weroansqua brushed away her tears, and Ellie said, "Can I tell Grandmom I saw my mother?"

"Yes, I think she would like that." The Indian held the child tightly, assuring her that all was in order, as it should be.

The two sat on the sofa in front of the warm fire while Ellie told Weroansqua all the times she had tried to practice her gifts—the whales, the animals, to Luke and Blake—and her conversations about it with Grandmom. They talked and talked until Weroansqua felt the little girl was ready for her next disclosure. The Indian chief was going to reveal and unlock the mysteries of the final powers Ellie was destined to possess. She again put her arm protectively around Ellie and drew her closer on the sofa.

The lamps flickered, the fire in the hearth sputtered, and seated in two of the chairs in front of the windows were figures of women, rather obscure, and not at all as easily seen as Annie had been. They appeared rather blurred. One was dressed all in black. Her clothing was made from rich-looking black lace, with a high neck, long sleeves, and an elaborate skirt that reached the floor. Her shoes were high-topped boots. She looked matronly, her dark hair, streaked with gray, was piled high on her head with ornate combs holding it in place. She had a kind face, chalk-white skin, and a pleasant smile.

"Ellie, meet a member of your ancestral family. Her name is Rhetta. Your aunt Jeanette carries her name: Rhetta Jeanette Gray. Seated in the chair beside her is her daughter, Sabra. They both lived their lives with the same gifts as we will bestow on you." Sabra had soft, slightly red hair.

She was dressed in a yellow dress and a bodice of lace fitted at the waist, with a black insert down the middle of the wide, billowing skirt. At the end of the three-quarter sleeves were lace cuffs. She also was smiling. They did not speak, nor did they motion for Ellie to come forward. They understood that this child must be scared. Taking that into consideration, they waited for Weroansqua to begin.

"This house was built by these women, along with Rhetta's brother, Jabez. They both lived here most of their lives and were happy. As I have told you, they shared many of the same powers as you possess, plus they also had the gifts that you have yet to be given: to move objects, see danger before it happened, and connect without audible sound to each other. Both were accompanied everywhere they went by the wolf, and Ellie, Sabra had a horse like your Pegasus. Pegasus is the descendant of Sabra's horse."

At that, Ellie spoke softly to Weroansqua. "I have a new horse. His name is Blue, and he is black."

"I have seen your new horse, child. He also is a special breed and can sense your heart. You will be happy with him, and he will take care of you. And, child, if you have wondered whether the new horse will tolerate the wolves, the answer to that is yes. They have already met." This was to be the chief's last visit to Ellie, and Weroansqua wanted Ellie to be informed about everything, knowing that in dreams she could reinforce whatever Ellie forgot.

Sensing Weroansqua's sadness about leaving her special child, and moving closer, Sabra finally spoke, telling Ellie that they would meet again—that she, Luke, and Blake would visit them in this house during her time in history, and it would be a similar adventure to the one they experienced with the Croatoans. Sabra told her that the years during which both Sabra and her mother had lived were important years for the island, and Ellie and her cousins would be allowed to travel back to that time—but not right now. They had much to do in their own time. Their grandfather and grandmother needed help, they would help their father, and on their own, their contribution to the island would be greater than both hers and that of Uncle Jabez. She told Ellie that she should become familiar with the house. It had many secrets, and when the time came, Sabra would help her uncover those mysteries. Sabra told her that both she and her mother, Rhetta, were now able to deliver messages to Ellie in her dreams.

Ellie became more comfortable as she sat beside the great chief. She was no longer fearful of the strange women sharing their thoughts with her. She listened intently, hoping she could remember, and hoping that she could learn to use her gifts. The women cautioned Ellie about use for good rather than evil, and the little girl understood. Everything seemed to be all right now that she had seen and hugged her mother. There was more of a completeness with her than before. She felt stronger, calmer, and more confident.

"Ellie," said Sabra, "put out the fire."

Ellie looked stunned. "How?" she said. "Do I know how to do that?"

"Think, sweetheart. Think hard, same as you did when you sent the dolphin to Blake. Think, close your eyes, and concentrate." Sabra looked kindly at Ellie and waited.

The child closed her eyes and, as was her style, suspended her breathing. She tried hard to concentrate on the fire in the hearth.

"Fire out," she thought, repeating it several times in her mind.

The fire sputtered, the flames lowered, the coals from the previously burning wood glowed red, and the blaze was suspended. Ellie was amazed, flashing the biggest grin as she looked up at Weroansqua.

"I did it! I think. Did I do it, or did you?" She was shocked at what had just happened.

"I only watched, my child. I only watched." Weroansqua was satisfied that her loving granddaughter would be fine. Her job was done.

Ellie awakened in her own bed, with Christo sending his shrillest crow, as if to say, "Snap out of it, girl!" Grandmom was leaning over her with her hand on Ellie's forehead.

"My goodness, child. You might have a fever. I think you had on too many covers last night. I should have checked on you. How do you feel? You can stay in bed today if you want to. I'll send everyone else to church and Sunday school, and you and I will stay home and try to bring that fever down." Odessa looked worried.

Ellie looked up at her grandmother and reached up to give her a hug. She was hot and sweating, and she really did not feel quite right. As her arms wrapped around her grandmother's neck she whispered in her ear, "I met my mother last night, Grandmom. I'm going to be fine."

★15★

The White Doe

T he boys came home from church and went straight to Ellie's room to check on her. They missed their sidekick and did not want her to be left out of whatever stories they had to tell about the Sunday school class and the antics that ensued during that hour. Georgie Tolson had more Old Christmas stories of the mischief he had gotten into. The girls asked about her, and Miss Arnetta, their Sunday school teacher, sent her love. Ellie was glad to hear the news, and she assured the two that she was only tired, and whatever Grandmom had felt was wrong was only temporary. Just in case, Grandmom wanted her to rest inside for the remainder of the day. The January air was beginning to resemble winter, and any chill might reactivate the fever Ellie felt when she awakened. The boys decided to stay inside with her to read their new library books. Blake was particularly happy as he and Ellie would read *The Black Stallion*.

They both changed their clothes and crawled into the bed with Ellie. Grandpop put coal in the potbellied stove in the hallway in an attempt to control the draft that ran through the second level of the keeper's quarters. Usually a blanket was placed at the top of the stairs, shutting off the opening to the second floor and keeping all the heat from leaving the rooms on the first floor. Today they would attempt to heat the entire house. Grandmom had the woodstove in the kitchen fired up, cooking dinner, which also helped keep the beach wind from whistling through the creaking walls. Luke was under his own blanket at the foot of the bed, and Ellie and Blake were at the other end. Luke appeared not to be bothered by Ellie's quiet reading aloud to Blake of *The Black Stallion*. At the good parts he suspended his search for information on Poseidon and listened to the adventures of the horse.

Grandmom and Nett came in with trays of food for dinner—fried chicken and sweet potato casserole with marshmallow melted on top—and also to check on how comfortable it was in that chilly room. They looked at the scene and felt the warmth of the stove and were satisfied that the kids were all right. Most of the afternoon was spent reading and napping, which was probably good for all of them, as most of the time they were going full speed ahead.

Downstairs, Grandpop was also reading his latest copy of the *Virginian Pilot* newspaper, delivered in a bundle to the porch of Mr. Eph's store the night before. Although it was not the thick Sunday edition, the Saturday paper would do. The Sunday edition would be there on the return trip that afternoon. Grandmom was reading the Bible, and Nett and Bill had gone into the village to visit Nett's brothers and their wives. Bill and Grandpop were planning to leave for Norfolk on Wednesday for Jack's first round of boxing on Thursday night at the naval base. The kids were on a countdown to snow, which in their calculations would come on the following Sunday night, or Monday at the latest. No one else was privy to that countdown, as the others had forgotten about the lightning that occurred just the other night. It was a chilly winter day, spent doing nothing—quite a change from most other days.

When Nett and Bill returned, Nett went upstairs and began her evening ritual of homework, both hers and the children's. It was decided that Ellie would probably be well enough for school on Monday. Blake was disappointed about not being able to continue listening and discussing horses, but his little snorting disapproval fell on deaf ears, as homework took precedence over everything in this family. Uncle Jack had taken care of Gus for the kids and was working on softening the saddle, only because Grandmom would not allow him to train on Sunday. "Fighting" was not considered respectful on the Lord's Day.

After homework, the children came downstairs for supper. Ellie needed to be observed in an upright position for Grandmom to assess her health and decide if she could attend school on the following day. Ellie was fine. She actually had not been ill. She was just emotionally drained after the dream travel that took her on the journey to meet her mother. Grandmom also knew that, but she was smart enough to realize that emotions have an impact on health, and she did not want Ellie to be affected by her dreams. She certainly had no reason to worry. The kids got to laughing and giggling at something—who knows what?— and almost couldn't contain themselves at the table.

Grandpop was the one for whom someone should worry. He seldom spent a whole day without the kids, and he missed them terribly. Bill was taking care of the duties tonight, going back and forth from the lighthouse to the assistant keeper's quarters, sneaking in some preparation time with Jack and Lindy. Grandpop decided to spend time in one of his storytelling moods.

"Okay, I feel a story comin' on," he said. "Have I told you the one about the crooked-foot deer?" That one was so familiar they could have repeated it to him, unless he had forgotten what he said and made up a new one.

"Grandpop, you said you had another story about a white dolphin," Ellie interrupted. They were really tired of the old deer stories.

"Well, how about the one about the white doe of Roanoke Island?" Grandpop was determined to tell a deer story.

"Great!" Blake chimed in. He had no interest in another white dolphin. After all, Grandpop didn't tell ones about his dolphin, James.

"Fine with me," Luke said. He wanted to make Grandpop happy, considering what he had done for them over the holidays. Also Grandpop was responsible for taking them back to the big house in the woods, so keeping Grandpop happy was in Luke's best interest.

Grandpop settled down in his special chair by the fireplace. Blake squeezed in there with him. Ellie and Luke stretched out at his feet on a blanket pallet Grandmom insisted on making to get them off what she considered the cold floor, and the story commenced.

"The first child born in the New World was named Virginia Dare," he began.

Blake cut his eyes and made his "Surprise!" face at the two on the floor. Luke punched Ellie, and they all listened up—so shocked at the subject Grandpop had chosen to use as his story. "She was born on the mainland, in a colony located where the *Lost Colony* outdoor drama is presented every year. The island is called Roanoke Island, and it's where the town of Manteo is located. Now, the town is named after the son of the great chief of the Croatoan Indians, the ones who inhabited our island."

"Was the chief a girl?" Blake chimed in, and Luke shot a look of disapproval at him, as did Ellie.

"Don't cause Grandpop to stop his story. We want to hear him talk, not you!" Luke said, also drawing a scowl from Grandpop, who didn't realize what they were arguing about. Grandmom, sitting nearby crocheting a doily for Nett's dresser, gave herself an inside smile at the sniping going on in front of her. She had to catch herself from laughing out loud. Instead, she kept her head down to cover the grin she couldn't stop.

"Well, son, as a matter of fact, you are right. Did you learn that at school?" Grandpop innocently replied.

"Yup." Blake narrowed his eyes in a satisfied, smirky look, glad he had wriggled out of trouble.

"Well, the chief of the Roanoke tribe, whose name was Wanchese, became unhappy with the settlers. To him, they were a nuisance, always depending on the Indians for supplies. The colony had waited for over two years for a promised supply ship to come from England, which never came. He planned to rid his island of the worthless white men and organized an attack to destroy them or drive them away from the island. News of his intentions reached Manteo, who had been baptized by the colonials on the same day as the new child, thus creating a special bond between him and the white settlers. He gathered some of his warriors. They organized and successfully executed a rescue of the few who were left in the camp. By the time Manteo and his tribesmen reached the colony, parts of the fort had already been burned. It was easy to persuade them to accompany him. They knew their time was short if they stayed, so the English gladly sneaked through the forest to the waiting canoes of the Croatoan.

"When the frightened colonials arrived on the shores of Manteo's tribe, most of the Croatoan Indians had never seen a little girl like the English baby who came with them. She had light hair, blue eyes, and unlike them, her skin was pure white. Many of the tribe thought of her as some kind of special princess, and over the years they began to treat her that way." Grandpop paused. "By the way, Ellie, her mother's name was the same as yours, Eleanor, although you were not named after her." He continued, "As Virginia grew, she played with the Indian children, but they gave her special treatment, thinking that her white skin was an omen from Dawnland, to be worshiped. They followed her most everywhere she went, fought over the right to sit next to her at festivals, and listened to her every word. She tried to teach them her language, and they in turn attempted to teach her.

"Over the years, the child whom they named Winona-Ska grew in beauty and stature until eventually she captured the heart of a young brave. The handsome young warrior's love was not returned by Winona-Ska, but he did not stop trying. He felt he could wait for such a prize as the fair maiden. Okisko, the brave's name, was not the only suitor the white princess had. There were others, all vying for her attention, but

Okisko was the most smitten, and therefore the most persistent. He tried in vain to gain her love. He presented flowers, special furs, carved items, and anything he could think of to attract her to him—all to no avail.

"It so happened that he and his friends were not the only Indians attracted to the beautiful young maiden. The conjurer of the tribe, Chico, was also planning to make Winona-Ska his squaw. He knew he was no match for the younger males, so he decided to enlist his black magical powers to help his cause. The dark forces were his tools. He set his fires and spent days and months calling on the evil powers of his visions to help him in his quest to own the maiden. He contacted the water nymphs, who had been banished to live in shells by the great god Poseidon in punishment for their deeds. Resenting their plight at being cast out of the ocean and into the smaller water, they listened. Chico promised them that if they would help him, he would restore the powers that Poseidon had taken away. Poseidon had removed their powers on the water, thus leaving them only powers on land, which were useless to them. They longed to gain access to water strength again.

"The plan was for Chico to trick Winona-Ska into accompanying him to visit Roanoke Island where she was born. In his evil mind, if he could not convince the beautiful young girl to fancy him, he would prevent any other man from marrying her. As she was not accustomed to evil thinking, she agreed to the venture. When she climbed into the canoe, Chico and the river nymphs were thus in control. As soon as they landed on the shores of Roanoke Island and her foot touched the soil of her birth, she was immediately transformed into a white doe. She turned and looked at the evil magician and leaped away into the forest, never to set foot on Hatteras Island again."

Ellie was so taken by the story that she began to not like this tale. She looked at Luke with such sad eyes that he scrunched next to her to comfort her. Grandpop was so enthralled in his magnificent story he did not notice, but both Blake and Grandmom did. Grandmom thought about stopping Charlie from his winding tale, but she did not know how, so she waited for him to finish. She knew she could fix things later.

Grandpop continued, "Turns out the sighting of a white doe darting to and fro through the woods caught the eye of the braves of Wanchese's tribe, and they began to hunt her. She, by that time, had also caught the fancy of the other deer, and they followed and protected her as she roamed the forests. She was elusive and could not be caught. Many arrows were fired off in her direction, but none found their mark. Seemed she knew the tricks of the Indians and was not fooled by their snares and traps to catch her.

"Finally, there was a contest among the Roanoke Indian braves: Whoever could kill the white doe would receive favor among all braves among the tribe. Wanchese, the son of the great chief with the same name, decided he would be the one to win the prize. He rummaged around the belongings of his father and found the silver-tipped arrow presented to his father when he and Manteo had visited the Queen of England. He put it in his quiver and joined the hunt. For a whole day and night the white doe eluded the hunters, being seen but never succumbing to the stings of any of the arrows. At last, she was sighted by young Wanchese, and he let fly the silver arrow from the container on his back. It found its mark and felled the doe. When the brave went to retrieve his valuable arrow, as he pulled it out, the shadow of a white deer rose from the lifeless body, drifted over the head of the startled Indian, and ran away. As the story goes, on many an occasion since, people living in that area have claimed to see the phantom spirit of the white doe, frolicking through the forest near the site where she fell."

A tear ran down Ellie's cheek, and Luke put his arm around her. "Don't cry, Ellie. It's only a story," he said.

Only then did Grandpop notice the effect the story had on his little girl. He picked her up, sat her on his lap, and said, "Sweetheart, you are so tenderhearted. It is only a poem I read. It isn't true. Nobody knows what happened to Virginia Dare, but this is one of the legends, and it was started by a woman who wrote a poem telling this story. There are many others, but people like a mystery, so they always relate to this poem. What was the name of that poem, 'Dessa, do you remember?"

"It was 'The White Doe: The Fate of Virginia Dare,' and the woman's first name was Sally. I can't remember her last name, but it was written 'bout fifty years ago, so you know she didn't know what she was talking about. She was just making up something. Don't worry, honey. In my memory from the Indians, passed down over the years, Virginia Dare married her young brave and they had many children. So don't fret. This woman even had the names wrong. The old magician's name was Sucki, not Chico. Shows how much she knew. Now dry your tears. Don't want you to get sick again. Come on, let's all go to bed. Grandpop won't tell any more sad stories, now, will you, Charlie?" She shot him a disapproving look.

Captain Charlie felt so bad about upsetting his beautiful child that he gave her a special hug, put her down, and whispered in her ear, "I don't know what I'm talking 'bout either." Ellie flashed her grandfather a smile of relief, gave him a much welcomed kiss on his cheek, and off to bed she went.

When Grandmom was listening to Ellie's prayers, and she got to the "God blesses," she blessed her grandfather, the white doe, and Virginia Dare, just in case. "Honey, you can't take these stories your grandfather tells seriously. He makes most of them up, and this one was just a tale he heard. Why, I even heard tell of someone who claims to be a descendant of Virginia Dare, just like we are of the Indians. So she must have married her brave. After all, people say the colony was 'lost,' and we know that wasn't true. So this is just another story to get people interested. Now, sleep well, have wonderful dreams of black horses, and Christo will wake you in the morning."

Odessa went downstairs to face a very sad captain. Never could he stand to see his little girl upset. She sat down in the rocking chair beside him.

"Now, Charlie, don't you go feeling bad about our child. We talked, and she knows it was just a story, like the one they tell about everybody being 'lost,' and anyway, you shouldn't think you can take away all her hurt. Children shouldn't grow up thinking life is always going to be great. She needs to know there is sorrow in life, or else how will you know when things are good? To appreciate light, there must be dark. That child is going to be all right. Sometimes she needs to be tough. We are not going to be around forever to protect her. She will need to learn to protect herself. We had a long talk, and she was asleep before I left the room." Odessa leaned over and patted Charlie's arm, and they both watched as the fire blazed, warming the whole room.

Ellie went to sleep, and in her dreams, she and Blake were racing across the beach on the back of the beautiful black horse whose name was Blue.

★ 16 ★

The Haunted House

When the children finished breakfast and had taken care of Gus, they dressed in their heaviest clothes and climbed into the car for school. Luke had his mythology book, trying to read on the bumpy ride. and the other two were looking at the pictures in Blake's pirate book. They assured Nett that they were ready with their studies and looking forward to the Monday morning assembly in the auditorium. They liked the group singing and getting to see all the other children in school before they parted to go to their respective classes.

After school, Luke—having planned the weekend in his head already—took the other two out to the barn and spent time with Ellie, teaching her how to put the bridle on Pegasus and, once accomplished, how to mount and ride, controlling the horse with the bridle. Ellie assumed he was readying her for Blue, but Luke was pretty anxious for the two youngest to get their own ride, leaving Pegasus to him. Blake, of course, learned everything at the same time as Ellie and was quite good. He, too, was thinking ahead, of times when he would be allowed to ride Blue by himself.

They were just getting the hang of it when Nett called them in for homework. All of them practiced riding bareback, as the saddle was not yet finished, and they were too small to lift it anyway. Grandmom's contraption at the back of Gus's blanket was satisfactory to serve as a back for the children to ride. For Luke, this was just passing the time until Saturday. They were going back to the mansion.

Every day they practiced putting on the bridle and mounting the horse on their own, without help from others, and the two younger children got better and better. They used the steps of the lighthouse, stepping up on the rings that tiered around the base, allowing them to perfect their ascent at the rear of the tower out of sight from the adults. Jack and Lindy coming back from one of their runs on the beach saw the action behind the lighthouse, investigated, and began to help them become more adept at climbing on the horses by themselves. They inquired about the reason for mastering the horse, and in true fashion the boys spilled the plan, which was to explore the house on the hill. The older boys approved, as it reminded them of when they were that age, remembering the mischief they invented.

They also had scouted the old mansion and had kept the secret of the loud organ. Jack and Lindy had gone one step further and dared other boys to visit, but only after they had rigged other booby traps to further scare the daylights out of any unwelcome visitor. Of course, the two older boys had gone with their friends and made sure the traps they set added to the scary event, thus ensuring the haunted house rumors that further resulted in keeping others away. However, even Jack and Lindy ran when they got a glimpse of the wolves' shadows moving around in the woods next to the house. Jack warned them about the presence of wolves, then remembered the encounter with Ellie. He noticed that the mention of wolves did not faze the three—unlike he and Lindy, who had no reason to trust the wild creatures.

The older boys were actually proud that these three would think of such an undertaking. He didn't think they would get in trouble if they were careful. They fine-tuned Luke's plan for him. After all, these young-uns had to do something to prove their sand as islanders, and this seemed mild compared to what Jack and Lindy had done growing up, as they, too, had a female partner in crime—Tinker, Mr. White's youngest daughter. So the plan was hatched, practiced, and perfected. Bring on the weekend. Had the adventure involved water, the older boys would not have agreed, but what kind of trouble could they get in on land?

The fighter, trainers, Dr. Folb, and the captain left Wednesday morning for the trials in Norfolk. Mr. Quidley had arrived at daybreak to close the curtains of the light, protecting the delicate and expensive prisms from the damaging sun. Then he went home planning to return for polishing, lugging up the cans of kerosene, and general maintenance for the next five days. He was happy to do it. Former lighthouse keepers missed the old tower and their days on the job. This made Mr. Quidley feel important to serve as the keeper once again.

Lindy, Cantwell Jr., and Jack traveled to the city in Uncle Baxter's side-railed truck. On Thursday morning while Jack and Lindy were at the naval base in Norfolk, practicing and studying Jack's opponents, Cantwell Jr., Captain Charlie, Bill, Baxter, and Baxter's other son, Mahlon, had an appointment at the Portsmouth Naval Shipyard to pick up the three diesel engines that were discarded after the new ones were installed.

They planned to park the truck with the valuable cargo at Mahlon's house in Norfolk to wait for the trip back home on Sunday morning, thus not having to leave the engines in a strange place, lest they be stolen. Everyone was excited. These engines meant electricity to three houses: the keeper's quarters, the house in the woods, and Baxter's house in the village. They would alter the lives of both families. It meant radio, lights, refrigeration, washing machines—taking away the washboard and galva-nized tubs that Grandmom and Nett slaved over each weekend, cleaning clothes—and things they could only imagine. Convenience, that's what they were bringing back: convenience.

Friday came soon enough. Colby and Thomas rode home from school with the boys, Nett promising to take them home before supper. The compound was as rowdy as Grandmom had ever heard—too rough for Ellie, who went to her room with her real dolls and cut-out paper dolls and furniture from the pictures in the catalogs. She played with her imaginary friends until supper. At supper, with company gone, the kids were unusually quiet. Something was up. Even Ellie had a hard time getting to sleep, for tomorrow was the great adventure.

Saturday morning after breakfast, Luke asked if they could take Gus on the beach, promising not to get near the water. They all assured Grandmom they would be careful and requested a bag of sandwiches for the day, "so they would not have to disturb her later." That was their story, and they were all sticking to it. Nobody was suspicious. Everything ready, they put the blanket on the horse, strapped on the saddlebag, climbed on, and sauntered across the dune to the beach, heading south. The trip to the house on the hill did not take long, even as they were only walking Gus. There was much anticipation, speculation, excitement, and of course giggle fits. They did not pass a soul on the trip down the southern side of the island, and finally they reached the area where they knew to turn right and go over the dune to the path in the woods leading to the mansion.

The house loomed large as they climbed toward the top of the hill. They tied Gus and went to shut off the alarm in the garage. Everything looked as before. Nothing had been disturbed. Luke uncovered the hidden key to the back door that let them into the kitchen. They entered and went up the several steps to the first floor. Once in the main entrance, they headed toward the wide double staircase in the middle, in between the two large rooms that made up the main floor.

They touched nothing, not even opening the curtains. The smell of dust and closure was still quite overwhelming, but it did not deter the children from their desire to see what was there. Reaching the middle landing where the stairs separated, they all went to the right. When they got upstairs, they examined the rooms. Ellie went straight to the round room and observed what she had seen in her dreams, but did not feel the same cold wind as before. *My mother is at rest*, she thought, and smiled inside.

Luke, still in the hall, opened one of the doors on the back wall. The door led to another set of stairs, which they had not had a chance to explore before, having been called away by their dad. When they got to the top of the stairs, there was a small landing, a table with a gold carved mirror above, and a pedestal displaying the bust of a pirate. A heavy wooden door had a fancy handle in the center of the door rather than on the side. Luke turned the knob to open the door. They viewed a large room that appeared to be a library or office. On the far wall opposite the door, there were two tall but small diamond-paned windows facing the ocean, and to the right on that wall was a large bookcase, filled with books and memorabilia. The windows of the entire house—as seen both inside and from the yard—were fitted with the same small diamond-shaped panes that withstood the elements of wind and rain, and were easily replaceable.

On the wall beside them were two more multipaned windows from which one could see the sound. From so high up, there was a clear shot of both. In front of the double windows facing the ocean, there were two plush chairs, and in front of the other two, facing the sound, was a window seat that had a cushion on top and doubled as a chest. There was a tall grandfather-style corner clock to the left of the door, and next to that a wall and another door. The left side of the room was a wall of bookcases located between the door and the east wall. The shelves ran floor to ceiling and were full of books, statuettes, and beautifully framed small paintings of pirates. Pirate artifacts were placed between books on both bookcases, along with the paintings and several small models of barkentine and four-masted sailing ships, with intricately carved mast-heads. But the dust was so thick that it was hard to read the titles of the books or distinguish the faces of the people.

The south wall, void of windows, was a backdrop for two beautifully carved Oriental chests, with large vases placed on top. The children only looked. They did not touch, as their fingerprints would show in the dust. They turned to the other door in the room. They opened this one, discovering what seemed to be another bedroom.

Most upholstered pieces were covered with cloth, so it was hard to see much. On the south wall separating the two rooms was what appeared to be a daybed, as it was too narrow for a real bed. Maybe it was a sofa, but was even too large for that, and from the lumps under the cloth, it looked to have several pillows on the sides and back. On the east side were two tall windows in the same manner as the ones in the first room, overlooking the ocean. On the west side were two similar windows overlooking the sound. On the north wall was a fireplace. They had seen the tall, wide brick chimney from the yard but did not realize there were fireplaces on every floor using that same structure.

On either side of the fireplace were bookcases or closets, this time with doors, which concealed whatever was behind. Under the two windows facing the ocean was an enormous and ornate mahogany desk. Whoever used that room was able to view the ocean and do business at the desk at the same time. On the west wall were two other tall windows from which one could see the sound. In the corner between the door and the windows on the west wall was another tall cabinet, maybe for clothes, and under the two windows was a window seat or chest similar to the one in the other room. The two rooms made up a great retreat—especially since one had to open a door at the bottom of the stairs to get there, and still another at the top of the stairs to get into the room.

"Wow, what a great place," said Blake.

They left the bedroom and went back through to the stairs, closing all the doors behind them. Their heads were almost on a swivel, trying to see everything as they walked down the wide staircase. They had not noticed the paintings lining the wall up to the third floor. The walls had inset paneling and pieces of railing protruding for gripping up and down the stairs, and the pictures followed the railing up the walls. They looked like they were old paintings, but again, dust covered everything. They were so beautiful, Ellie wanted to wipe away the dust to protect them.

"Look what I found," said Ellie as she looked back up at the boys descending the stairs. She was at another door, the one on the other side of the double chests separating the door leading to the third-floor stairs. Upon opening the second door, she was looking at yet another set of stairs, not leading up, but down. At the bottom of these stairs was another door. When opened, it revealed the kitchen. They realized that the people on both the second and third floors could go to the kitchen without being seen by anyone on the ground floor. It was the back stairs. They loved it.

They had explored the second and third floors and were now standing in the kitchen, which ran across the back of the entire house. It obviously had been added at a later time than the first building, as it was quite different in style from the rest of the first floor. From the outside, even the roof was not the same. This room was made of rough exposed timbers, with a brick fireplace cooking area and an iron curved rod suspended from the top for hanging a pot over the fire.

Running down the center of the kitchen was a long, thick wooden table—no chairs, just a work area. Most of the walls were exposed brick, not wooden panels like the rest of the house. The kitchen had lots of iron rods from which hung pots, sinks with side-handled pumps like Grandmom's, and cabinets with doors, and near the end of the wall facing the ocean was a single multipaned window that looked like the other windows in the house but was set horizontally rather than vertically. Once in the kitchen, Blake, of course, had to go look at the indoor privy and decided to use it. He approved.

"Come on, Blake! Keep up. I'm not going to look for you if you get lost. We can't stay all day. Grandmom will get worried." Luke was barking out orders again. But Luke had seen other places he wanted to explore before they left to start back. They walked up the several steps leading again to the main floor and the two gigantic rooms located here. There were many windows in all the rooms, and they were tall. At least they looked that way, judging from the curtains hanging from ceiling to floor.

They decided to take one more look around before going home. They started up the double staircase on the second floor. When they reached the landing leading to the staircases on either side, the huge, ornately framed door that served as part of the back wall—also with a round, ornate wooden frame in the middle—looked a little like the one that led to the tower room, but with no knob. As the other two ascended the two staircases—Luke going up one side, and Ellie the other—Blake decided to touch the round wooden piece in the middle of the framing on the back wall. To his shock, the entire door moved back, exposing another hallway, which looked to be between the walls.

"Luke, Ellie. Lookie what I found!" He screamed so loud the other two raced down their respective stairs to the middle of the landing. There was indeed another hallway, behind the walls, leading to the left of the opening. They all just stared.

"I'm going in," said Luke. "Come on, let's see what this is."

"I'm not going," said Ellie. "What if you get inside there and can't get out? You'll be sorry. I'm staying here. If you get lost behind there and can't find your way out, at least I'm here to let you back into this side."

"Yeah, that's a good idea. We don't know where this goes." Luke and Blake went into the hallway behind the door. "It's dark in here!" Luke called back.

Almost as soon as he said that, Blake, who was following behind, turned around and went out the secret door, yelling back at Luke who was still behind the wall.

"Just a minute. I'll be right back!"

"Don't tell me you have to go to the bathroom *again!*" Luke yelled back. "Hurry up! I'm not waiting here forever!"

Blake raced down the stairs, out the back door, and across the yard to Gus, who was patiently waiting in the yard, maybe asleep standing up. Blake reached up, dragged down the saddlebag, pulled out a flashlight, and—leaving the bag on the ground—hurried back to the house where the other two were yelling at each other on the middle landing leading to the second floor. Luke had obviously not waited for Blake and was feeling his way down the hall between the walls. He thought he felt another door or framed structure on the right, but in the dark he couldn't tell and continued going straight. Blake turned on the flashlight and followed Luke.

"What?" Luke was shocked. "Where did you get that? Is there no end to what you carry with you when you leave the house?" He was both happy and surprised.

They started down the lit hallway, fighting their way past cobwebs, dust, and everything else time had contributed to the musty, smelly hallway. At the end of the hallway was a set of stairs, also between the walls. They started down the stairway, slapping at the webbing that hung from the ceiling and obscured their view. The stairway went down, way down. The flashlight flickered on and off like it needed new batteries. As they descended the stairs they kept shouting back at Ellie to come join them, but she would not. She was so afraid that they would get stuck between the walls of the house, she just couldn't talk herself into leaving her post.

The boys went down and down, coming to another small landing where the stairs turned and went down again. It proved to be a nasty descent, with cobwebs and dirt all around, and it began getting colder and for sure damp. Both boys thought about turning around, but neither would admit it, so they just kept going down until they reached a dirt bottom. Blake shined the light ahead, seeing that they were in a tunnel with a ceiling taller than a man and wide. From the vantage point where they stood, they saw a running stream. At that time the light went out. Blake banged the flashlight, and it flickered again and went out.

"Blake, gimme that light." Luke took the tube from Blake's hand and slapped it on his hand, gently, and still it would only flicker. They could hear Ellie yelling to come back, but they were too far gone. The glow from the water gave just enough light for them to follow it. They knew where they were. It was the stream and grotto they had explored when they were visiting with the Indians. They felt like they could find the end if they kept going. They knew there was a waterfall and pool at one end and an exit leading to the sound at the other. They just did not know which end they were headed toward.

"Luke, something just touched me." Blake froze. He was scared to death. "*Luke!*" He was in a panic, and he grabbed in the dark in front of him for his brother's shirt or arm or whatever he could find. He was afraid to step, because every time he did, something crunched. The walls were nasty to touch, so he tried to stay away from them, and now something was in there with him.

Luke began to back up, and he also touched something that was not Blake. He stopped and was too afraid to turn around. He just stood there, breath suspended, wondering what was going to happen to them, and feeling just a little sorry they had been so bold as to venture into this underground tunnel. Luke could hear something. It was breathing heavily. It touched him again, this time giving him a little push.

"Blake, stop that!" but Blake did not answer.

He then heard Blake's voice much farther behind than he thought, and he knew he was not alone. Luke had gotten too far ahead of his little brother and needed to get back to save him. It was Luke's fault that he was down there. Luke slapped the light once more, and it flickered, revealing a huge wolf standing behind him. In the dark he slapped the light again. This time it stayed on for a while, and he recognized Rafe. Luke's sigh of relief echoed down the dark passageway, and he yelled out to Blake.

"Turn around, Blake. I think what touched you was your wolf!" Luke was hoping he was correct.

Blake backed up just a bit and felt the object again against his back. By that time Luke was closer, and he and Rafe were together now, standing in front of Blake. He slapped the light again, revealing the huge form of Theo standing behind Blake, patiently waiting for the little kid to move forward. The light stayed on just long enough for Blake to turn his head to see his beloved companion's golden eyes shining behind him. Without a thought of danger, Blake wrapped his arms around the huge animal's neck and gave him a hug.

"Careful, Blake," Luke cautioned. "Remember, we aren't supposed to touch them."

"He touched me first," Blake shot back, not sorry he had hugged his protector. "What do you think they are doing down here? They couldn't have come down the steps, could they?"

"I'm sure they came from another passage, maybe the one near the sound, and remember, there were lots of caves down here. Anyway, let's get outta here. Ellie is probably headed toward Gus right now going for help. We have to stop her. We will come back when we have light. Let's go back up."

Blake moved over, gave one more touch to Theo, and with Luke ahead of him—slapping the light for a flicker once in a while—they headed toward the steps and safety.

When they reached the hallway between the walls, and the door leading to the inside of the house, they could finally see that the wolves had not followed them, but Ellie was nowhere to be found. *Oh, no!* She had gone to get the horse and find help. They began yelling her name frantically, and they ran down the staircase and were almost in the kitchen when behind them they heard Ellie yelling back. They turned around, headed back to the middle stairs, only to see Ellie standing at the top of the stairs to the right, holding a lit lantern.

"You should have taken this," she said calmly. "There are lots of these in the pantry of the kitchen, and Grandpop or somebody left matches. I went down to the stairs but didn't want to miss you, so I came back and have been waiting for you. Did you find anything?" she asked innocently, obviously not in a panic at all.

The boys breathlessly told of their adventure—the wolves, the grotto, the stream, the nasty stuff they were stepping on in the dark—as both were tumbling all over each other's speech to get the information out as fast as they could. Their hearts were still racing from being scared and happy all at the same time. They had discovered the most amazing thing they would ever see, and it was not a dream.

"Why weren't you scared for us?" Blake asked.

"I saw you and the wolves," said Ellie calmly. "I just learned how to do that. At first I was scared, then I remembered that I could think where you were, so I sat down on the stairs and concentrated hard to picture you. I went looking for a lantern and was going to follow, but I didn't want to get spiders in my hair, so I waited. I could see you beside the stream, and I knew where the stream ended up, so if you didn't come back I would have ridden Gus to the sound, where we used to see the Indians wash clothes."

The three kids sat down on the top of the wide staircase, wondering how they could get the door closed. This would be a dead giveaway to Grandpop or anyone else who came into the house that there had been intruders, and it was them! Luke got up and looked inside the open panel, to the inside wall, and there was a large, round piece of wood on the wall, obviously another way to close the door, but it was inside, used for closing the door and leaving someone on the other side. So that was not good. They needed to find out how to close the door from the living room side. They ran their fingers along the wall on the front side to find a way to get the door to slide back.

They were beginning to panic. Finally, Luke stepped inside the hallway and pushed the door-paneled circle, and the door began to move to its original position. Luke jumped back to allow the door to close. The trigger was the door handle. Both ways.

Relieved, and worn out from their emotional adventure, they decided they had experienced enough for one day, and it was time to go home. In a way, they could hardly wait to get outside and in more familiar territory. They left the same way they came in, locked the kitchen door, and as Luke replaced the key and turned on the generator again, they moved Gus to the fence, crawled on, and begin their journey back through the wooded path to the beach. As they started their trip home, they caught a glimpse of the three wolves, shadowing them from the nearby trees, and Ellie waved to Twylah to let her know she was sorry she had not been able to be with her today, but acknowledged her presence anyway. She was having second thoughts about not having followed the boys down to the stream, but she would be sure to go next time.

They finally smelled the sweet salt of the ocean, dismounted Gus, and walked him over the dunes to the beach. It was much colder than they remembered it being, and dark clouds were beginning to form in the west over the sound. The air had a fresh, sharp smell—sort of like a shift of wind, but not exactly. The ocean was a little rough, the waves were bigger, and the incoming wash was beginning to breach the strand of shells that had been left from the receding tide earlier during the day. There was not much hard sand for Gus to trot on, so they moved nearer the dunes and slowed Gus to a walk. As he sauntered along, Blake reached around behind him and retrieved the saddlebag. Holding on with his knees, he extracted the sandwich Grandmom had packed for them and passed one forward for Luke and one for Ellie.

After they ate, they were feeling much better—relieved and happy and proud of being brave. They started laughing, telling each other what they thought of this thing or that. Then they began to wonder about all the pirate artifacts that had been on the third floor. They could not figure out how to approach Grandpop about that, because if they asked, he would know that they had been there. They decided that they would just have to wait until they accompanied Grandpop to the old house and somehow got him upstairs, allowing them to make a "natural" discovery.

Their curiosity was killing them. They had seen swords, flintlock pistols, and lots of things they associated with pirates. They wondered, *What was the fascination with pirates in that house?* They thought it was built by Grandmom's uncle Jabez. *Was he a pirate?* There would be no answers for a while.

When they came over the dune to the house, they walked Gus around to the barn and began cleaning him up from the trip he had taken. They wiped him down, brushed him good, gave him water, which he was glad to get, and left him lots of hay to eat. They also fed Ol' Tony and Big Roy, and stayed a little while to talk to all of them. Twinkle was quietly standing in the first stall, maybe making more milk.

By the time they got back in the house, it was getting dark, and Grandmom and Nett were in the kitchen making supper. Usually, supper was sort of leftovers from the large dinners that were served in the middle of the day, but this was something fresh, as with only Grandmom and Nett in the house they probably had not made much for dinner, so the children got in on a rather large supper. Luke and Blake could not seem to get enough milk, prompting their mom to question where they had been all day. They told the story they had all agreed upon, about finding a huge shark washed up on the beach and extracting a tooth. It sounded good enough, and everybody was satisfied.

During supper, the familiar ring that belonged to the keeper's quarters—one long and two short jingles—sounded, and Nett answered. Her side of the conversation led everyone to believe that it was Grandpop, causing them to crowd around to listen. Uncle Jack had won his first and second rounds of boxing and was headed to the final round tonight. The diesel engines were safely in front of Mahlon's house in Norfolk, and everybody would be home tomorrow night, depending on when they caught the ferry. Uncle Jack so far was not hurt, and excited about the final bout tonight—and no, he did not have another black eye. Grandpop was bringing gifts from the city back to everyone, which he kept as a surprise. Over all, it had been an exciting day.

Ellie awakened in a start. It was still dark, and the house was quiet. The only sound was the wind beginning to howl. She wanted to scream out, "Uncle Jack won!" but instead of making a sound, she dropped back to sleep. It was only a dream.

★ 17 ★

Convenience

It was Sunday morning, and the wind had grown really cold during the night. Nett had to make a fire quickly in the old potbellied stove in the hallway upstairs. The children would never be able to get dressed in this cold room. She hesitated in waking them until the rooms had warmed up a bit. It was early, but she heard Odessa moving around downstairs, and Nett went down to help her with those fires also. As they were getting heat going everywhere, the phone rang—their ring. Nett picked it up and listened. As she held the horn from the hanger at the side of the box, she turned with a big smile toward her mother and said, "Mom, he won." Odessa did a jig right there in the kitchen.

"Go wake the kids," Grandmom said. "This is something they will want to carry with them to Sunday school. We might be the only ones who know."

Nett went upstairs to kiss each covered head with the news. She could hardly find any of them, they were so buried down in their covers. The weather had definitely taken a turn toward the cold. She whispered the news in the boys' ears, and Luke sat straight up, threw off his covers, and pranced around in shadow-boxing mode until Blake joined him. When she went to Ellie's room, the same whisper gathered a different response.

Ellie said, in a muffled sleepy voice, "I know." Then she snuggled under with Sweetie Pie until it sank in. At that moment, she also sat straight up in bed, with the most surprised look on her face. "He did?" Now that was really a surprise. She thought she had dreamed that very thing. Did she dream it, or did she *know*?

By the time they all washed up in the wash basin bowls that were placed on each bedroom dresser, the water was still warm from Nett's having filled them from a kettle that she kept on the upstairs potbellied stove, usually to keep moisture in the dry air. The house was warming up. The children dressed, and they had gone to the potty bucket on the back porch, then threw it in the bushes, feeling the extremely cold wind. The same dark clouds that had been drifting their way from the sound yesterday were now both dark and lined with that blue-gray color in huge scalloped tufts, drifting toward the sea. The smell of the air was fresh and crisp, and actually stung their noses inside. It was a different smell. What they did not know was that this was the smell of impending snow!

Everybody was excited at church with the news of Jack's victory, and as Pop was not there to lead everyone in singing, Mr. White took over. His great booming voice could be heard over everyone else's, including Miss Myrtle's. No contest, everyone liked Mr. White's voice. The only thing for the kids was that he didn't go up and down on his toes when he hit a high note like Pop did, so there was a trade-off: Pop's little style and Mr. White's big voice. Church was fun.

On the way back, there was so much hopping around in the back of the jalopy that Nett had to turn around and threaten to stop if they didn't calm down. They all could hardly wait for the travelers to return. The news that Pop was bringing home surprises was a thing to speculate over. Grandmom said it was not toys, so after that disappointment, the guessing started.

Dinner was fried chicken, everybody's favorite and the fastest meal to get together. Grandmom's biscuits still melted away when eaten, and Nett had to caution the kids not to fill up on the biscuits. They also had collards, which were the island's seasonal cold greens, with luscious dumplings, Ellie's favorite. One time she asked Grandpop, when they were cutting collards from the garden, if he could possibly grow some dumplings. Grandpop was always repeating that story, he thought it was so funny. He took her down to the windmills in Kinnakeet to show her about grinding corn. There was also going to be lemon meringue pie, Luke's favorite. They ate their fill, not afraid to finish one off, because there must be several others on the porch, waiting for the hungry travelers to come home.

The day was spent cleaning up Gus from his trip the day before, then reading their books. It was too cold to stay outside. Luke had persuaded his mom to teach him the piano, so he also got a lesson. His practice and enthusiasm caused the other two to want to learn, so Nett spent most of the day listening to scales on the piano. Anything to pass the time.

It was dark when the trucks turned into the compound. The kids had been at the back window for so long that the dark had settled in, and they had to move back to the living room. They heard the commotion and quickly grabbed their coats to greet the caravan. Even Odessa was bundled up on the porch to give Jack a hug and examine his face. There was so much hopping around, the men could hardly get into the house for the kids "wanting to see."

"Isn't anybody glad to see me?" asked Bill with his arm around Nett. "Don't I get a hug?"

At that he was attacked. He picked up Blake and swung him around.

"Me, too!" said Luke, but he was too tall, so Bill gave him a special handshake and threw a boxing move at him to let him know that he was getting to be a young man now, and some things had changed. Luke was satisfied and kind of felt great that his greetings from now on were going to be like those for the older boys.

Not too much time passed before the kids were jumping from one foot to the other to see what the surprise was. Grandpop told everybody to keep on their coats, and they all went outside again to the big truck. Of course, the huge diesel engines were pushed up next to the cab, leaving little room for anything else, but there were two other tall things in big boxes, one that read "Frigidaire." Grandmom squealed, and the kids looked around in total surprise. They had never heard Grandmom utter such a sound, and she was hugging Grandpop like she had seen something amazing. What the heck was it?

"What's that, Grandpop?" Ellie questioned. She wondered what was making everybody so happy. Even Aunt Nett was prancing around, and Uncle Bill had the biggest smile.

"It's an icebox," said Grandpop.

"But we already have a big one on the back porch," added Luke. *What was so special about another one?* he was thinking. Blake was not even paying attention. He had crawled up on the back of the truck by the rails and was looking around for something else. He saw a smaller box that looked like half a trunk and yelled out, "What's this?" as he was trying to find some words on the box that had been strapped down next to the larger boxes.

"It's a radio," said Bill. Now that got a response, as the three kids really got animated.

Then something very unusual happened. Blake felt something on his face, and when he went to wipe it away, he screamed, "*Snow!*"

Everyone stopped marveling at the boxes on the truck and realized it was indeed beginning to snow. This homecoming had just amped up. Could it get any better? The snow was soft and flaky, drifting down slowly, but it was coming, and the air was getting colder, so it was going to keep on coming. Tomorrow everything would be covered in white. They could already see it on the walkway and the steps of the house. There would be no sleep tonight. From the steady beam of the lighthouse, they could see it coming in fast. And that smell that tickled their noses before was the smell of snow.

There was so much snow on the ground the following morning, it was almost impossible to unpack the truck. The engines and iceboxes had been covered the night before, and it would be impossible to unload them until the weather changed. Nett tried to get the jalopy started early, before breakfast, but it refused, and a call came that there would be no school, as the buses also were having trouble. Mr. Austin was the only one in the building, and his call to the stores and Coast Guard station canceled school. The place was too cold for anyone to learn anything.

At breakfast, Grandpop explained what the diesel engines would mean to all of them, but the kids hardly listened. All they wanted to do was eat and get outside. After breakfast, everyone was quickly getting bundled up to go outside, even Grandmom, who insisted on checking on the chickens and Twinkle the cow. The kids went with her to examine Gus, Ol' Tony, and Big Roy, who all seemed not to care about what was going on outside. By the time they all made the rounds, big military trucks were showing up in the compound—not to see Jack or Lindy, who were still asleep in the assistant keeper's quarters, but to see the kids. Lots of these guys were from up north and hadn't seen wonderful weather like this for a while, and probably at company mess they discussed just where the snow would be the most fun. The lighthouse kids!

The boys from the station started throwing snowballs when their feet hit the ground, and before Luke and Blake could turn around, they were pelted with the soft orbs, which fell apart on impact. Forts were built, teams were organized, and Lindy and Jack awakened and joined the fun. Grandmom began to put together a massive dinner. They were certainly about to have company. She started making pies—pecan, lemon, sweet potato—all for the crowd of boys she would be feeding. Nett was up to her elbows in flour, and everybody was laughing about everything, as Blake's sleeves began to get stiffer and stiffer. Nett called the kids in, put heavy scarves around their necks, and tried to stop the nose dripping. Then she gave up, knowing there was going to be some heavy washing later. She made them change clothes for dry ones and sent them out again.

It was hard to get the children to eat. They loved the company, laughed all during dinner, got teased, loved that, and went back out for more punishment. Finally the boys knew that the children needed to get out of the snow and wet. They had changed their clothes three times, and it was getting toward dark. The seamen knew the kids would not quit until they did, so they reluctantly left the compound to go back to the station. The kids—tired and wet—came in for the last time to change into dry clothes to eat and supper. It had been an overly active day, so Nett suggested they go to bed a little early. She got no argument.

When morning came, the children anxiously checked out the window, only to discover that the snow had melted and disappeared as fast as it had come. There were patches of white in the bushes and the shade, but it was going fast. The kids were hoping that there would be some left in the schoolyard, and there was, as the trees prevented the sun from melting the last of the pretty white stuff. At recess, there were attempts at snowball fights, but it was not happening. By that time, midday, everything was back to normal. But the most important thing was that Grandpop was right.

Lightning in January produces snow within ten days. It was a fact!

When they got home, they found that Grandpop and Bill had unloaded one of the diesel engines and the icebox, and they finally got a good look at the radio. Everything would depend on the wiring of the house from the structure to the generator. Pop said it would be finished by the weekend, and they would be going to the house in the woods to unload the diesel and check on how to wire that area. Radio by the weekend! It was almost too good to be true. People in Hatteras had some electricity, and those who listened to the radio talked like it was just the best!

Each day when they came home, they watched all the activity involved in getting electricity. It set in motion Charlie Gray's vow to make sure the island was able to share in the good fortune that Bill had brought to them. He began a campaign of writing letters and going to meetings. He even traveled to Washington, DC, over the next year to petition the government on behalf of the island for consideration in helping light the island. He and his friends were successful in getting the Rural Electrical Cooperative Association to join with them, and within five years after their efforts began, the island had access to electricity. Tall poles went up everywhere, and wire was strung from pole to pole down the still sandy two-track "inside" road, but one hurdle had been jumped. There were more to come, with talented men like Charlie Gray and E. S .White, the Midgetts, the Williamses, and others who helped all along the way.

The house was wired, the Frigidaire was in operation, the milk was extremely cold, and the kids could not get enough of it. Grandmom thought there was not enough milk on the island to fill the bellies of these three. Plus she couldn't stop grinning. The radio was tuned to the news every night, with Grandpop and Bill sitting so close to it and looking at it so hard that one would think it was expecting them to answer back. They almost found out more than they wanted to know, but that was communication at its finest. Sometimes it was just too much information.

The cabinet-style box was pretty, made of mahogany and having a knitted cloth screen framed in the same wood. It really was a piece of furniture. Grandpop liked *Burns and Allen, Amos and Andy, Lum and Abner*, and *The Charlie McCarthy Show*. Bill liked *The Great Gildersleeve* and *The Life of Riley*. The kids liked *The Cisco Kid* and *The Lone Ranger*.

Grandmom and Nett didn't get to choose. They just listened to whatever was on. Grandpop did not allow the radio to play except at certain times. He did not want to replace books in the lives of the children, so only particular programs were playing on certain nights. It was fun, but the only thing that played every day was the news in the early evening. After the initial introduction, the kids did not obsess over it. They went about their adventures as usual, as well as their constant plotting concerning the mansion on the hill.

Finally, the work at the keeper's quarters was done. The diesel was being delivered to the big house in the woods, but nothing was to be connected yet. Uncle Baxter's house was the next project. Bill's time on the island was now short, only a few weeks left, and he wanted to wire electricity to Pop's brother-in-law. He assured Captain Charlie that his services would not be needed. There were enough men living at Baxter's house to complete the job in half the time it had taken to do the keeper's quarters. He assured his father-in-law that he and the Miller boys would be at the mansion before dark to unload the last diesel and give Uncle Backy his truck back. So Charlie and the kids took the jalopy to the old house for the day. The children were overly anxious to "help" their grand-pop with anything he needed to get done, promising not to be a bother. Grandmom made a picnic basket for everyone, and the adventure began.

The security turned off and the house wide open created a feeling of freedom for the kids, who had sneaked around and observed everything in the musky odor of staleness when they explored the inside of the house earlier. This time, the doors were flung wide, open letting the chill of the January day flow throughout, and the children roamed around the house freely. They did not try to open the secret door and were careful not to tell Grandpop where anything was. They acted surprised at everything. The winter air felt good in the house, and Grandpop started a fire in the kitchen to keep the children warm. It was not needed, as warmth was not even a problem. Looking around was the rule of the day, and they made the most of it.

If Pop had thought they would help with anything, he was sorely mistaken. He couldn't even find them. Blake got to climb his tree and considered staying up there until he remembered the pirate things he had spied before. Now he needed to get Grandpop up to the third floor in order to "discover" the things he was curious about. Grandpop was busy messing around the barn and the boathouse, looking for a proper home for the huge diesel generator.

As he rambled around talking to himself, he noticed Blake was hanging around his knees everywhere he went. They talked, Grandpop did his thinking out loud, and Blake listened. Sometimes Pop would ask him what he thought, and Blake agreed with whatever the subject was. He was playing the game. He felt that if he spent time hanging around, maybe he would get his grandpop to follow him to the third floor.

Meanwhile Luke was making the rounds of all the rooms, peeking under cloth coverings and discovering just exactly what was there. The big pipe organ was fascinating. Without touching anything, he gave the place the once-over. He opened drawers, looked behind doors, stayed away from the hidden door, and also explored the yard and surrounding buildings. He was getting the lay of the land. He climbed up into the hayloft and checked out all the equipment. Most needed to be thrown away, as it was so old it was falling apart anyway. He was curious about the boathouse and the tools he found there. Meanwhile his mind was working and planning, dreaming of how to use the things he saw. Luke was thinking of his time exploring the island with Powwaw, looking for herbs and special plants. He would get to do that again.

Ellie was in the round room with the door closed. She was channeling Sabra. She lit the fire again but quickly put it out, realizing her grandpop would see the smoke. But she was satisfied that she could do it. She tracked both Luke and Blake in her mind, and saw where they were. She was practicing, and this place conducted her thoughts well. It seemed easy to do things that up to this point had required total concentration. She finally left the room and went back up to the third floor, sitting on the window seat, staring at the sound, and attempting to re-create the life that Sabra had when she was trying to do secret business during the time the English were watching the house.

She saw Sabra's workers as they channeled out the tunnel under the stairs to meet with the one she knew already existed from the Indians. She also saw things under there that the boys had not described, and she knew things that were old. The water was pure, and she also thought she saw something that was sunk in the grotto in order to hide it. She just could not figure out what it was, and whether Sabra or Uncle Jabez put it there. In her mind, she met Uncle Jabez and knew that he had taken Sabra into his confidence, like Grandpop had done with her. In her inner eye, she saw that they were partners in some things secret. She saw Sabra and her wolf walking the woods, and she felt a kinship. The house was talking to her.

Her mind shut off as Grandpop and Blake came upstairs. Luke was not far behind, and he looked at Ellie like he might know something—like maybe he had seen some of the things that she had seen. He gave her a *knowing* smile, and she knew they had things to talk about. Maybe the house was also talking to him. Blake and his chatter shattered the moment.

"Grandpop, why are there so many things here that look like pirates?" he asked.

"Like what, son?" This was not a conversation Grandpop wanted to have with this little kid.

"You know, like the swords and the pistols and the hats and—well, Pop—almost everything," he answered.

"Your uncle Jabez," began Grandpop, "who built this house, sold pirate booty."

EPILOGUE

Jack Gray won the Golden Gloves in Dallas, Texas. Lindy accompanied him as one of his trainers. Bill went to war. He shipped overseas and survived the European theater. His ship spent the later part of the war in the Pacific. Wallace was also in the Pacific and had a ship shot out from under him. Jack went into the Coast Guard and later went back to college and became an educator. He served as the principal at a large high school near Washington, DC. Lindy's daughter won Miss U.S. World and placed fourth in the Miss World pageant held in England. Miss Sweden won that year.

The island continues to honor Reginald Fessenden, Major General Billy Mitchell, and others who found the serenity of the place conducive to their success.

The children began to use their mental powers around each other. They had a feeling, in the adventures to come, that they were going to need them to survive. Blue became part of the family later in the spring. The children took over caring for the entire horse population, allowing their grandpop to concentrate on other duties. Captain Charlie was the sole keeper of the light, as war threatened to move the family away from the beach. There was much activity near the lighthouse compound, as several navy officers moved into one side of the assistant keeper's quarters until they could be housed. Two young men from the Coast Guard moved into the other side and were assigned to help Captain Charlie with his responsibilities.

The house in the woods took on a new importance as the kids learned more about its history. The house began to display a personality once Uncle Jabez returned.

In the next book the kids meet Uncle Jabez and spend time on the island with the pirates he dealt with. They are transported to the 1700s and meet the burly men who roamed the sea.

They enjoy each adventure, learn a new language, and practice their skills.

ABOUT THE AUTHOR

Jeanette Gray Finnegan Jr., Torok is a tenth-generation islander whose childhood was spent on Cape Hatteras when it was totally independent of mainland amenities. Jeanette—Jaye to friends—graduated from East Carolina University with a double major in English and history, and she did extensive graduate work at Old Dominion University in photography. After thirty years teaching both English and Advanced Placement U.S. Government, the author came home, back to the island, to live.

Jaye and her husband own the Dolphin Den Restaurant in Avon, one of the villages, and both spend the off-season writing. The five books in this series have been in the works for at least ten years. Previously Jaye photographed and produced a calendar of the island, from one ferry to the other.

The island is changing, and multigenerational families are dwindling. These books recall those moments that made life solid and depict a proud and innovative people, living on the edge of the world.

The stories are events that actually took place while growing up here. We know our history, and we found enough evidence of it as children. We would like to share it with you.

Enjoy the sights, sounds, and smells of this strip of land you obviously feel connected to also. This is what it felt like to live a natural life, surrounded by family and friends, few strangers, and lots of excitement. Growing up island was a special privilege with some unusual memories.